A PLUME BOOK

A DRUNKARD'S PATH

Allison Stedman

CLARE O'DONOHUE has been a television writer and producer for more than a decade. She spent four seasons as a producer on HGTV's *Simply Quilts*, and is still trying to use up the fabric she was given while working on the show.

A Drunkard's Path

A SOMEDAY QUILTS MYSTERY

Clare O'Donohue

A PLUME BOOK

PLUME
Published by the Penguin Group
Penguin Group (USA) Inc., 375 Hudson Street, New York, New York 10014, U.S.A. •
Penguin Group (Canada), 90 Eglinton Avenue East, Suite 700, Toronto, Ontario, Canada
M4P 2Y3 (a division of Pearson Penguin Canada Inc.) • Penguin Books Ltd., 80 Strand,
London WC2R 0RL, England • Penguin Ireland, 25 St. Stephen's Green, Dublin 2, Ireland
(a division of Penguin Books Ltd.) • Penguin Group (Australia), 250 Camberwell Road,
Camberwell, Victoria 3124, Australia (a division of Pearson Australia Group Pty. Ltd.) •
Penguin Books India Pvt. Ltd., 11 Community Centre, Panchsheel Park, New Delhi – 110 017,
India • Penguin Group (NZ), 67 Apollo Drive, Rosedale, North Shore 0632, New Zealand
(a division of Pearson New Zealand Ltd.) • Penguin Books (South Africa) (Pty.) Ltd.,
24 Sturdee Avenue, Rosebank, Johannesburg 2196, South Africa

Penguin Books Ltd., Registered Offices: 80 Strand, London WC2R 0RL, England

First published by Plume, a member of Penguin Group (USA) Inc.

First Printing, October 2009
10 9 8 7 6 5 4 3 2 1

 REGISTERED TRADEMARK—MARCA REGISTRADA

LIBRARY OF CONGRESS CATALOGING-IN-PUBLICATION DATA

O'Donohue, Clare.
   A drunkard's path : a Someday Quilts mystery / Clare O'Donohue.
       p.   cm.
   ISBN 978-0-452-29558-2
   1. Quiltmakers—Fiction. 2. Quilting—Fiction. 3. Murder—Investigation—Fiction. I.
Title.
   PS3615.D665D78   2009
   813'.6—22   2009004345

Printed in the United States of America
Set in Granjon • Designed by Eve Kirch

BOOKS ARE AVAILABLE AT QUANTITY DISCOUNTS WHEN USED TO PROMOTE PRODUCTS OR SERVICES. FOR
INFORMATION PLEASE WRITE TO PREMIUM MARKETING DIVISION, PENGUIN GROUP (USA) INC., 375
HUDSON STREET, NEW YORK, NEW YORK 10014

To my dad, who loved a good story

$\mathcal{A}$CKNOWLEDGMENTS

I had a lot of fun writing this book, the second in the Someday Quilts series, and I have a lot of people to thank for making the work easier. First, my wonderful editor, Branda Malholtz, for her help with the manuscript. The incredible publicity team of Mary Pomponio and Marie Coolman. My amazing agent, Sharon Bowers of The Miller Agency, for answering every question and helping me navigate the world of publishing. Thanks also to Illinois Crime Scene Investigator Howard J. Dean for his invaluable help with the blood-spatter section of this book. Special thanks to my mom for helping me proof the manuscript. To my book club, Kara Thomas, Allison Stedman, and Joscelynne Feinstein, for our fascinating discussions on books I never would have found without them. Maria Kielar, for her friendship, photos, and for keeping me from being a starving artist. Alex Anderson, for her incredible support and enthusiasm. The gang in LA, including Laura Chambers, Mary Margaret Martinez, Alessandra Ascoli, Cam Frierson, Kelly Mooney, and Celia Bonaduce. The Chicago crowd (though some have moved on since), including my cousin Margaret Smith, Kevin Dorff, Ewa Tchoryk-Bardwell, Kelly Haran, and Karen Meier. The New Yorkers, including Amanda Young, Aimee Avallone, Bryna Levin, and Joi DeLeon. My dear friend Peggy McIntyre, her husband Jim, and kids Matt and MaryKate. V, for being there. My tea buddies and best friends, Mary, my sister, and Cindy, my sister by marriage. And my family, Dennis, Petra, Mikie, Jim, Connor, Grace, Jack, and Steven.

A
Drunkard's Path

CHAPTER 1

"Can I get you a glass of wine?" The waiter smiled.

I looked at my watch: 8:35. "No, thanks," I said. "I don't think my friend is coming."

I got up from the table and walked out of the restaurant with as much dignity as I could muster. I had been stood up. Stood up on our first date.

As I walked toward home, an icy wind slapped me across the face. January is just a miserable month. The holidays are over and there is nothing but snow, cold, and long, lonely, dark nights. Now the one thing I had been looking forward to was over before it could begin.

I reached Main Street, the center of Archers Rest, and had a decision to make. I could go home, or I could walk down to the police department and find out why the local police chief, Jesse Dewalt, had left me sitting in a restaurant for more than half an hour without even a phone call.

He was supposed to be my friend, and he was the one who'd asked for this date. Actually, he'd asked me out three times before I finally said yes. But clearly it was a bad idea. I was getting over a broken engagement that had left me unwilling to trust my own judgment when it came to men. It was the reason I'd come to Archers Rest from New York City. After things fell apart, I realized that, even at twenty-six, I wasn't sure what to do with my life. All I knew was that I wanted a fresh start. And I had one—new friends, new job, new home, and tonight, a possible new romance. But that hadn't exactly worked out, had it?

Maybe Jesse was still mourning the death of his wife, Lizzy. For two years, he'd been a single dad raising a five-year-old girl. Maybe it was too much for him, I thought. Maybe he wasn't ready.

If that was the case, what was the point in talking to him about it? I could just forget the whole thing and head back to my grandmother's house where I was a non-rent-paying tenant. It might have been the sensible, even dignified, thing to do, but I couldn't move my feet in that direction.

It's not that she wouldn't be on my side, but Eleanor Cassidy is not what you would call a cuddly woman. She would wonder why I hadn't confronted Jesse, why I scurried home instead of standing up for myself.

A third alternative was to go to her quilt shop and sit for a couple of hours. I started working at the shop part time after I moved to town, and I had a couple of unfinished projects waiting there, which I could work on to pass the time. Then I could go home and mumble something to Eleanor and pretend the whole evening had gone as planned.

It took a moment for me to realize that, as my mind was wandering toward quilting, my feet were headed directly to the police station. My feet were clearly braver than my head.

Well, why not? I'm a modern woman in charge of my own destiny. "If a man stands me up, he is damn well going to hear about it," I muttered to myself, even as I wondered if I could get past the station unnoticed.

I couldn't.

"Hi, Nell."

I turned to see Greg, the youngest of the twelve uniformed officers in Archers Rest. He was also the most eager. Jesse once told me that Greg gave out more parking tickets than all the other officers combined. It was a source of amusement for Jesse until the day he found a parking ticket on his own car. It seems that Greg had spent twenty minutes waiting for the meter to expire, just so he could ticket the boss's vehicle. Greg told me later that he was hoping Jesse would admire his diligence and promote him. Instead Jesse confined him to desk duty.

"Looking for Jesse?" Greg asked.

"Um, I guess," I managed to get out.

"He's down by the river. He sent me back to the station to pick up some walkies." Greg held up two walkie-talkies. "But I'm going back to help with the investigation."

"What investigation?" I asked, but Greg was in too much of a hurry to answer. I followed him for two blocks, from the station to where Main Street met the Hudson River. Then I kept following as he walked down the river's edge for a quarter mile to the end of town. All the while I struggled to keep up with him without breaking into a full-out run or stopping to catch my breath.

"Stay here," Greg shouted when we reached the crime scene. "I'm going to find out what's going on."

He had the energy and excitement of a kid showing off to his friends, and it got me a bit excited too. What was going on? I waited impatiently for Greg to come back with all the answers, but he returned a moment later, a failure.

"Everything okay?" I asked.

He shrugged. "I'm supposed to do crowd control." He pointed toward the twenty or so people standing near the police barricade. "I thought this was my big chance to help with the investigation."

"You are helping."

I tried to be supportive even as I saw how defeated he looked. More than that, I understood. Standing on the sidelines wasn't exactly my favorite activity either. I walked away to see if I could get a glimpse of any of the action.

The river, normally a black hole on a cold January night, was bathed in light. The police cars had their lights flashing and their headlights on, and three twenty-foot temporary klieg lights were flooding the riverbank. In the middle of the light, Jesse and another man were standing next to something on the ground. I moved closer to get a better look but was immediately stopped by an officer I didn't recognize. And after five months of living in Archers Rest, I'd met all the full- and part-time officers in town.

"I'm Nell Fitzgerald," I said. "I'm a friend of Chief Dewalt."

"He's a little busy right now, miss," the policeman said, obviously not swayed by my small-town connections. "Why don't you call him later?"

I looked down at the patch on his coat. Morristown Police. "You're not from here," I stated the obvious.

"No, miss. We're here to offer our assistance to the Archers Rest Police Department."

I nodded and moved about ten feet away, toward the area at the edge of Main Street where the crowd was gathering.

"What is it?" I turned and saw Bernie, a member of my grandmother's quilt club or, I should say, my quilt club, since the women had officially taken me on as a junior member. Junior, that is, until I finished my first quilt.

"I have no idea. I can't get in there to talk to Jesse."

"Whatever it is, it sure put a crimp in your date," she said.

I nodded. I hadn't told Bernie I had a date with Jesse. In fact I'd sworn my grandmother to secrecy, but I wasn't entirely surprised that word had gotten out. Archers Rest was a small town with a means of communication faster than the Internet—gossip. My guess was that when Jesse asked his mother to babysit, she told her good friend Bernie. And by now, I was sure, Bernie had told everyone else in the quilt club. I knew right then that our Friday meeting would be less about piecing and more about my love life. I'd have been annoyed, but, considering how things were going, I could use the advice.

I tried to see what Jesse and the other man were talking about, what they were looking at, and why officers kept walking over and walking away, but I couldn't see anything. Frustrated, I was about to give up and go home when I had a better idea.

"I'm going to find Greg," I said to Bernie.

"Don't do anything I wouldn't, dear." She smiled.

I laughed. Bernie was the ex-hippie of the group and even now, in her sixties, was known for her outrageous behavior.

"That leaves me a lot of room," I said.

I headed toward Greg, who was standing near an empty ambulance with two other Archers Rest officers.

"Hey, guys," I said. "Jesse and I had a date tonight. He stood me up and I'd like to yell at him."

It was a little embarrassing to admit that publicly, but I wasn't about to stand around with the crowd when a little embarrassment might get me closer to the action. The three men laughed, exchanged looks, and seemed about to turn me down when Greg took a few steps toward me.

"I'll get you within yelling distance," he said. "But put in a good word for me. You know, to get me back on the streets."

I nodded. Greg and I walked past the barricade and the officer from Morristown. Greg pointed me toward Jesse and then turned and walked back to the barricade. Whatever happened now, I was on my own. I took a few more strides, then stopped when I was about three feet away from Jesse and got my first look at what lay at his feet.

It was the body of a young woman. She was pale and wet, I assumed from being pulled out of the river. Her pink dress clung to her. Her eyes were open and blank except that she looked, at least to me, frightened.

"Oh my God," I said.

Jesse looked up. "What are you doing here?"

"Well, I waited at the restaurant and you didn't show up, so . . ."

Jesse walked over to me. He leaned in and said, almost too quietly for me to hear, "I'm sorry. There's no excuse for not calling you."

"I don't know. That looks like a pretty good excuse." I nodded toward the body.

He glanced momentarily back at the dead girl and then moved in front of me, blocking my view. "I'm going to be here all night, Nell. Go home and I'll call you tomorrow. I promise."

I looked up at his earnest, intellectual face. His dark hair was rumpled and his glasses were perched crookedly on his nose. Something about the sad, serious expression and the way he squeezed my hand made me want to kiss him. But there was no point in wasting our first kiss in front of a corpse, the police force of two towns, and a growing crowd of spectators.

"Get some sleep if you can," I said.

He smiled a little. "I will. Get a deputy to take you home."

I let go of his hand and started to turn, but I had to ask. "Who is she?"

He shrugged. "I have no idea. No one from town. And Chief Powell doesn't know her either, so she must not be from around here."

I looked at the man I'd seen Jesse conferring with. He was large, over six feet tall, and looked to be in his forties, but with a crew cut that made him seem older. "Is he from Morristown? One of their cops tried to stop me from coming down here."

"He didn't know who he was dealing with." Jesse smiled. "But I do. And you're not getting your nose in this. It's probably just a suicide anyway, so I'll wrap this up before I need your keen investigative skills."

"Are you making fun of me?" I smiled.

He leaned toward me, his lips moving toward mine. Then he must have thought better of it. Instead he moved his mouth close to my ear and whispered, "Go home before I arrest you."

"Empty threats," I said. But I moved back from the scene. I walked up from the river's edge onto the pavement of Main Street, past the twenty or so people who were still watching, and toward the safety of my grandmother's house.

As I pulled my wool coat snugly around me, I found myself smiling at the thought of Jesse's warm breath against my cheek. But before I lost myself in images of him, I remembered something that made me feel suddenly cold—the sight of that poor young woman lying on the bank of the icy Hudson River. I wondered what had made her do it. Or who.

CHAPTER 2

"Doesn't that thing ring if someone's calling, like a real phone?" my grandmother, Eleanor, asked.

"Yes, unless it's broken."

"Is it broken?"

"Not as far as I know," I sighed.

"Well, then put it down. He'll call when he gets to it." She shook her head. "Besides, you want to make a nice impression on the people here, don't you?"

Reluctantly I dropped my cell phone into my purse and looked around. It was the sort of event I'd often dreamed of—an art opening, with some of the coolest, hippest artists in New York State in attendance. But instead of feeling excited, I felt out of place: an artist wannabe standing in the corner between my grandmother and her best friend, Maggie Sweeney. A week ago I'd read in *The New York Times* that the Coulter Art Center, the school I planned to attend, was holding an open house/art show. The article teased that a famous area artist, Oliver White, would be making an announcement regarding his collection. I desperately wanted to go, but I didn't want to go alone, so Maggie and Eleanor volunteered.

I was worried that they would feel bored, but while they made themselves at home among the crowd, I stood, like a kid on her first day of kindergarten, unsure of how to join in.

"Which one is Mr. White?" Eleanor asked me.

"I'm not sure," I admitted.

I didn't know anything about Oliver White, but, judging by the excitement in the room, I guessed he was a pretty big deal in the art world.

Maggie's deep green eyes pierced through me. Even in her seventies, she had a withering authority that must have come in handy in her years as town librarian.

"Why don't you get out there and meet some people?" she scolded me. "There's no point in coming to a place like this if you spend your time talking to a couple of old ladies."

With that she nudged me forward. I moved three inches and took a deep breath, then changed my mind. Too late, though. When I turned around, Maggie and Eleanor had disappeared into the crowd. I stood self-consciously for a minute, but that only made me feel worse, so I tried, unsuccessfully, to break into a conversation three men were having. Then I got a glass of wine from a passing waiter. That helped. I wasn't normally a wallflower, but so many of these people were artists. They did what I only dreamed about doing. I couldn't imagine any conversation in which I wouldn't sound like an idiot.

The only thing left to do was to look at the paintings. And it was quite a collection. Hung around the room were more than thirty paintings, mostly of women, covering nearly fifty years of White's career.

According to the exhibit brochure, in the late fifties and early sixties Oliver White painted musicians, drug addicts, and beatniks in New York's Greenwich Village. These early works were, to quote the brochure, "full of the pain and confusion of a man at odds with himself." Whatever that meant. There were only a few examples from that period, but each was full of emptiness and anger.

One, called *Nobody*, was of a nude woman who at first appeared to be sleeping but was, on closer inspection, passed out in vomit on a dirty bed. I wondered what kind of person would paint this woman rather than help her, but I was strangely filled with envy. There was an energy and emotion in White's work, a franticness to it. Any artist, or aspiring artist, would kill to be as good.

I took a few more steps and saw that his work had completely changed. These paintings and charcoal drawings, from what the brochure called "his pastoral period starting in the late seventies," were mostly of people from small towns and farms in upstate New York. There were still nudes, but these women were actually awake and seemed a million miles away from that girl on the dirty bed. Still, there was something sad or even resentful in his depiction of them.

"Cool, huh?"

I turned to see a woman of about twenty, with a shock of long and seemingly unmanageable copper red hair that fell in her face. She was wearing jeans and a bright green cardigan over an orange T-shirt and tugged at a chunky pink plastic necklace that made loud noises as she moved.

"I'm Kennette," she said brightly.

"Nell," I replied. "It's so different from his earlier stuff."

"He got sober," she said. "He was a drunk or an addict, or both, when he was painting in the city."

"That explains it, I guess." I turned back to the painting in front of me. "There's something about his stuff . . ."

"I know," she said. "It's almost violent, which is weird, since he looks like such a sweet old man."

She turned and nodded toward a very tall seventyish man with white hair and a neatly trimmed beard. He stood in the center of the room, smiling at two older women. It took less than a second for me to recognize them as Eleanor and Maggie.

"He's talking to my grandmother."

I was embarrassed, but I was also ashamed of myself for feeling embarrassed. Eleanor and Maggie were great, cool people. It was just that now I would meet the great Oliver White as a granddaughter and not as an artist. On the other hand, without Maggie and Eleanor, I would probably never have the chance to meet Oliver White at all.

Kennette was already walking over to join them, so I followed as quickly as I could.

"Nell, we've been talking about you." Eleanor smiled.

"That's what I was afraid of." I knew I was blushing, but Oliver was holding out his hand, so there was no time to run.

"You are Nell," he said in a warm English accent. "I'm so delighted." He held my hand in both of his and studied my face with his soft gray-blue eyes. "You would make a wonderful model."

"You apparently say that to every woman," Maggie said.

Oliver nodded. "I believe it about every woman." He moved from me to Kennette and gave her the same attention.

"So lucky am I," he sighed. "I get to stare at women all I want, and no one can accuse me of being anything but professional." He turned back to me. "Nell, I understand you're also an artist."

"No," I said.

"Not yet," Eleanor corrected. "She's going to take art classes here."

Oliver's eyes widened. "How wonderful. I'm always envious of talent as it emerges. I can't wait to see your work."

I found myself a little off balance. The intensity of his stare made me feel as if he had discovered all my secrets.

"I didn't realize you were English," I said to change the subject. "I thought you were a local artist."

"I came here from London in '57, so I suppose I am a local artist, but I haven't managed to lose the accent." He smiled at me, then at Eleanor. "I guess I spend too much time alone to practice my American."

"That's not what I've heard," Kennette jumped in. "I've heard you've dated everybody."

Oliver nodded. "That was a long time ago. It's now all fading memories and regrets, I'm afraid."

"Not all regrets, surely." Eleanor smiled. "You've created masterpieces."

Oliver seemed to blush a little. "That's very kind of you." He stared at Eleanor long enough that Maggie and I exchanged looks, though my grandmother seemed neither embarrassed nor intimidated by the attention. Eventually Oliver turned back to us.

"Well, I have to take care of some business," he said, "but I hope to talk to all of you later."

As he walked away, the four of us openly stared at him. "He's quite something," Maggie said, summing up what we were all thinking.

"Ladies and Gentlemen: I want to thank you for coming to the opening of this exhibit of the works of Oliver White," a man said into a microphone. "As you know, Oliver White is a renowned contemporary artist, best known for his paintings of the female form. His works hang in museums and private collections across the world, and they sell for tens of thousands of dollars. We are very proud to have him honor our small school with his presence and his work." Around the room, people burst into applause. Oliver smiled and nodded. "And today," the man continued, "he is bringing us even more."

Oliver smiled, nodded again, and took the microphone. "I have spent the better part of my life trying to express myself in paint. I have sometimes failed," he said to protests from the audience, "and I have sometimes succeeded." He paused. "I have done so to the detriment of my personal life, leaving me with money but no one to share it with. This is my biggest regret."

I thought his eyes moved toward our little cluster, but maybe I was imagining it.

"However," he continued, "my regret is the Coulter Art Center's good fortune. In my will, I have made the school my largest beneficiary. It is my plan to leave it the collection you see in this room, along with perhaps my greatest work, a piece I call *Lost*.

The room burst into applause as a large painting of a woman was revealed. It was all very dramatic, and, despite my resistance to anything that seemed too smooth and charming, I found myself caught up in the excitement.

Oliver stared at the painting, as did everyone else. From where I was standing I could barely see it, but it looked like a woman in a blue dress, looking out a window.

"I hope that it will inspire students for years to come," Oliver said and laughed. "And if not, sell the whole damn collection to buy some brushes and see what the young folks can come up with." More applause.

It looked as if he were finished talking, but instead of handing back the microphone he paused. "And I intend to do one more thing. I intend, if I am allowed, to teach two classes this semester. In one I would like to invite advanced students to join me in figure drawing, and in the other," he looked around the room, "I would like to teach aspiring artists, those taking their first steps into the deep, dark waters where I have spent my life."

Gasps and applause drowned out whatever was said at the mic after that. Oliver looked around, smiling, while the crowd, and even the man who had introduced him, seemed stunned by the announcement.

"Did you hear what he said?" Maggie practically shouted. "You can take his class."

I nodded, but inside I was trying to decide if I was excited or terrified at the idea.

CHAPTER 3

By the time we got home it was late, and Eleanor went straight to bed. I sat in the kitchen, drinking tea and wondering if I would one day be an artist as celebrated as Oliver White. It was a little difficult to get swept away in fantasy, however, because Barney kept nudging me to pay attention to the real star of the family—him.

Barney, a golden retriever, had just celebrated his twelfth birthday. His gifts from the quilt club—three dog-size quilts, several chew toys, and a large bone—cluttered up his bed and spilled onto the kitchen floor. He was nearly deaf and increasingly, I was beginning to think, forgetful. I watched him wander the kitchen as if he were looking for something, then stop, stand for several seconds, give up, and drop onto his bed. Once there, he discovered a squeaky rubber fish and began happily playing with it as if he'd been reunited with an old friend. He had the telltale gray hairs of an old golden but the enthusiasm of a puppy.

"You okay, old boy?" I patted his head, and he wagged back a yes. I gave him one of the dog biscuits that Eleanor had stopped feeding him, since she felt he was getting a little fat. But what's wrong with being a little fat if you're the dog equivalent of about a hundred years old? For that matter, what's wrong with treating yourself to a real cookie if you're scared about starting classes for the first time in five years? Since my grandmother wasn't around to disagree, and Barney didn't seem to mind, or would soon forget anyway, I dipped my hand into the cookie jar for one of Eleanor's famous oatmeal raisins. I was about to take a bite when the ring from my cell phone made me drop the cookie like I'd been caught in the middle of a burglary.

I saw who it was on the caller ID, so I waited until the third ring and answered. "Hello," I said, trying to sound casual and even a little bored.

"Hey, Nell. I'm sorry, the day just got away from me." Jesse's voice sounded exhausted. "Is it too late to call?"

"No. What happened?"

"Just a busy day."

"What happened with the girl?"

I heard him make a grunting noise. "It's going to be all over town tomorrow anyway," he sighed. "It wasn't a suicide, or it least it's not looking that way. The coroner found red marks on her wrist."

"Someone had tied her hands?"

"Something like that."

"Did you find any rope or anything?"

"No, nothing."

"So someone tied her hands, brought her to the river, then untied her and threw her in?" I asked. "That doesn't make sense."

"Not so far," he said. "Do you mind if we don't talk shop?"

I settled into a kitchen chair. "Nope. What do you want to talk about?"

"Do I get a rain check for last night?"

I paused to make it seem like I was actually debating my answer. "I guess so." I smiled. "As long as you show up this time."

"Friday, then."

"Quilt club," I reminded him. "What about Saturday?"

"If I can get a babysitter. My mother is going to a wedding. The daughter of someone in her bridge club."

"I'll get a babysitter," I said. "I'm sure I can find a volunteer from the club for such a good cause."

"They consider our long-postponed first date a good cause?"

"Our long-postponed first kiss."

He laughed. "I don't care how many bodies are floating in the river. I'm not missing that." I could hear the smile in his voice, and I wondered if he knew how happy I was to hear it.

After we hung up, I went upstairs to bed. I set the alarm for six, with a plan to be at the school no later than seven, even though registration didn't begin until nine. Oliver's offer would, no doubt, bring aspiring artists out of the woodwork. Scared or not, I didn't want to miss out.

I thought I would have trouble falling asleep, with the excitement of registering for classes filling my head. Instead I was out the minute I pulled my lover's knot quilt over me. But it was not a restful sleep. All night I had dreams of falling out of a vomit-covered bed into deep dark water, my hands tied, the current pulling me farther from shore.

When my alarm went off the next morning, I was so sleepy I had to wonder for a minute why I'd planned to get up so early. But as soon as it hit me, I jumped out of bed and into the shower. I was dressed and in the kitchen before Eleanor or Barney woke up, which was no easy feat.

I made myself some coffee and toast, left a note saying "Wish me luck," and headed out the door. I knew I was going to be ridiculously early, so I brought a book, an apple, and several quilt blocks. I'd painted the blocks months ago but never got around to sewing them together. Waiting for registration, I decided, was as good a time as any to get started.

When I arrived at the Coulter Art Center, I expected to be the first person there. I wasn't. About a dozen other students, ranging from their early twenties to their late sixties, were already waiting outside the office for a chance to register for class. I took my place in line behind them.

"Are you here for Oliver White's class?" I asked the forty-something man in front of me.

"We're all here for White's class," he said, a little frown on his face. "And I heard he's only taking fifteen students."

I quickly counted. I was number fourteen. "Well, then we're all in," I said.

He shook his head. "Several of the slots have already been filled by people who work at the center."

I stared down at my class schedule, wondering if I should start looking for a backup. "How many slots are filled?" I asked.

"I don't know," he said. "But I think it's more than one."

The excitement about registering for art classes suddenly deflated, I tried to console myself with the two courses I was sure to get. I looked through the schedule once more and saw that two other drawing classes were being offered.

"One's as good as another," I told myself. But I didn't really believe it.

After about twenty minutes of standing, one by one the prospective students sat. I put down my tote bag, ate my apple, and recounted the line just in case there were fewer people now that we were seated. No luck.

As the line behind me grew, and word got out that White's class was probably filled, I decided to distract myself. I got out my hand-sewing project and started piecing together the little squares. Before the holidays I had painted snowmen, Santas, reindeer, and poinsettias on six-inch squares, with the plan of sewing a red batik sash between each square to make a cheery little Christmas wall hanging, but I hadn't finished it in time. I slowly poked my needle in and out of the fabric, following the line I'd drawn on the back of the sash, and wondered if at this pace I'd have the thing done by next Christmas.

At nine the door to the registrar's office opened. Everyone in line got to their feet and moved a few inches forward. As my turn came to move into the office, I didn't have time to put my sewing away, so I scrunched the blocks in my hand, repeatedly sticking the needle into my thumb.

Though it was my turn, a woman a few years older than me refused to move away from the registrar's table. She was wearing an insanely out-of-season sundress, military boots, a leather jacket, and a wool cap. The whole look screamed "I'm cool and alternative and way better than you." I immediately felt annoyed and inferior, and then annoyed at myself for feeling inferior.

"What do you mean I can't get a slot?" she was saying to the registrar behind the desk.

"Look, miss, I've said it ten times," the registrar, a woman of about fifty, responded. "The class is full. You can stand here all afternoon but nothing will change that." Then she leaned over and looked at me. "Next."

I pushed ahead of the cooler-than-thou chick and took my place in the front of the line. "Hi," I said, smiling and trying to look as friendly and cooperative as possible.

"What classes do you want?" The registrar peered up from her glasses. I showed her my registration form, already filled out. "White's class is full," she said. "The other two are open. Do you want a different class?"

I looked over at the sundress lady, who was still standing at the desk. Clearly she had already fought the fight.

"I guess so," I said. "I can take the other Thursday drawing class."

She nodded, scratched out White's class on my form, and added the other one. "The teacher for that course is really very good," she said, and gave me a sympathetic smile.

I handed her a check, took my completed form, and vowed to console myself with a big breakfast before heading to work. I made my way past the line that had formed behind me, just in time to hear another disappointed budding artist plead his case to the registrar.

I was heading into the parking lot and toward my car when I caught sight of an older man walking to the school. Without any idea what I was going to say, I ran over to him.

"Mr. White?"

He looked down at me. "And who would you be?"

"Nell Fitzgerald. I met you last night at the opening."

I reached out to shake his hand, but I realized too late that I was still holding my quilt blocks.

"Ouch." He pulled back and removed a needle from his palm. "What's all this?" He took the blocks from my hand. As he examined my snowmen and Santas, I briefly considered running. Instead I stood there, staring at the ground, humiliated by the idea that my silly little paintings were being seen by one of the best artists in the country.

"These are on fabric," he said. "What are you going to do with them?"

"I'm making a quilt," I said quietly.

He looked at me. "You make quilts?"

"This is going to be my first, if I can get it done."

"Are you self-taught or do you have a teacher?"

"My grandmother. You met her last night."

"I remember."

"She owns a quilt shop in Archers Rest," I said. "I work there part time, and I'm trying to take some art classes." Stop talking, I kept saying to myself. He doesn't care about my grandmother or my ambitions.

He took one more look at my blocks then returned them to me. "You should take my class, then."

I nodded. "I tried. It was all full up."

He took a deep breath. "And that stopped you? How disappointing."

He started to walk away. My embarrassment was overtaken by my curiosity, and I followed him.

"Did I have a choice? I can't just show up at the class."

He stopped. "You want to learn. I want to teach. It seems like a perfect match to me." He sighed. "Of course if you don't want to play . . ."

"I do," I insisted. "I came here two hours early, and I still didn't get in. Are you saying I should just show up?"

"When I was a young artist I didn't let anything stand in the way of my dream. It mattered more to me than anything in the world. Perhaps that isn't the case with you. But in my experience a truly dedicated artist doesn't allow for any interference in his dream."

He walked away, leaving me wondering if he was issuing a dare or a warning.

CHAPTER 4

"I'm looking for a batting that will give this an old-fashioned look." A woman spread a flying geese quilt top across the counter. It was made of reproduction fabrics that I recognized from our inventory.

"Civil War collection," I said confidently. "One of my favorites."

The woman smiled. "I was in here a few months ago, and I was telling an older woman about my love of antique quilts. But the good ones are getting so expensive."

"So she told you, just because you hadn't inherited one didn't mean you couldn't own one," I said. "That was my grandmother."

I walked her over to a large built-in bookcase that had been subdivided into sections. It held all the batting we carried, and we carried it all.

"We have polyester, cotton, poly-cotton blends, silk, wool, and bamboo," I said. "Silk is wonderful but pretty expensive. I'd suggest using a cotton batt and then washing the quilt after it's been quilted. It will give it a puckered antique look."

"Wash it?" She practically gasped.

I smiled. "First quilt? Don't worry, quilts are like babies," I said, repeating my grandmother's mantra. "They're a lot hardier than they seem." I pulled down a full-size cotton batt and walked back to the counter. "Anything else?"

"I guess I need quilting thread," she said as she stared, blinking, at two large racks of thread.

I walked her through the difference between hand and machine quilting threads, helped choose a color that would blend into the material and hide a first-timer's mistakes, and rang up the sale, all with the confidence of an expert. And I was an expert, as long as no one else was in the shop.

I'd been working at Someday Quilts for only three months, but I'd spent much of that time listening to my grandmother advise customers. The rest of the time I leafed through quilt books and rearranged fabrics, getting ideas for my first quilt—or first through fiftieth since there were already more quilts I wanted to make than I would ever have time for. "Sign of a true quilter," Eleanor often said to me. Another sign would be actually finishing a quilt.

Since the shop was quiet, I sat behind the counter and picked up my Christmas blocks to finish piecing them together. Five more blocks and the quilt top, a simple four-by-five block arrangement with sashing, would be done. Or almost done. I still had to add borders and quilt it. Everyone in the quilting group told me how much faster the process would be by machine, but, in truth, the sewing machine intimidated me a little. My grandmother owned several, and while one was a simple Singer Featherweight, the other two were computerized and, to me, complicated. One could even embroider without anyone sitting at the machine, for heaven's sake. Eleanor, who had never learned to set the clock on her VCR, could operate both as if it were child's play. One of these days, I promised myself, I would sit down and figure them out.

I comforted myself with Maggie's advice that every quilter should learn how to hand piece first. And I had to admit, I was getting the hang of it. I added a reindeer block to a sashing strip in record time.

"Pretty good there, Nell," I congratulated myself, and looked up just in time to see someone familiar pass the shop.

I headed to the door as the Morristown police chief paused to light a cigarette a few feet away from Someday Quilts.

"Hi," I said. "Nice to see you again."

He looked up, utter confusion in his eyes.

"I'm a friend of Jesse's," I tried to clarify, sounding more like an idiot with each word. "I was at the murder scene the other night." Ridiculous. I was making it sound like we'd met at a party.

He walked toward me and held out his gloved hand. "Marty Powell," he said as he shook my hand. "You're Dewalt's girlfriend."

I blushed. "I'm . . . I don't know" was all I got out. That stumped me. I needed a change of subject. "How's the investigation going?"

He took a puff of his cigarette. "Slow, but we did get one break. The victim's name was Lily Harmon. Ever hear of her?"

"No. But I've only lived in town for a few months," I said. "I'm sure if she were local Jesse would have—"

"He doesn't know her either. No one around here does." He took one last drag and threw his cigarette on the ground. "Strange that she'd come down here to kill herself among strangers."

I nodded and said good-bye. I watched him walk in the direction of the police station and I went back inside. I stood in the middle of the shop, staring blankly at the walls. I was supposed to be getting it ready for the quilt club meeting. That meant I was supposed to grab a bunch of chairs from the classroom and put them in a circle and throw on a pot of coffee, but instead I kept going over the conversation in my mind. Or, actually, just two words of it: "down here." If Powell didn't know who she was, why did he think she came from north of town?

"He probably just used it as an expression," Natalie said when the quilt meeting was under way. She was tired, but these days she was always tired. Natalie had just announced that she was eight weeks pregnant with her second child, and after we'd exhausted baby name ideas, I told them about running into Chief Powell.

Natalie sat, munching on cookies, next to her mother, Susanne, a former beauty queen turned doting, and in Natalie's eyes, too-involved grandmother. Bernie had closed up her pharmacy early, as she always did on Fridays, and was sitting next to Susanne. Maggie and my grandmother rounded out the circle. I hadn't even bothered to sit down yet because I was busy getting everyone coffee and passing out cookies, which Natalie was eating as fast as I could get them to her. Carrie was the only member of the group not yet in attendance.

"What kind of an expression is 'down here' anyway?" Bernie asked.

Susanne nodded. "I agree. It's a bit suspicious." She leaned forward. "And he wasn't very nice to my nephew, Richie."

"Rich found the body, along with a couple of his friends," Natalie offered before her mother could finish.

"What were teenagers doing by the river on a January night?" Eleanor asked.

"Something they didn't want anyone to see," I suggested. "You know, the kind of thing you wouldn't admit to a cop."

"Maybe that's why Powell wasn't nice to Richie," Eleanor said. "Maybe he knew he was up to something."

"Richie's a good boy." Susanne's voice raised a little. "It's that cop. I don't like him."

"I'm surprised Jesse is working with him," Maggie added.

"Why is Jesse working with him?" Bernie turned to me.

I was a little embarrassed to admit it, but I did anyway. "I don't know. Jesse hasn't told me anything."

"Well, he will tomorrow." Natalie smiled, and with that the conversation turned to where Jesse and I were going on our date, what I was wearing, and whether it would actually happen this time.

Quilt meetings, I'd learned in the last couple of months, were almost never just about quilting.

"How late am I?" Carrie burst through the door, carrying a half-finished star quilt.

"You missed the discussion about the girl in the river, but we're still on Nell's love life," Bernie said cheerfully.

"Good, then I'm right on time." Carrie dropped her quilt in a heap and grabbed a cookie.

"Why don't we talk about quilting?" I offered, to everyone's general amusement. "I'm having trouble keeping the sashing straight as I sew." I held up my Christmas squares.

"It'll iron out." Susanne smiled a slightly mischievous smile.

"Will it? That's good news," I said.

"No, it won't." Eleanor shook her head at Susanne. "That's just the lie we tell ourselves so we don't unsew everything. The truth is, when you sew your nose is six inches from the fabric. You notice every imperfection. But once it's finished, and you take a step back, you won't remember what was wrong in the first place."

"And no one else will either," Maggie offered.

I leaned back in my chair as far as I could and stretched the arm holding my blocks. I could still see the imperfections.

"Are you sure that isn't another lie we tell ourselves?" I asked.

Bernie leaned back in her seat. "Speaking of lies, I think it's interesting that the other sheriff said the girl killed herself."

"Don't start that again," Eleanor said. "It'll only encourage her." She nodded toward me.

"It will not," I defended myself. "Besides, I thought of that. He didn't realize that Jesse had already told me it wasn't a suicide."

Bernie nodded. "I just don't like the idea of Jesse having his investigation interfered with by an outsider. I think he's trouble, that sheriff."

"Is that a psychic prediction?" Susanne laughed. Bernie often talked about her psychic abilities but rarely was able to demonstrate them.

Bernie leaned forward toward Susanne. "Mark my words," she said. "This is the beginning of more trouble."

"That's enough about dead girls and police officers," Eleanor declared. "Honestly, you would think we got together to gossip."

"God forbid," Natalie said, laughing, "when we really get together to dissect Nell's love life."

"Then why do we bother bringing fabric and thread?" I asked.

"It's our cover, in case the police bust in." Bernie smiled. "Who would suspect a bunch of quilters to be up to no good?"

CHAPTER 5

Eleanor was quiet the entire way back to her house, which made me a little suspicious. When we pulled up in front of it, she didn't get out. Instead she stared out the window into the clear night sky.

"I agree with Bernie," she said nearly in a whisper.

"About what?"

"About you staying out of the investigation. You have nothing to do with this case."

"I don't think that's what Bernie said," I laughed.

"I won't split hairs with you, Nell," Eleanor snapped. "I'm telling you to stay out of it."

I was about to point out that I was, in fact, a grown woman and therefore too old to send to my room. But I saw the worry in her eyes and softened my approach. I took her hand and held it. Though her hands were wrinkled and covered with spots, they were strong and beautiful. They had made thousands of meals, hundreds of quilts, held her children and grandchildren, and survived more than seventy years of life. Next to hers, my hands, though unblemished and youthful, didn't seem nearly as lovely.

"I'm not doing anything, Grandma," I said. "I'm just a busybody like everyone else in town."

She nodded. "Anyway, you have to concentrate on school. And Jesse."

"It's just a first date, if we ever actually go on it. Don't go imagining we're in love, because we're not."

Eleanor let go of my hand and reached for the door. She got out of the car before she spoke again.

"Don't be so sure that love isn't important," she said. "Love is the most important thing in the world."

Before I could answer, she slammed her door and headed toward the house.

The next night I was in my bedroom, wondering if love *was* the most important thing in the world—or if the most important thing was the right pair of shoes. I held up the black boots I'd worn for my original date with Jesse, along with the black check skirt and pink sweater I'd been wearing that night. It was a perfect date outfit, but I figured it was bad luck to wear the same thing I'd been wearing when Jesse stood me up, so I went through my closet in search of something else. After trying on three pairs of pants, two skirts, and a dress, I was back in the black check skirt but paired this time with a light blue sweater. That is, until I noticed the sweater had a spot on the sleeve, and then, after trying on nearly every top I owned, I settled on a black cashmere cardigan over a black silk tank.

When I put on my mascara, it left goop under my left eye that made me look like I'd been in a bar fight. In an effort to fix the problem, I ended up making it worse and had to do my makeup all over again. By the time I was searching for my favorite earrings, I was nearly in tears. What was the point of this anyway? I was a disaster in relationships, and this one hadn't exactly gotten off to a good start. I was about to give up and call off the night when I heard an odd knocking at my door. Barney was pushing his head against it until he had enough room to nudge his entire body through. He walked over and sat in front of me, expectantly.

"I don't have any cookies, old friend," I said. He pushed his head under my hand. "Oh, you want a cuddle, do you?" I asked, but I already had my answer. I scratched his ears as he wagged happily. He rubbed his head against my skirt, and I couldn't bear to push him

away even though I knew I didn't have time. I stayed five more minutes and petted the old dog, then frantically tried to brush off the
evidence of our encounter.

As always I learned a little something from Barney. Happiness is a
thing you have to go find for yourself, but dog hair is something that
finds you.

When I arrived at the restaurant twenty minutes late, Jesse was looking at his watch.

"I'm sorry," I said quickly. "I couldn't figure out what to wear."

He stood up as I got to my seat. "You look great."

Then he paused and so did I. We couldn't exactly shake hands, but
should we kiss or touch or something? It was clear that neither of us
knew what to do, so we sat down in embarrassed silence, grabbing
menus to hide behind.

"How's the investigation going?" I asked as soon as the waiter had
taken our orders.

"It isn't," he admitted. "We found out that the woman was from
Kitchener, in Ontario, Canada."

"So that's what Chief Powell meant by 'down here,'" I said.

Jesse smiled. "Already on the case, I see."

I knew I was blushing. "No, I just happened to chat with him
outside the quilt shop yesterday, and he mentioned something about
the girl coming down here to kill herself," I said. "Only, he didn't acknowledge that it wasn't a suicide."

Jesse nodded. "We still have no idea why she was in Archers
Rest."

"But you know that she was," I said as the waiter put my salad
down. "I mean, you know she wasn't in a neighboring town."

"No, I don't. I just mean in the area." Jesse took a stab at some let-
tuce. "Don't look for hidden meanings in everything I say, Nell."

"I wasn't. I was just asking." I went back to my salad, feeling a
little scolded. Several minutes of silence passed. This date was not go-

ing well. "I signed up for classes," I offered as a conversational olive branch.

Jesse's face brightened. "Did you get that class you wanted?"

"No, it was all filled up. But I ran into the teacher outside the school, and he sort of suggested I just bully my way in."

Jesse smiled. "Sounds like he's figured you out."

"So you think it's a good idea to push my way into places I don't belong?" I smiled. "That's good to know."

He laughed. "What did I tell you about finding hidden meanings?"

After dinner we walked toward the river. I waited for Jesse to take my hand, but he didn't, so after a few blocks I put it in my pocket. All through dinner I got the feeling that we were more like friends out for a bite than people on a first date, and I was about to say that to Jesse when his phone rang.

"Now?" he said into the receiver. "All right. I'll be there in a minute." He hung up and looked at me sheepishly.

"Police business," I said.

He nodded. "I'm sorry. I hate to cut the evening short."

"It's okay. We weren't really planning anything else anyway." I knew the disappointment I felt had crept into my voice, but I didn't care.

Jesse stared at me for a long minute, then turned and walked toward the street. He stopped—his back to me. I wasn't sure what to do, so I just waited. Finally he turned.

"Do you want to come?" he asked.

We walked into the state police lab just after ten o'clock. A large man with uncombed hair and thick glasses came toward Jesse at full speed.

"It doesn't make sense," he said as he handed Jesse a manila folder.

"What doesn't make sense?" I knew I should probably keep quiet, but Jesse was studying the papers in the folder and the large man seemed anxious to talk.

"She was asleep. She had been given a double dose of diphenhydramine hydrochloride."

"What's that?" I asked.

Jesse looked up. "An over-the-counter sleeping medication." He glanced toward me, then closed the folder and looked at the large man. "Dr. Parker, you're saying that she was unconscious when she drowned."

Dr. Parker's eyes sparkled. "That's exactly what I'm saying. I've rerun the tests just to be sure. Come with me."

Without waiting, he started walking toward a double door at the back of the hallway. Jesse followed him, and since no one said I couldn't, I did too.

Immediately upon entering the room, I regretted my decision. On a slab in the center of the room was the girl that had been taken from the river. A sheet covered her body but her head and shoulders were exposed. I had seen dead bodies before, I had even seen this one before, but this was different. A person who has just died still looks like a person, but this girl looked both real and artificial, her skin almost translucent. Never had death seemed as transformative as it did when I looked at the way her brown hair framed her frail features. Whoever Lily Harmon once was, she deserved better than to end up here so young.

"And then there's this." Dr. Parker directed Jesse closer to Lily's body. He pulled the sheet back and I saw where she had been cut open for the autopsy and sewn together again. I wanted to throw up but I just took a deep breath.

"It's a scar," Jesse said as he stared at Lily's body.

"We should go." Jesse's warm breath startled me back from wherever my mind had wandered. Even though I knew he was right, I lingered just a minute longer, staring at her, feeling oddly protective of this stranger. "Nell," Jesse said.

I nodded and followed him out of the room and out of the building. After the chill of the morgue, even the frigid January temperatures didn't seem so bad. I stood just outside the door and took a deep breath.

"I'd tell you that you get used to it, but you don't really. You just pretend to," Jesse said. "I'm sorry. I shouldn't have taken you here."

"No. I'm glad you did. I like seeing you at work. You're so sure of yourself."

Jesse blushed. "It's a nice contrast to how unsure I am everywhere else."

He stepped closer and took my hand. We had barely moved off the steps of the morgue before Jesse stopped and turned toward me. He swept my hair off my face and smiled. I knew what was coming, and suddenly I felt out of breath. He leaned in and bumped my nose.

"Ouch," I laughed.

"That was supposed to go better." He pulled away slightly. His right hand was cradling my head, so I knew he wasn't going too far.

"You can give it another shot," I said. "And if you—"

He leaned in again. "Shh." He planted his lips on mine.

We kissed for five minutes, until the sounds of a coroner's van reminded us of where we were.

CHAPTER 6

"If I talk to the registrar again, maybe I can imply that Oliver White wants me in the class," I said to my grandmother over breakfast on Thursday morning. "It wouldn't exactly be a lie." I took a bite of toast and swallowed some coffee before I changed my plan again. "Or I could go to the class today and see if anyone's dropped out."

"Or you could ask him," Eleanor said flatly.

I looked up from my toast. "I can't do that." I searched for a reason why not and only came up with, "It's too simple."

Eleanor shook her head. "I forgot. You like to keep things complicated."

"Well you can't really spare me at the shop anyway," I added. "It gets busy enough for two full-time people."

"Don't use me as your excuse."

Eleanor got up and took my half-finished breakfast, giving the lone slice of bacon to Barney. My grandmother was about to celebrate her seventy-fourth birthday, but she had more energy and nerve than I ever did. She'd had a rough life. She lost her husband in a car accident and was left with two small children to raise and no money. Yet she built a successful business and a good life. Maybe she had learned somewhere along the way that, sometimes, you just have to ask.

✂

"I'd like to join your class, Mr. White—Professor White." I stumbled on my words, but my feet were planted firmly in front of the door to his classroom, blocking his way.

He smiled and peered down at me through his glasses and beard. "Oliver," he said. "It's just Oliver." He looked me up and down in what was either a creepy old man's assessment or a way to amuse himself while adding to my tension. "What makes you think that you can just join my class?" he finally said.

"Why not? I want to learn how to paint and you want to teach. It seems like the perfect arrangement," I blurted out, echoing White's words in the parking lot.

His smile widened into a Cheshire-cat grin. "I'm sure you can find a spot."

As I entered the studio I saw nearly twenty students, more than were supposed to be allowed in the class. Including, I noticed, the pushy girl from the day of registration. I guess I wasn't the only one with a grandmother.

Everyone was standing behind an easel, arranging their drawing pads and nervously shifting their feet. I quickly found an empty space, wondering if I looked as excited as everyone else.

"How many of you are artists?" Oliver asked the class. A few hands went up. Oliver nodded. "Well, I can tell you right now that I doubt any of you are really artists. Being an artist takes time, patience, work, study, and sacrifice. By the end of this class you'll have a taste of what I mean, and perhaps it will inspire one or two of you to continue on this path toward being an artist. But I warn you, it may not be worth the price."

After such a pretentious opening, I wondered if I'd fought to get here for nothing, but I seemed to be alone in my assessment. All around me people were leaning forward, caught up in the excitement of being on the starting line of their dream.

We first went around the class, saying our names and explaining our reasons for being there. Though it was supposed to be a class for beginners, several of the students were already selling their work at local art or craft shows. My guess was that the class White was offering for advanced artists had filled up the night he made the announcement, leaving several people to crowd into the beginner's course. Those of us who really were beginners were divided into two categories: people that said "I've always liked to draw" and the more annoying "I feel I need to do this for my soul."

The pushy woman from the registrar's office said her name was Sandra, and added, "I took this class on a lark because ceramics was already filled." An odd answer given how desperately she wanted to get into the class. Oliver smiled at her, but there was no warmth in it and he moved to another student without comment.

Then Oliver turned to me. "You're the quilter," he said.

Was that a bad thing? "Yes," I said. "I work in a quilt shop anyway. But I'm here because I've always enjoyed drawing and painting and I want to see if I'm any good at it."

"You learned from your grandmother, if I recall," he said.

"Yes."

He nodded and moved past me to an older man who had been a reporter for years before retiring to Archers Rest and finally taking up his lifelong dream of becoming an artist.

After he was finished, a familiar voice started speaking behind me. "I'm Kennette and I just like to draw," she said.

I turned around and waved. She was wearing the same bright outfit she'd worn to the opening and a huge, eager smile on her face.

To assess our artistic abilities, we started the class by drawing a group of bottles that Oliver had placed on his desk. I pulled out my drawing pad, a piece of vine charcoal, and a kneadable eraser and arranged them on my easel.

"Do you have a piece of paper I could borrow?" Kennette tapped my shoulder.

"Yeah. Sure." I tore a piece of paper off my drawing pad and handed it to her.

"Cool," she answered. "Do you have some extra charcoal?"

I nodded and handed her a piece. "Do you have an eraser?" I asked.

"No, I don't need one." She smiled. "I'm very free-form."

She immediately started drawing bottles on her paper without bothering to look at the arrangement.

I, on the other hand, spent most of the class struggling to re-create the bottles in exacting detail, making liberal use of the eraser. Oliver walked around, stopping at each student, making comments or suggestions, and filling me with terror. When he stopped at Kennette's easel, I saw out of the corner of my eye that he was smiling approvingly.

"You've really found the essence there," he said to her.

How do you find the essence of bottles? I wondered, feeling as completely inadequate as I ever had.

Then he walked over to me. He watched me for what seemed like an eternity before he quietly said, "Nice, but very restrained. Let yourself be wrong because it will allow you to take more chances."

He moved away from me and on to another student before I had a chance to respond or even to think about his assessment.

When the class ended I lingered a minute. The "let yourself be wrong" comment stung since I knew that was not my strong point. Besides, wasn't the point of the exercise to draw the bottles? How could getting them right be the wrong thing to do? But those questions weren't the reasons I waited to speak with Oliver. More than anything, I wanted confirmation that I belonged in this class with all these eager wannabes.

In doing so, I realized that it had only been two hours since his annoying opening speech and I had already fallen for it. When there were only a few students left, I made my way over to Oliver, but it was almost too late. He was already heading out the door. I followed him and quickly realized I wasn't his only stalker. Sandra was closing in as he reached his office. I held back and watched as the two stopped and talked quietly for a second before Oliver let her into his office and closed the door behind them.

"He's amazing, isn't he?" Kennette was behind me, staring at the door to Oliver's office the way a puppy stares at a chew toy.

"He's interesting," I replied. "I wonder why he's talking to that woman Sandra."

"She's a weird one, huh? Who dresses her?"

I glanced over at Kennette's mismatched outfit and smiled. On second look, it had a kind of charm to it. "I think she has an ulterior motive for being in the class," I said. "She was desperate to get in."

"We were all desperate to get in." Kennette shrugged. "And she probably has the same ulterior motive as half the class—she's hoping Oliver will discover her."

"I guess." I nodded. "Still . . ." I let the sentence trail off because I didn't actually have anything to add. I just didn't like Sandra, and I wondered if I was jealous of the impression she was obviously making on Oliver.

"Where are you going from here?" Kennette said as we walked out of the building into a bitter cold January day.

"Work. I work at my grandmother's quilt shop in Archers Rest."

"If she's hiring, let me know. I need a part-time job." I nodded a good-bye and headed toward my car. After a few steps, I realized Kennette was following.

"Do you quilt?" I asked.

"I'm a fast learner." She bit her lip and looked at me hopefully.

Before I had a chance to think about it, I spoke. "Well, if you want to follow me to Archers Rest, you can meet her," I said. "I'm pretty sure she can use an extra hand. I'm only there part time."

"I'll just go with you," she said. "I walked here."

"Where do you live?" I asked.

"Nearby," she said and hopped into my passenger seat.

CHAPTER 7

Eleanor was in the classroom area of the shop, leaning over a quilt that had been stretched across a table. Susanne was with her, and they were busy putting pins through the layers.

"What are they doing?" Kennette whispered as she stood behind me.

"Pin basting," I said. "It's when you layer the three parts of a quilt—top, batting, and the back—and get it ready for quilting. You have to temporarily hold the layers together so when you quilt them they don't shift.

"They're doing it with safety pins," she said.

"Yeah, you can do it with thread or little plastic thingies, but for machine quilting, safety pins work fine." I was a little proud of myself for being so knowledgeable.

Kennette tiptoed over and examined the work reverently. My grandmother looked up and smiled.

"I remember you. How are you . . . ?" my grandmother's voice trailed off into a question.

"Kennette. I'm great."

"What a lovely name, dear," Susanne said. "What's your last name?"

Kennette looked down for a moment then smiled. "Green," she said.

"It goes with your outfit." Susanne smiled. "It's lovely to have you here."

Kennette dropped her tote bag and moved closer to the quilt. "Can I watch? I don't want to be in the way."

"You're not in the way," Susanne said. "We're just prepping this big old thing for quilting."

"You're pin basting." Kennette smiled.

Eleanor's smile widened. "You're a quilter."

"Not really," Kennette answered. "But I've always loved quilts. They're such an amazing combination of utility and art."

"Would you like to help me baste this?" Susanne handed Kennette a curved safety pin and explained to her that the shape made it easier to get through the layers of fabric.

"How far apart do you put them?" Kennette looked absolutely thrilled at the prospect of jumping into the project.

"It depends on the batting," Susanne explained. "On this one we need to put a pin every three or four inches. About the width of your hand."

At that Kennette put her hand down next to an area that had been pinned and began to add her own safety pins.

"Good work," Eleanor said. "We got lucky that you happened by today. This is the most tedious part of making a quilt."

"That's why you do it in a group, I bet," Kennette said.

"You've figured out our secret." Susanne smiled.

I coughed, since no one seemed to notice I was there. "She's looking for a job," I said.

Susanne looked up and saw me standing in the background. "Hi, Nell. I was wondering if you were coming in today."

"I came in with Kennette."

Eleanor glanced up and smiled, then turned back to Kennette. "Are you an art student as well?"

"We're both in Oliver White's class," she said.

I moved toward Eleanor. "I was thinking that with me only here part time, maybe you could use another hand for a few hours a day."

"That's a wonderful idea," Eleanor said. "Let's look at the schedule and see if it will work out."

"Should'nt we finish the pin basting first?" Kennette grabbed a handful of pins and started carefully putting them through the layers of fabric. This move delighted Susanne and Eleanor, who cheerfully went back to basting the quilt. I knew before she did that Kennette had gotten the job.

There clearly wasn't anything for me to do, as I certainly wasn't about to get involved in the very boring job of basting the quilt. "Why don't you take Kennette on a tour of the shop," I suggested. "I'll go across the street and get some coffee to celebrate this occasion."

Eleanor nodded. "Carrie is there. I saw her earlier. Ask her if she can spare a few small cups." Eleanor and Kennette headed to a wall of books at the back of the shop.

I walked across the street to a store closed for remodeling. The shop, until recently a failing pet store, was slowly being transformed into the sort of hip café that was around every corner in my former Manhattan neighborhood. Since moving to Archers Rest, I hadn't missed my old publishing job, my ex-fiancé, or the out-until-dawn lifestyle of New York City, but I did miss coffee shops like the one Carrie was planning. I knew I would be a loyal customer when she finally opened its doors.

As I reached Carrie's shop, I saw Jesse heading toward the river. I started to wave, and even though I could swear he saw me, he didn't acknowledge that I was there.

"Hey there," Carrie said as she opened the door.

"You don't happen to have any coffee, do you?" I asked.

"That's a dumb question," she laughed. "I'm on my third pot."

I walked into the shop, more puzzled than hurt by Jesse's behavior. But once in, I was struck by the transformation from pet shop to, there's no other way to say it, huge mess. The floors were dirty, the place smelled of wet fur, and Carrie was still finding bird poop whenever she cleaned. The biggest change was on the walls. She was painting them a soft brown—the color, naturally, of milky coffee.

"They look great," I said as she poured me a cup from a home coffeemaker she was using until a professional machine was installed.

Carrie beamed. "Thanks. I think they're almost perfect."

"Almost? What more can you do to them?"

"I was thinking . . ." She paused. Her face scrunched up, and she looked at me for so long that I began to worry I had something in my teeth. "I was thinking that maybe you could paint something on the wall." She gestured toward the large blank wall directly opposite the front door.

"Paint what?" I was now the one with the scrunched-up face.

"Whatever you want. Something to do with the shop, or whatever." I could see she was hopeful.

I stared at the wall. A mural. Suddenly I was filled with ideas—coffee cups and a New York skyline, blacks and browns and creams, with bright colors like teal showing up in unexpected ways. But when I glanced away from the wall at Carrie's excited face, reality set in.

"What if I screw up?"

"You're an artist. You won't screw up."

"I'm an art student."

Carrie wasn't going to take no for an answer; I could see it in her eyes. "There's no pressure. I'll paint over it if you don't like it," she said. "But I won't have to, because it will be amazing." She put her arm around my shoulder, and we both stared at the wall, imagining the possibilities. "Do you think you can have it done in four weeks? With school and everything."

I nodded.

"Then at least *something* will be ready for the opening." She sighed and took a sip from her coffee.

Carrie was in her forties, a former hotshot stockbroker who had moved to Archers Rest, married the local pediatrician, and now had two kids. After years of talking about it, she was finally opening her own business. But her ever-present insecurities were getting the best of her. I smiled as reassuringly as I could.

"You'll be fine. The opening will be great, and the place will be a huge hit," I said.

"Well, you're my role model."

At that I nearly did a spit take. "Me? Good Lord. You have Bernie with the pharmacy, my grandmother with the quilt shop, Maggie who raised seven kids and served as town librarian for something like forty years, and I'm your role model?"

"You came up here a heartbroken wreck of a thing, jilted by your fiancé, bored with your life," she said. "And now look at you."

I got up and gave myself an exaggerated once-over in the store's window. "All I can see is that I could use a facial," I said.

She threw a napkin at me. "You're going after your dream. That's huge. When I saw that you were willing to do whatever it took—"

"You said, 'If that idiot can do it . . .'"

She laughed. "Exactly."

Of course I hadn't really done anything yet, except attend one day of class. But I didn't bother explaining that to Carrie and dampening her hero worship.

I headed back to the shop with two paper cups of coffee balancing in each hand. When I saw Susanne out front, I was relieved. But then I saw the near-panicked expressed on her face.

"What? Is something wrong? Has Kennette done something in the shop?"

"No, heavens. She seems lovely. Don't you like her?"

"I guess. I don't really know her. She needed a job and I figured—" I couldn't get the last words out before Susanne interrupted.

"That's nice of you, dear." Susanne pulled me farther from the shop. "I've been mulling this over all afternoon. I knew I couldn't say anything in front of your grandmother, so I've been waiting for you to come in."

"There is something wrong." I tried to wriggle out of Susanne's grasp but couldn't. She was holding tight.

"No. I don't know. I want you to talk to my nephew."

I stopped struggling. "The one who discovered the body?"

Susanne nodded. "I'm not going to say anything. I don't want to color your view of what he told me. I want you to listen to Richie and judge for yourself."

"If he knows something about the girl's death, he should go to Jesse," I said. I was curious, and even a little tempted to run over to see her nephew immediately, but I also knew that if I did Jesse would kill me.

"That's the thing that's so weird," Susanne whispered, as if the whole town were bugged. "He tried. Jesse won't believe him. In fact he just ignored him."

I nodded. It seemed Jesse was doing that a lot lately.

CHAPTER 8

The teenagers of Archers Rest had no mall to hang out in, so they usually gathered by the river in the summer and the local bowling alley in the winter. At least that's what Susanne told me as we drove to the alley after closing up at the shop.

It had been difficult enough to convince my grandmother that I needed to take Susanne home, especially with Susanne's car parked right out front. Add in Susanne's nervousness, and I worried that Eleanor was on to us. If not for Kennette's presence, I don't think we would have gotten out of there.

And I had another problem. I knew it was going to be difficult to keep the conversation I was hoping to have with Richie from getting back to Jesse. Archers Rest is a small town where gossip is king. The hope that somehow it would escape Jesse's notice vanished when Greg walked into the bowling alley not a minute after Susanne and I arrived.

"Hello, officer," I said, trying to seem casual and not up to anything he would have to report to his boss. "Has Jesse given you the night off?"

"Wish he hadn't," Greg lamented. "There's a full-blown murder investigation going on, and he won't let me be any part of it. He doesn't know what a keen investigator I am."

"He'll see it eventually. Jesse's a pretty smart cop."

Greg scowled. "He's not as smart as he thinks he is." Then he turned and walked toward the snack bar.

"Come on," I said to Susanne. "Let's try to do this without drawing too much attention." I nodded toward Greg, who was comforting himself with a beer.

Susanne nodded. "I won't interfere. I'll stay completely out of the way."

"You don't think he'll talk in front of you?"

Susanne hesitated. "He's a teenager," she said, obviously choosing her words carefully. "I think he'll be worried about saying something in front of me that might get back to his mother."

"Doesn't his mother know that he found a body in the river?" It was bad enough that Jesse and Eleanor would be mad at me for talking to this kid. I didn't need some irate mother coming after me as well.

"Yes," Susanne said. "She knows about that. She just doesn't know everything. She's kind of a nervous person."

"Runs in the family." I smiled, but Susanne looked confused, so I dropped it.

She spotted her nephew in the middle of a group of boys laughing into their Cokes and trying to look above it all. Not that it was working. I think you can only look so cool in bowling shoes.

"Richie," Susanne called out.

I could see him blush even from across the room. He looked up and nodded, said something to his friends, and made his way through the crowd to us.

"Hey, Aunt Susanne," he said. He was an average-looking kid with a friendly, unassuming smile.

"Richie, this is Nell. I was telling her about you," Susanne whispered. "I want you to talk. I won't interfere."

"I'm Rich." I noticed how strongly he emphasized that his name had only one syllable.

Susanne looked around before shepherding Rich and me into a corner. "I'll get us something to drink," she said, then stepped away as if she didn't have security clearance for the conversation.

"She's a little dramatic." Rich rolled his eyes.

"You must trust her," I said. "You told her stuff you didn't tell your own mother."

Rich blushed. "I told Natalie. She told Aunt Susanne," he said, "which is cool. Aunt Susanne doesn't get on my case about hanging out."

"Is that what you were doing at the river?"

He nodded.

"She said you saw something, and she wanted you to tell me."

He shrugged. "It's no big deal. I don't know." Now he looked as uncomfortable as Susanne. "My friends and I were just . . . hanging out there that night."

"The night the girl was found."

"Yeah. We weren't doing anything."

"It's January, and you were hanging out by the river." It was my turn to roll my eyes. "You must have been doing something."

He sighed. "A few beers. That's all. Aunt Susanne thinks that's why Chief Dewalt didn't take me seriously."

"He thought you were drunk."

"But I wasn't."

"Okay." I could see that whatever it was weighed heavily on him. "What happened? Just go through it step-by-step."

"Artie Collins, Blimper, and I were hanging out, just having a couple of beers . . ."

"These are friends of yours?"

He gestured back toward a group of boys. "Artie had a flashlight, 'cause it gets pretty dark by the river at night."

"Pitch-black," I agreed.

"So he's flashing the light and we're drinking. Nothing serious. And he sees something in the water. So we walked over to check it out." Rich stopped and took a deep breath. "And it was, you know, that lady."

"The woman they fished from the lake?"

He nodded. "So I called the cops from my cell phone and we waited until they came. In case, you know, she floated away or something."

"Did you touch her?"

He shook his head. "We could tell it was too late to help her." He sat up and looked at me. "We would have helped her if, you know, she was alive. We're not jerks."

"I know," I said. "You waited for the police, which was the right thing to do. And then you told Jesse what happened."

"We didn't tell him about the drinking. In case."

"I don't think he would have done anything, Rich. He had his hands full that night."

He shrugged again and looked back toward his friends. "I guess."

"Is that it?" It hardly seemed like the kind of information worth all the fuss Susanne had made.

"No." Rich looked down at his shoes for a moment. "I'm not making this up, so I don't care if you believe me. When we were waiting for the police, I saw this picture—a photograph—on the ground. When they all got there, this cop from Morristown made us go wait on the street and no one would talk to us until they got the lady out of the water."

"I think I met that cop." I smiled. "He's very insistent."

"When they finally came over, I told Jesse about the picture and he made me take him to exactly where I said it was." He paused. "But it wasn't there."

"Maybe someone picked it up. One of the other officers."

"He said it wasn't in evidence, and it wasn't any big deal anyway, since he doubted it had anything to do with the case."

That seemed odd. I knew Jesse was a thorough officer, a good cop. Why would he dismiss possible evidence so quickly?

"What did the photograph look like?"

"Old, really old. Ancient."

I could see Susanne hovering within earshot. When she caught my eye, she used the excuse to jump in. "He's sixteen. Anything from the eighties he considers ancient," she said.

Rich frowned. "No, really old. Black and white."

"A black-and-white photo of what?" I asked.

"A woman. She was kind of like your age. And wearing this big dress, sitting on a bed or something and staring, like, far away." He stopped for a moment. "She had kind of a weird expression."

"What do you mean?"

"I don't know. Weird." He took a cola from Susanne and took a long sip.

"Do you remember anything else?" I asked. "Anything specific about the woman or the room or what she was wearing?"

His stared into the air for a moment. "Yeah. She had dots on her dress."

"Polka dots?"

He shrugged. "I guess. That's all I can think of." He nodded to me and took off toward his friends.

"He said all of this to Jesse and got nowhere," Susanne said. "Don't you think that's strange?"

"Well, maybe Jesse's right. Maybe the photo has nothing to do with the woman in the river," I said.

"Then where is it?"

Good question. And I had another one. I walked over to Rich and his friends.

"Did anyone else see the photo? Artie and . . ."

"Blimper." A tall, thin kid with a wide smile reached out his hand. "Pleased to meet you."

"You're Blimper?"

He patted his flat stomach. "It's meant to be ironic."

I nodded. "Well, Blimper, did you or Artie see the photo that Rich saw?"

"No. Once I saw the body I couldn't see anything else. And Artie was busy trying to keep in his lunch."

"Screw you," said a kid I assumed to be Artie.

"Did you tell anyone else about the photo?"

"Like who?"

"One of the other officers at the scene," I said. "Maybe Chief Powell."

"The guy from Morristown?" Blimper laughed. "He's a piece of work."

"What do you mean by that?"

"My sister's boyfriend got caught drunk driving in Morristown." Blimper leaned in as if telling me a state secret. "And the guy wouldn't cut him any slack. He's like some ex-military guy turned cop and he's hard core. Strictly by the book."

Rich looked at me as if he were about to cry. "I swear I'm telling you the truth. I don't care what the cops believe."

"I believe you, if that counts for anything," I offered. "And your aunt believes you."

"So why doesn't Dewalt?" asked Blimper.

"The guy's got a stick up his ass," Artie laughed.

"He's a really good police chief," I jumped in, a little too defensively. "He just has his hands full right now."

"Or he doesn't know what he's doing," Artie said. "How else do you explain ignoring a perfectly good witness?"

"I don't know," I admitted. "But he must have a reason."

I just couldn't figure out what it was. And I knew there was no way Jesse would tell me.

CHAPTER 9

For three days I debated what to do with Rich's information. I took a walk by the crime scene and, as I expected, found absolutely nothing. The place had been picked clean by the police. I doubt there was a stray leaf that hadn't been bagged as evidence.

It didn't make any sense. Why would Rich make up a story about a photo? And even if he had, why would Jesse be so dismissive? I knew I would have to confront Jesse about it. It was just a matter of figuring out how.

He had been almost impossible to reach for days. Every time I called he said he was just on his way out. He'd promise to call back later, and he would, but it was always late. After work, after he'd put Allie to bed. I could hear the exhaustion in his voice and I felt like I was just another item on his "to do" list.

"I want a second date," he said on Wednesday night just as we were about to hang up. "Anytime you're ready."

"I'm ready anytime," I answered.

"We'll have to figure something out."

With that, he said good night and hung up. It was perplexing. He was nice, he was interested, but he was also distant and unable to commit to even a second date. It was the sort of male behavior I used to spend hours discussing with my girlfriends when I lived in New York City. I didn't know if I actually had girlfriends in Archers Rest, though I was pretty sure Bernie, Maggie, and the rest would happily have debated the issue with me if I wanted.

Not that I had much time for it. I was at the shop about thirty hours a week and feeling overwhelmed and excited by my art classes. On Mondays I took ceramics. On Tuesdays I studied color theory, and on Thursdays I had class with Oliver.

"We're going to reverse draw," he announced at the start of class. "Everyone take some vine charcoal and cover your entire page."

As she had done in the previous class, Kennette leaned over to borrow paper. This time I gave her several sheets, though I was a bit annoyed.

She must have sensed it, because she smiled. "When I get my first paycheck I'll be able to afford my own pad," she said.

Her good nature made me feel ashamed. "It's okay," I said.

Here I was living for free in my grandmother's house, and I begrudged poor Kennette a few pieces of paper—Kennette, who was wearing the same outfit for the third time, making her either highly eccentric or very broke.

"Is everything okay?" I asked.

She smiled. "Yeah. Great. How are things with you?"

"I don't know. Okay, I guess."

"Do you ladies have some questions?" A booming English voice rang out from the front of class.

"No, Oliver. Sorry." I shrank next to my easel and started covering my paper with charcoal. As I did, I saw out of the corner of my eye that Sandra was moving slowly away from her easel. I watched as she picked up several pieces of vine charcoal from one of the other students and put them in her pocket. It was odd since she already had several pieces of her own, but Sandra was odd, and I added it to the list of things I needed to look into.

We were supposed to draw the fruit that was arranged on a small table in the center of the easels, but I just couldn't make it work.

As if he knew what I was feeling, from across the room Oliver said, "Stop trying to draw the fruit. Draw the form as values. Lights and darks. See that and not the color."

I had to laugh. It was something I heard over and over from the quilt club. To them fabric was a palette. A sometimes distracting palette. They held the fabrics at a distance and squinted, separating them into lights, mediums, and darks.

"Colors don't matter as much as contrast," Maggie once instructed me. "Light and shadow: that's what's important in an interesting quilt."

And so it was, apparently, with fruit. As soon as I applied this quilting logic to drawing, the process became less intimidating.

"Don't see the color," I told myself. "See the value. The banana is light. The green apples are medium. The deep red strawberries sitting in the shadow of the bowl are dark. Simple."

"See the sensuality in all the objects you draw. The life," Oliver instructed as the class drew. "They are not lines; they take up space."

I could see him walking behind each easel, nodding approval or making a suggestion. It was so important to each student that Oliver like what he or she did, and I could see the disappointment in those who didn't hear "lovely," his official endorsement.

When he stopped next to me, at Sandra's easel, I couldn't help but watch. I was hoping, stupidly, that he would hate what she had done, if only to prove that buddying up to the professor didn't get you a free pass.

"It's charming," he said. "Quite a lovely interpretation. One of the best in the class." He smiled at her and lingered near her easel. Though Sandra said nothing, she touched his arm in a way that seemed more intimate than a student and teacher should get.

I took the chance to step back from my work and glance over at Sandra's. I'm not an art critic, but it was hardly charming—certainly not one of the best in the class. Neither was mine, to be honest, but Sandra's drawing was almost unrecognizable as fruit.

Oliver came to me next. "Lovely. You have mastered value," he offered. I wanted to be thrilled, but after Sandra's evaluation, his praise felt flat.

He stopped next at Kennette's easel. He studied it much longer than the other students, standing back, then moving in close and standing back again.

"I'm not finished," a nervous Kennette explained.

Oliver shook his head. "You have talent, Kennette," he said with a quiet certainty but also a hint of surprise. Then he walked to the front of the class.

"He knew my name!" Kennette nearly jumped when class ended and we packed up our supplies.

"He said you have talent, which is a much bigger deal."

"Everyone in class has talent. Your drawing is way better than mine."

I looked at my sketch pad, then hers. I was getting better, I thought, but I was still controlled, even timid. Kennette's work had a confidence about it.

"He's right," I admitted. "You're really good."

She shrugged. "I'm supposed to open up with your grandmother tomorrow, so I figured I'd head to the shop tonight, if that's okay."

"Yeah, it's fine," I said. I was trying to figure out if it was rude to ask any of the obvious questions, but I couldn't help myself. "Where do you live?" I finally asked.

Kennette blushed. "I don't have the most ideal living situation," she said. "And I'm kind of broke, so I don't have a lot of options."

"I'm sure it wouldn't be a problem to stay at my grandmother's tonight."

She lit up. "That would be great."

"Where were you planning to sleep anyway? I mean, if you came to Archers Rest tonight."

"I don't know. I would have figured out something."

I stood back in awe. Awe and fear. With a little bit of envy thrown in. Could I be so free-spirited? And if I was, would I be as good an artist?

As we left the classroom, I quickly dialed the shop but got no answer. I knew it wouldn't be a problem with Eleanor to bring home a guest, but I was starting to wonder if Kennette had the common sense to work in a quilt shop. Not that I could stop her at this point. She was a stray cat, and having fed her she was going to come back, day after day, looking for more. And just like a stray cat, there was something endearing in that.

We were heading toward the car when we both suddenly stopped. At the far end of the parking lot Sandra was in tears while Oliver tried, apparently in vain, to comfort her.

"What do we do?" Kennette whispered to me.

"Leave, I guess. I doubt they've even noticed we're here."

"Why is she crying?"

"Maybe because your 'talent' trumped her 'best in class,'" I suggested.

Kennette looked surprised. "Oh, I hope not. I wouldn't want something I've done to have hurt anyone."

I laughed—probably not the right thing to do because it confused Kennette and caused Oliver and Sandra to look our way. It was just that Kennette's words were so sincere, and so kind, and so unlike anything I would have said.

As soon as Sandra spotted us, she jumped into a car and sped away. Oliver seemed embarrassed, but in seconds his mood had changed.

"Ladies, how did you enjoy class?" he called out cheerily as he approached.

At this Kennette immediately swooned. "It was great. I learned a lot. I couldn't believe how much I learned."

I was mortified. "I wasn't laughing at Sandra," I tried to explain. "I was laughing at something Kennette said."

Oliver waved it off. "We artists are excitable creatures. It's what makes us interesting lovers and terrible spouses. Where are you off to, then?"

"Work," I replied.

"At your grandmother's shop," he said. "Isn't that where you work?"

"Where we both work," Kennette jumped in.

He looked over at her. "How lovely. And you're both going there now?"

"Yes," I said, amazed that he would take the time to chat.

"I'm absolutely fascinated by quilting. A wonderful and underappreciated art form. I've always wanted to study a quilt up close and really see the workmanship of a master."

Really? I thought. Because if that were true, there were quilt shows.

But what I said was, "It's really endless, what you can do with fabric."

"You should see Nell's grandmother's quilts," Kennette said. "She's really wonderful. She has them all over her shop."

I was about to point out that Oliver was too busy to bother with my grandmother's quilts when he turned to me.

"Mind if I follow you there?" he asked.

"To the shop?" I couldn't believe what I was hearing. "It's in Archers Rest. That's about a half hour from here."

"Lovely day for a drive." He smiled.

"That's our car," Kennette offered, pointing to my mine, just a few feet away.

"Fantastic. I'll be right behind you." Oliver practically ran off to his car.

CHAPTER 10

A half hour later we were parking in front of Someday Quilts. In my rearview mirror I saw Oliver patting his hair.

"What is he up to?" I asked.

"He's just interested in quilting." Kennette jumped out of the car, all enthusiasm and excitement.

I could see Oliver get out of his car, straighten his jacket, and move toward the shop. Kennette stopped him, and he smiled and seemed to be listening, but I could see him glancing toward the shop door.

What is he up to? I asked again.

Oliver and Kennette walked into the shop before I even got out of the car. A part of me wanted to avoid the train wreck that was almost certainly about to happen, but then—as is the case with actual train wrecks—curiosity got the better of me. I knew I had to see this through, so I went inside.

"These really are magnificent," I heard Oliver say from the back room.

I walked to where I could see Oliver, Kennette, and my grandmother looking at the quilts that hung on the back wall.

"Oliver is a big fan of quilting," I said, a bit too sarcastically for Eleanor's taste. I could feel the disapproval boring into me.

But Oliver apparently didn't notice. "Great art is great art, regardless of the medium," he said and turned to face another wall. "Amazing. May I touch?"

"Of course. Quilts are meant to be touched," Eleanor said.

"That's the thing I love about quilting. It's so unpretentious."

"It can be," Eleanor laughed. "But, believe me, we have our prima donnas too."

Oliver smiled at her, and for a moment seemed to stare into her eyes. Eleanor must have noticed it too, because she did something I'd never seen her do before. She blushed.

"This is your work?" he asked, pointing to a large winding ways quilt that hung on the wall. "It's really magnificent. I love your use of bold colors and this design is so exciting."

"It's actually a classic pattern," Eleanor explained.

"It's got so much movement. But that's due to your use of color," Oliver gushed as he moved close to the quilt. "And the workmanship is really something. I can tell that I'm in the presence of a master."

I looked at Kennette to see if she shared my nausea at all the blatant kissing up. Of course Kennette was eating it up as much as Eleanor.

"Does anyone want anything? Coffee or anything?" I asked, looking for an excuse to get out of there.

All three of them turned to me, smiling.

"Lovely. Black, if you don't mind." Oliver walked toward me. "But my treat." He reached into his pocket and handed me a hundred-dollar bill without even looking at it.

"Kennette, you want something?" I asked. She was staring at Oliver as if he were George Clooney.

"No," she said. "I'm fine."

"Do you want to help me get the coffee?"

"No. I'm fine."

I looked over at my grandmother in the hopes that she was still a little sane, but Eleanor wasn't looking at me either. She was smiling at Oliver, who was—and this is where things started to get weird—smiling right back.

✂

"My grandmother has a boyfriend." I slammed the hundred-dollar bill on the table as soon as I walked into Carrie's coffee shop, which was still very much in the midst of remodeling.

"Eleanor?" Carrie looked up from cleaning.

I heard something fall in the back room, and Natalie came running out, a mop still in her hand. "What did you say?"

"My art professor followed us to the shop today."

"Us?" Carrie interrupted.

"Kennette, the girl I take classes with."

"She's going to work at the shop." It was Natalie's turn to interrupt. "My mom told me about her."

"How come I don't know about her?" Carrie asked.

"I forgot to tell you," Natalie answered. "She takes classes with Nell and she wears funky clothes and she's very nice. At least that's what my mom said. She sounds interesting."

I threw my hands up. "She's not as interesting as this," I shouted. "Oliver, the art teacher, he followed us to the shop and is now in there hitting on Eleanor."

"How do you know?" I could hear the shock in Carrie's voice. "What exactly did he say?"

"He said he liked the quilts."

Natalie laughed. "Of course he liked the quilts. They're great quilts. And since he's an artist, he'd know."

I shook my head. "It was the way he said it. He praised every little thing. And it was more than that." I paused for dramatic purposes. "He smiled at her."

I expected more laughs, but neither woman moved.

"What did she do?" Carrie finally asked.

"Smiled back," I said.

We all stood in silence in the middle of Carrie's shop.

Finally Natalie said, "I want to see this."

We were almost out the door when I remembered the reason I supposedly came over. Carrie poured coffee into three disposable cups, and we headed across the street to Someday Quilts, trying to look casual, and absolutely failing.

Nothing had changed in the few minutes I was gone. Eleanor and Oliver were standing by the quilts, smiling. Kennette was a few feet away, staring dreamily. I gave Carrie and Natalie my best "I told you so" look.

"Here's the coffee," I announced.

"And it came with friends," Oliver said happily. In seconds he was charming the new arrivals and asking to see their quilts, which were also on display. It gave me a chance to pull Eleanor aside.

"What's going on?"

Eleanor the unflappable had returned. "Your teacher has a good eye for quilts," she said, and then went to the counter for her coffee.

"I would love to sit with you sometime and discuss the techniques you use," Oliver said to Eleanor as he followed her to the counter.

"That would be fine. And I'm sure there's a lot I could learn from someone in your field that would apply to quilting."

"No doubt." He smiled. "Tomorrow perhaps. Dinner?"

"We have quilt club," I cut in. "Every Friday."

"Saturday, then?" Oliver's eyes never left Eleanor.

"I close up the shop about six," she said.

He nodded. "I'll pick you up at eight?" He squeezed Eleanor's hand. "It was lovely to meet you ladies. I'm sure we'll see each other again."

"At class," Kennette jumped in.

"Yes, of course. And perhaps before then."

We stood at the door and watched him get into his car and drive away. Everyone but Eleanor. She was busy stacking some newly arrived magazines.

"You have a date!" Natalie shouted. "A date with a handsome, successful artist."

"It's not a date," Eleanor scolded her. "He's interested in talking about quilts, that's all." And with that she disappeared into the shop's office.

"Wow" was all Carrie could say.

"Isn't he wonderful?" Kennette asked. "He's so sophisticated and charming. Like an old-fashioned movie star."

He was. I had to agree. And so did half the women taking his class, including the annoying Sandra. Even in his seventies, he had a sexy, bad-boy quality about him. It seemed clear that he had spent a lifetime playing by his own rules and was celebrated for it.

So why was a man like that hitting on my grandmother?

CHAPTER 11

"It's off the table," I whispered. "No one can bring it up. Trust me."
Though Oliver had been in the shop only twenty-four hours before, every member of the quilt club arrived for our usual Friday meeting knowing word for word what had happened. And everyone was dying to talk about it. Except Eleanor.

Kennette and I had tried to broach the subject when we were sitting in my grandmother's kitchen having dinner a few hours after Oliver's visit. The stone silence we got in response made it clear that this was not an open subject.

All day at the shop Kennette and I made pathetic attempts to look busy while Eleanor waited on every customer who came in, unwilling to let us handle even the easy sales. When we were finally closing up for the night, Eleanor suggested that Kennette stay for the meeting. There was nothing unusual in that, the quilt group was extremely welcoming. But I felt that my grandmother wasn't just fostering Kennette's interest in quilting. She was hoping that the presence of a newcomer would draw attention away from her.

It didn't work. Ten minutes into the meeting Bernie teasingly asked about Eleanor's plans for the weekend. Eleanor remembered something she needed in the office and disappeared.

"She must be terrified," Bernie said. "It's been years since she's gone on a date. When did her husband die?"

"Almost forty-eight years ago," Maggie said. "Joe died just weeks after Eleanor's twenty-sixth birthday."

I'd never done the math before. It took me a second to digest the fact that my grandmother was my age when she was widowed with two small children.

"And she never went on another date again?" Natalie asked quietly, in case Eleanor emerged.

Maggie took a deep breath. "She had . . ." Maggie was choosing her words carefully. "Interest." She stopped for a moment, and then added firmly, "But she had children to raise."

"Getting remarried would have made that simpler," Susanne whispered, sitting forward in her chair.

Bernie shook her head. "I think she was mad at Joe for getting drunk and wrapping his car around a tree."

"And leaving her broke," I added. "I know she was really blindsided when she found out that he had lied to her."

"About what?" Natalie asked.

"He'd wanted her to think they were doing better financially than they actually were," Maggie answered. "Nell's right. I think she was more upset about the lies than about finding out after he died that she had no money."

Bernie sighed. "I think she was just afraid to get hurt again."

Carrie sat back in her chair, stunned. "I can't imagine Eleanor being afraid of anything."

As if on cue, Eleanor walked back into the meeting and sat in her chair. "We've been asked to donate some quilts to the fire department, if anyone's interested," she said. "They find it very helpful to have warm quilts waiting for a family watching their house go up in flames."

We all nodded and murmured our willingness to participate. But Kennette sat up and looked straight at Eleanor. "I think it's wonderful that you have a date with Oliver White. I think he's a fascinating man, and he clearly has great taste." She looked around the room. "We all think it's wonderful."

Each member of the quilt club sat silent in her chair, waiting for

Eleanor's reaction. But before she could say anything, Kennette spoke again.

"But that's not what we're here to talk about," she said, "so I was wondering if you ladies could help me choose a pattern for my first quilt?"

Having a new quilter in the group broke the tension. Bernie jumped up and headed to the rack to choose a quilt book. The rest of the women scattered throughout the shop, looking for the simplest patterns. Kennette got up and wandered around, examining the finished quilts that hung around the shop with the same dreamy attention she seemed to give everything.

Eleanor and I stayed in our seats but said nothing. What was there to say? Kennette had gracefully opened the topic and then closed it. I wondered if Eleanor was as relieved as I was.

"That one," Kennette said, pointing to a blue and white quilt Maggie had made.

"It's called a drunkard's path," my grandmother told her. "It's simple enough, I suppose, but it's all curves."

A drunkard's path quilt is made by repeating one simple block, a square with a quarter circle of a different color sewn into one corner. By repeating this block and moving the squares the quilt develops a zigzaggy look. Maggie once told me that the pattern went by many names, but during the beginnings of the temperance movement, in the late 1800s, it was renamed drunkard's path. And it was easy to see why. The undulating effect of the semicircles did sort of remind me of a drunk staggering home.

"I like it. It feels playful," Kennette declared. The rest of us walked over to the quilt and stared at it.

"It does feel playful," Bernie agreed. "I never really thought about it. I guess it's because I hate curves."

"Nothing to them," Maggie said. "A little more work maybe, but Kennette's up to the task, aren't you?"

Kennette beamed at the praise. "With help," she said.

"You have said the magic words," I laughed. "You're going to get more help than you know what to do with."

And, just as I predicted, the rest of the meeting was taken up with helping to choose the right fabrics for the quilt. Kennette quickly found a bold purple paisley that she loved. Though the pattern was too large and busy for the small drunkard's path blocks, it was the perfect backing to the quilt—and the inspiration for the other fabrics. The group spread out to find light yellows, creams, and whites for the square part of the blocks and purples and blues for the quarter circles.

Then, using the acrylic templates my grandmother sold in the shop, Susanne showed Kennette how to cut the two pattern pieces.

Next Natalie showed her how to cut slits in the curve's seam allowances to create more give and, she explained, "To make the block lay smooth."

Once dozens of block pieces had been cut, Carrie used one of the shop's sewing machines to help Kennette sew them together.

We all got so carried away in the excitement that we forgot about anything else. Susanne and I cut out the rest of the blocks, while Maggie, Eleanor, and Kennette sewed them together. Carrie and Bernie carefully pressed each block, and Natalie placed them on the design wall.

By eleven that night we had all Kennette's blocks sewn and ready to be pieced together to make a quilt top.

"It's amazing!" Kennette was almost in tears. "I can't believe you guys did this."

"You did it too," Carrie said.

Kennette nodded. "I can't wait to finish it."

"Don't get so caught up in the end result that you miss out on the fun along the way," Maggie warned. "The real joy of quilting is in the process."

"I suppose," Kennette said, "but I still can't wait."

"Well, when things are slow you can use one of the classroom sewing machines to piece the squares together," Eleanor said. "And in no time you'll have a top."

"And then we'll help you quilt it," Bernie said.

Kennette came back to the house with Eleanor and me, thanking us the whole way. Once home she went upstairs to Eleanor's office and went to sleep on the pullout sofa. I walked Barney. When I came back, Eleanor was at the kitchen table, pouring tea into two mugs.

"She's an interesting little thing, isn't she?" Eleanor said.

"I bet there's a great story," I said. "I'm betting on a bad breakup and that the boyfriend threw her out without her stuff."

"You don't think she has a place to stay?"

"I don't know. Or maybe where she's staying is really horrible, 'cause she never seems to want to go there."

"Poor thing." My grandmother sipped her tea.

"If she stayed here . . . ," I started.

Eleanor looked up. "Of course she'll stay here. It will be easier for her to get to the shop and you can drive her to class. And see what you can do about lending her some new clothes."

"I just can't imagine what she's doing," I said. "What happens to people who live like she does?"

"They end up like that girl in the river," she said. "With no one to claim them."

I stared at my grandmother as she stared off into space. Kennette might have been a lost sheep, but she was, at least temporarily, safe— which was more than I could say about Lily Harmon.

CHAPTER 12

"Leave me alone," Eleanor snapped. "I don't need you to put jewelry on."

I dropped her pearl necklace onto the dresser. "I'm just saying it looks nice on you. And when you have dinner with a friend," I said carefully, "you want to look nice."

Eleanor grunted, picked up the pearl necklace, and fumbled with it. Then she dumped it in my hands. "Put it on me," she said.

I did as instructed. "You look great."

"Honestly, Nell, it's not a date. It doesn't matter if I look great."

"Haven't you told me it's always important to look great?"

"Make sure Barney gets his dinner," she said. "And a short walk. It's cold outside and I'm worried that he'll get sick."

"I'll take care of him." I smiled. "It's not like I have anything else to do tonight."

"Maybe Jesse is working."

"He's not," I admitted. "I called the station. He left at five."

Eleanor furrowed her brow. "Then I can't understand why he didn't call you. I know his mother is home tonight, so he could have gotten a sitter."

I shrugged. "I think maybe he's not interested."

"Nonsense. He's had his eye on you since the day you moved into town. He's just scared, that's all." Her face softened, the nervousness seemed to melt away, and she smiled at me. "We all get scared, you know."

"Not you," I said, laughing.

"No." She added her own laugh to mine. "Never me."

And then the doorbell rang.

We both took a deep breath. "Stay here," I said. "Let me answer it."

I sprinted down the stairs but I was too late. Our houseguest, Kennette, had already answered the door to an obviously surprised Oliver.

"Kennette, I didn't know you lived here," Oliver said as he walked inside.

"Oh, I don't. I'm just"—she hesitated—"I'm just here."

"That's lovely," he cleared his throat. "Is Eleanor ready?"

"Almost," I said. "I'll get her."

Oliver nodded and cleared this throat again. "Lovely." He looked nervous, and when Eleanor descended the stairs a minute later, he looked even more nervous. After a moment of awkwardness, they were gone.

"Don't they seem like Cinderella and the handsome prince heading to the ball?" Kennette asked once we were alone.

I nodded. "And we're the ugly stepsisters." I threw my arm around her shoulder and we went into the kitchen for dinner.

I was, under my grandmother's tutelage, getting pretty good at cooking. I could now just pick one of her recipes and, if it was simple enough, make it without supervision. Earlier in the day I'd made a quiche with asparagus and mushrooms, and as I heated up a couple of pieces, Kennette played with Barney.

Kennette seemed perfectly at ease in the house and in the clothes I'd lent her. She'd paired my gray argyle V-neck sweater with a pair of brown cords and tied a light blue silk scarf around her neck. They were probably the most boring clothes in my closet and yet, on her, they looked artsy and cool.

"I need to go out after we eat," I said, trying to sound casual. I didn't want any questions because Kennette didn't seem like the type to keep a secret.

"Okay. Can I take Barney for a walk while you're gone?"

"He'd love that. In fact I think he loves *you*." Barney's leg was shaking in that blissful doggy way as Kennette scratched his ear. "Just be careful."

She smiled. "We'll be fine. Barney will be my attack dog if anyone tries to approach us."

I nodded. I didn't want to remind her about the dead girl. I had a feeling that Kennette was just beginning to feel at home, and I didn't want to take that away from her. Still, I said it again. "Just be careful."

As soon as Kennette and Barney headed toward the river for their walk, I jumped into the car. I didn't exactly know what I was going to say, but I knew I had to say something. When I parked the car outside Jesse's house, I could see through the window that the TV was on and there was movement inside.

I was pretty sure I would look foolish no matter what excuse I came up with, so I didn't bother. I just took a deep breath and headed for the door.

"Hi," a surprised Jesse answered.

"Is it all right if I come in?"

"Yeah, of course."

He opened the door and let me walk past him into the living room. In the months I'd lived in Archers Rest, I'd been to Jesse's house twice. His living room was comfortable and lived in, with his daughter's toys all over the place. It was welcoming except for the five pictures of his dead wife, Lizzy: their wedding photo, a vacation snapshot, and three photos with their baby. They made me feel like the other woman.

"You want something to drink?"

Jesse was already heading toward the kitchen without waiting for a response, so I sat on the sofa. When he came back, he handed me a beer and sat very close to me.

"Where's Allie?" I asked.

"In bed. Your timing is perfect."

"I was driving around and I thought . . ."

"No you weren't." Jesse grinned. "I know exactly why you're here."

I sat up. "You do?"

He nodded, then leaned in and kissed me. It was the kiss of a man who was very sure of himself, and it sort of threw me. Still, I stayed kissing him for several minutes before I offered a protest.

"What are you doing?" I said when I finally pulled away. "I didn't come here for that."

"Okay. That's fine." Jesse took a slug of his beer. "So what did you come over for?"

"I don't know. I kind of forget now," I laughed.

"Let me know when you remember."

He leaned in and kissed me again, but before things got out of hand I stopped him.

"How's the case going?"

"Aren't you a little warm in that coat?"

"No, I'm fine," I said. "Did you find anything else about that girl?"

"I think you should take your coat off." Jesse reached over and started easing it off.

"Have you figured out where she lived?"

Jesse began kissing my neck.

"What's gotten into you?" I got up. "Where's my shy police chief?"

Jesse stood up, inches away from me, and took a deep breath. "The case is going slowly. Is that really what you came over about?"

The truth was that, yes, it really was what I came over about. But now it seemed like a bad idea to admit it.

"No, I came over because it's a Saturday night and Eleanor and Oliver went on their date and . . ." I shrugged. I knew playing insecure female would get me in less trouble than amateur detective.

Jesse nodded and took my hand. "I'm sorry. I've been spending a lot of time at the station. And I hadn't spent any time with Allie in over a week, so I figured I'd give her my Saturday night. I should have just told you instead of making you wonder what was going on."

"It's okay. But you can talk to me about things, you know. I am your friend."

"Got it," he said. "Take your coat off and tell me everything that's been going on."

We sat back on the couch, and I filled him in on class, Kennette, and my grandmother's big date. He told me about the coffee machine breaking at the jail and finding a dirty pink backpack downriver from the crime scene.

"Maybe it belonged to that girl Lily," I suggested.

"We're looking into it."

"The 'we're' means you and Chief Powell?"

He nodded. "He thinks she was murdered in his town."

"He just wants an excuse to muscle in on your case."

"She was found near Morristown."

"But in Archers Rest," I pointed out.

"Yeah," he agreed. "But based on the current of the river that night, Powell might be right."

"But that would give him jurisdiction, wouldn't it?"

He sat up a little and looked at me. "Not that you care, right?"

"I'm just expressing an interest in your work." I tried to sound as innocent as possible. "In fact I heard that some kids may have found a photo and I thought it might be something."

"Yes. I think it is something."

"Really?" I brightened. "Because I got the impression from Susanne's nephew that you had sort of dismissed it."

He laughed. "I knew it. You've been poking around."

"I have not. Susanne came to me and told me what Rich had said, so I talked to him."

"That's poking around."

"Jesse, I talked to a friend of mine's nephew. That's it. And you think it's something."

"I think it's none of your business."

"I'm a citizen. I have a right to know if there's a crazed killer on the loose."

"Well if there is, you are putting yourself in danger."

"Then tell me why you didn't take Rich seriously and I'll stay out it. We can go back to kissing."

"That sounds suspiciously like you're trying to bribe an official."

I smiled. "What if I am?"

"If I tell you, then you have to stop interfering. You leave the detective work to me."

"A counter bribe."

"A threat, actually."

"Okay. No more interfering." I knew I was lying. I assumed Jesse did as well, but I knew it made him feel better to think, at least for a while, that I was staying out of it. "You said you thought there was something to the photo," I reminded him. "What?"

"I think it's a waste of time." He took a sip of his beer. "Rich and his friends like to get high down by the river. They also like to break into houses. He has a long history with me, and one of the things I've learned is that he likes to embellish."

"You think he's lying."

"I think that a dozen police officers from two towns went over that crime scene for days and no photo was found."

"But someone could have taken it. The killer could have seen that the boys discovered the body and when they called the police—"

Jesse stopped me. "You're assuming that the photo, if it existed, has something to do with the murder. And you're assuming that the killer was standing around watching the action and then moved in and took the photo while the boys were waiting for the police. Except no one saw the killer."

I could see his frustration.

"The photo doesn't exist," he said firmly. "End of story." He shifted his body toward me. "We're done with this, Nell."

I wasn't getting more information, and I certainly didn't want to fight, so I dropped the subject.

"You want your bribe?" I asked.

He nodded. "I don't want you to think this will work every time."

"If you'd rather not—" I started.

Rather than let me finish, Jesse leaned in and kissed me.

CHAPTER 13

Eleanor said nothing about her evening with Oliver except, "It was nice," and Kennette and I decided to leave it alone. Every morning Kennette went to the shop with Eleanor. I went with them, but instead of going to Someday Quilts, I went to Carrie's coffee shop across the street. The idea of doing a mural still intimidated me, but Carrie liked my sketches so I bought the paints and prepared to move forward.

I lightly sketched out my idea on the wall. The plan was a cartoonish skyline of New York "poured" from a giant coffeepot. One of the buildings, of course, would feature the exterior of Carrie's coffee shop; that is, if she could come up with a name.

"I don't think it should be Carrie's," she said. "That seems a bit too arrogant, don't you think?"

"I don't know. I think it's cute. In fact the whole place is cute."

Carrie had been making quite a lot of progress on the shop. Now that it was painted, she was slowly bringing in furniture. It was all mismatched, bought from yard sales and secondhand shops. She arranged the chairs and tables toward the back, leaving the front open for the counter and a large couch. Maggie had given her an old sofa from the seventies that was ugly but still in good shape. Carrie reupholstered it in bright purple velvet, which gave the place exactly the funky East Village coffee shop look she wanted.

It must have seemed that my time was completely taken up with work, school, and the mural. And it was. But that was only because

I was completely stuck on what to do next about the murder of Lily Harmon. Jesse wasn't going to let me tag along on his investigation, and my grandmother would put me in the morgue if she thought I was out chasing a killer. But I knew I had to do something. Rich had seen a photo on the ground, and if it meant nothing, it would have been in evidence. So either it had been taken by the killer, lost somehow, or—and this nagged at me—Jesse was lying about it.

✄

On Thursday I drove with Kennette to class. I wasn't much in the mood to talk, which wasn't a problem since Kennette tended to go on and on about Oliver—what he might say, what we might learn, even what he might wear.

"Does Eleanor have competition in you?" I asked, only half joking.

Kennette blushed. "Do you think he's called her since their date? She hasn't said anything."

I noticed she hadn't answered my question, but she had raised an interesting, and embarrassing, point.

"It's going to be awkward if he hasn't," I said, almost to myself.

"He must have," Kennette said firmly. "He's too good a person to hurt Eleanor."

"He'd better be." I felt like I had another mystery to uncover. What was going on with my grandmother and my teacher?

Once in class, I didn't have to wait long. Oliver came over as I was setting up my easel and smiled.

"I'm so looking forward to dinner on Saturday," he said. "I have a feeling your grandmother is a wonderful cook."

"She is," I stumbled. My surprise was obvious.

"You should ask your young man," he said. "Eleanor told me that the two of you make a fascinating couple."

"She used that word?"

He laughed. "Not exactly. She said she thought you would be good for each other if you got out of your own way."

"That sounds more like her."

Oliver smiled again then moved on to another student. I turned to Kennette, who had been pretending to arrange her pencils during the entire conversation.

"Dinner on Saturday. That's cool, huh?" she said.

"Why wouldn't she mention it, though? Do you think she doesn't want us to know?" I asked.

"Should we be there?"

"I don't want to be there. You, me, them. We would be sitting there while they giggled and stared at each other."

"They won't giggle. They're in their seventies," Kennette whispered.

"I don't care what they do," I told her. "I'm going nowhere near the house on Saturday."

Kennette looked disappointed but smiled. "I could hang out at the shop. I'm only half finished piecing the top for my drunkard's path."

"I'll help," I offered. "Anything not to be at the house when Oliver arrives."

I was emphatic with Kennette, but as class went on I started to lose my certainty. Once again Oliver spent just a little more time with Sandra than he did with anyone else in the class, and once again he praised her a little more than she deserved. Worst of all, once again as he walked to his office after class Sandra followed him.

If he really was getting involved with Eleanor, he had better be worthy of her. And as he let Sandra into his office and closed the door behind him, I felt more and more sure that he wasn't.

"I have to do something," I said to Kennette. "Can you wait for me to drive to the shop?"

"What do you have to do?" Kennette had become like my little sister. Always tagging along, both a welcome friend and a tiresome pest.

"Nothing special. I just want to talk to Oliver."

"You want to ask him about your work?" she said. "It's really good, you know. Especially when you paint on fabric. You are freer on fabric than you are on canvas."

I looked at her. "How do you do that?" I asked.

She blushed. "What?"

"I've been trying to figure out what's wrong with my work and you nailed it. I'm trying too hard in class. When I paint on squares to make a quilt, I figure if I make a mistake, who cares? I'm learning."

"Aren't you taking this class to learn?"

"Yes but when I work on fabric I don't have Oliver White standing there judging me."

"I don't think he's judging you. I think he's guiding you. He's trying to make all of us better. Just like when Maggie helps me with a seam or Bernie suggests a color. They're all so excited to have other people interested in the thing they love."

"But they're not Oliver White," I insisted. Except, I wondered, who is Oliver White anyway?

And then his office door opened. I grabbed Kennette and pushed her against the wall around the corner.

"Shh," I instructed. She nodded.

Sandra walked out first, with Oliver right behind her. He wrapped his arms around her and held her against him for a long time. It seemed as though she had been crying. She said something to him but I couldn't hear it. His voice was louder, deeper, and slightly easier to hear.

I thought he said, "I've never wanted anything more in my life."

Then he reached into his pocket and took something out. It looked like money. She took it and nodded. Then she walked down the hallway and he went back to his office.

"Give me a minute," I whispered, leaving Kennette in the hallway.

"Oliver," I stood in the doorway. Oliver was sitting at this desk just a few feet away, but it seemed as if he didn't hear me. "Oliver," I said again.

"Sorry. Yes, Nell." He stood.

"Is everything okay?" I had no idea how he would react but I was going to say it anyway. "I saw Sandra leave your office in tears."

"She does cry a lot," he sighed. "Poor girl."

"It's just that she has so much attitude with everyone except you."

Oliver's face was a blank. I tried to read a little guilt or fear or something in his eyes, but there was nothing but a pleasant and empty smile. He reached into his pockets but came out empty-handed. Then he looked around his desk, confused.

"Missing something?"

"A pack of cigarettes. Not important." He sat back and looked up at me. "Your grandmother is quite a woman. She seems to have overcome a lot and with such grace."

"Yes," I said. "She believes in doing the right thing. No matter how tough it is."

"I imagine she's instilled that in you."

"She wouldn't want to be around someone who wasn't good and decent and responsible."

I wondered if he heard my warning. He just smiled. Then he placed his hand on my back and walked with me out of the office, locking the door behind him.

Kennette had disappeared, so I walked down the hallway to find her. I was about to give up when she came walking out of the ladies' restroom.

"Ready?" She smiled.

I nodded. "Give me a minute."

I was surprised to see that my hands were shaking. What was it about Oliver that so unnerved me? It made me admire my grandmother more that she seemed able to hold her own with him. I walked into the ladies' room to wash my face, but before I had a chance, I saw Sandra at the mirror.

"What do you want?" she shouted.

"It's a bathroom. What do you think I want?" I snapped back. Oliver might intimidate me, but she didn't.

I turned on the sink and washed my hands, but I kept my eyes on the mirror. Behind me Sandra was smoking a cigarette and staring at the ceiling, anger all over her face.

"Oliver is really getting to you," I ventured.

"Meaning?"

"You always seem to be upset around him."

She shifted her weight. "Screw you."

Charming. I wasn't going to be able to match her attitude so I went a different way. "I'm just saying that if Oliver is doing something he shouldn't . . ."

"He's not."

"He's doing something."

She threw her cigarette in the sink. "Jealous?" She swept passed me and out the door.

It was a dramatic exit, to be sure. But as far as I was concerned the conversation wasn't over. Next class, and every class, I was going to push them both until I found out what was going on.

"He's paying her to be his lover," I said on the drive to the shop.

"That makes no sense," Kennette said. "He's not like that."

"Okay, so she's in trouble and he's helping."

"Much more likely."

"What if she's pregnant with his child?"

"Gross!" Kennette shouted. "He's not going around getting some student in . . . that way."

"Come up with a good reason why he keeps having these secret meetings with a student, then hugs her and gives her money."

"He's nice," she sounded exasperated. "He's just nice."

"Well even if he is the nicest man on the planet, I am not leaving him alone with my grandmother. I'll tell you that."

"So we're going to be there on Saturday?" Kennette smiled.

"You, me, and the chief of police."

CHAPTER 14

If Eleanor was annoyed to have her romantic dinner for two turned into a family meal for five, she didn't show it. She stayed home on Saturday to cook, which left the shop entirely to Kennette and myself.

And it was probably a good idea. About once an hour a member of the quilt club came in to get the scoop on the plans for the evening. I had no news to tell them, but at least we could talk openly on the subject. The night before, at our regular Friday meeting, we'd all stepped around it. Instead we spent the evening finishing Kennette's quilt top and discussing the importance of an accurate seam allowance.

The only subterfuge was when we arranged for Carrie's husband to call with a crisis at home, entirely false, so that she would leave early. Her shop was opening in a month, and we were planning a large group quilt for the blank side wall. As much as we were keeping it a secret, I was pretty sure Carrie knew. After all, she had me painting a mural on the back wall. She had cool mirrors and paintings ready for the area behind the counter. But one large wall was left blank, and Carrie was quiet about what she planned to put there. I assumed she was holding the space for her "surprise" quilt.

We had decided on something modern and abstract, and Susanne was putting together sketches for approval. She had said it might take her a week to get truly inspired, but she showed up Saturday afternoon with three beautifully realized ideas.

"These are gorgeous. I'd vote for any of them," I said.

"Keep them with you and make sure everyone gets to look at them," Susanne told me. "And take notes."

"On the sketches?"

"On what happens tonight."

I leaned in so Kennette, who was straightening fabric, would not hear. "I don't think I trust him."

"You don't have a reason, do you?"

I did. At least I thought maybe I did. But I couldn't say anything. If I mentioned Sandra to anyone without first telling Eleanor, I would be a bad friend to the one person who had been there for me when my life had fallen apart. So I shook my head.

"I guess I'm just annoyed that her love life is moving along more smoothly than mine," I said.

"Maybe having dinner with Oliver will teach Jesse a thing or two about romance." She smiled. "Besides, I hear we're up for a big snow storm this evening, so maybe they'll both have to spend the night. That will be cozy."

I smiled but the thought made me a little sick.

Once dinner started, a hearty meal of my grandmother's special meat loaf and mashed potatoes, romance seemed to be the last thing on anyone's mind. Jesse and Oliver were good-naturedly arguing about English football, which, I found out, Jesse actually followed.

"Anytime you put two guys on a field with a ball, I'll watch it," Jesse admitted a little shyly.

"Good for you," Oliver said. "Though you really should support Liverpool over Manchester United."

"You're nuts" was Jesse's response as he stuffed more potatoes in his mouth.

On the other side of the dining room table, Eleanor, Kennette, and I were pretty much left out of the conversation, so we ended up discussing Carrie's quilt. The separate conversations continued for more than ten minutes, until a beeping noise from Oliver's jacket interrupted. He reached in for his phone, looked at it for a moment, and frowned.

"This text messaging is a bother," he said, and he put the phone back in his jacket. "Doesn't anyone want to have a conversation anymore?"

"Isn't that what we're having?" Kennette asked.

"Well, we're actually having two conversations," I corrected her. "You guys are talking sports, and we're talking about abstract quilt designs."

"We're making a quilt for one of the club members who's opening a coffee shop," Eleanor explained.

"And it's abstract in design?" Oliver's interest was piqued. "What are your influences?"

"No one person, as far as I know. Susanne just drew several designs," I said. "One is pretty much boxes of colors. It's kind of a variation on a log cabin design. The second is appliquéd circles and semicircles on squares made up of strips, and the third is an Amish-style quilt with lines of bright fabrics alternating with background stripes of black.

"I like the second," Kennette offered.

Oliver leaned toward her. "Why?"

I felt suddenly like we were in class, but Kennette was relaxed. "I don't know," she said without a hint of insecurity. "I just like it."

Oliver smiled and leaned back. "You have a clarity of vision that one rarely sees in a new artist."

Kennette beamed and Jesse winked at me. It was, I had to admit, a nice evening.

"Dessert anyone?" Eleanor jumped up. "I've made an apple pie."

"Let me help," offered Oliver. The two left the room for the kitchen and were gone for just a little longer than it would have taken to bring in the pie, plates, and a pot of tea. When they came back, they were both smiling. Watching the way Oliver shyly moved around Eleanor, I was a little jealous of their smooth romance. But not for long. I reached out and took Jesse's hand.

"Well." Kennette got up from the table. "I think it's time my date and I went for a walk." She patted Barney and he jumped up and headed for the door.

"What about dessert?" Eleanor asked.

"I won't be long."

"Take my wool coat." Eleanor disappeared into the hallway and came back with a teal blue coat. "It's very cold outside tonight. The wind is howling something fierce."

Kennette was swallowed by the large, heavy coat as well as the scarf and hat Eleanor had brought for her, but she didn't seem to mind. I think she enjoyed being the center of so much fussing. Once fully enclosed in the winter getup, she patted Barney's head and he followed her out of the dining room.

"We'll be right back," she said.

"We'll have hot tea waiting for you," Eleanor called after her.

"And keep a cup hot for me." Oliver grabbed his coat. He reached into the pocket and pulled out a pack of cigarettes. "Nasty habit. I'd like to tell you I'm giving them up, but I've already given up too many delicious cravings. I'm keeping the ones I have left, no matter how ill-advised."

He opened the back door and stepped outside.

"Stay on the back porch," Eleanor said to him. "It's protected from the wind and snow."

"A smoker," I chided Eleanor once Oliver was gone.

"A man's allowed his vices," she said. "Jesse, you look like you could use a piece of pie."

"Yes, ma'am." Jesse gave me a look that said he'd noticed what I had. Eleanor was smitten.

Ten minutes later when he came back into the dining room, Oliver's hands and face were wet.

"See, I told you it was cold outside," Eleanor said as she gently touched his cheek. Oliver took her hand.

"I washed up a little to keep that nasty cigarette smell from ruining the scent of your pie." He kissed her finger and she smiled at him, while Jesse and I pretended not to notice how happy they both seemed.

Oliver, Jesse, and I each had two slices of pie before Eleanor took the plates away. "Save some for Kennette," she scolded as she put the kettle on for a second time.

"Where is she?" Jesse asked. "It's been at least half an hour."

"Maybe we should go out and look," I said.

"Barney's with her," Eleanor tried to reassure us, but she looked worried. "He has some sense, that dog."

"If he had any sense he would have come in twenty minutes ago. It's cold out there," I reminded her.

"I'll go." Jesse got up.

"I'll go with you." I stood next to him.

He looked like he was about to protest, but then he nodded. "Oliver, you and Eleanor hold down the fort. If I can borrow a flashlight, that will help. Nell will take her cell with her, so call her if Kennette or Barney comes back."

"What do you mean Kennette *or* Barney?" Eleanor asked. "They'll be together."

"Then why aren't they back?" I asked.

"Barney just got interested in some squirrel, that's all." Eleanor took a deep breath and Oliver put his arm protectively around her.

Jesse and I wrapped up warmly and headed out. It was snowing, but for a while Jesse was able to find a set of human tracks and a set of dog tracks. Then, near the river, both sets disappeared.

Ice crystals were forming on my face, and the wind was making it hard for me to keep my eyes on Jesse. I was getting confused even though I knew the area, and Kennette had only been at the house for just over a week.

"Stay with me," Jesse shouted. "Stay right next to me but look in the opposite direction."

I nodded and stood with my back to him. I could see nothing but snow, and I could feel nothing but cold mixed with a growing sense of panic.

"What could have happened to them?" I asked Jesse.

"Barney probably ran after something and Kennette got lost looking for him." Jesse sounded so sure. I leaned my head against his shoulder just for a moment of comfort. As I did, my phone rang.

"She's back?" I asked before Eleanor had a chance to speak.

"No." Eleanor's voice sounded frantic. "Barney is back. He's covered in ice and snow. And he's soaking wet."

"And he's alone?"

Her voice was almost a whisper. "He's alone."

I hung up and started to tell Jesse, but it was clear he had figured out the situation. "She's lost out here, that's all." Jesse turned toward me and held me. "Don't get scared. It takes longer than a half hour to freeze to death in this weather."

"You're right. It's just that it's easy to get lost."

"But she'll walk toward the light coming from the house. She's got common sense, right?"

Against my better judgment, I laughed. "Not really. But she's got a way of getting herself help."

Jesse grabbed my hand and started to walk toward the river, shining the flashlight on the water. "If Barney is wet, maybe he walked into the water. Maybe she followed him."

With the snow and the incline, walking became nearly impossible. I grabbed Jesse's coat and held on. I knew I was slowing him down but I couldn't turn back. If Kennette was in trouble, then I was partly responsible. I'd brought her to Eleanor's house, I'd insisted she be here for this dinner party, and I'd let her go out into the cold alone so I could sit with Jesse.

"It's not your fault, you know," Jesse said.

"How did you know what I was thinking?"

"I know you," he said.

I smiled. He did know me, and that was pretty cool. I looked up at him, his glasses frosting over in the cold, and I thought how lucky I was to have found such a good man. But before I had a chance to say that, something flashed behind him.

I stopped and took a deep breath. "Something's in the water," I said slowly. "I don't know what it is."

"Stay here," he said. "Stay right here." He moved slowly, deliberately, toward the water.

"What is it?" I shouted.

For what seemed like an eternity, Jesse said nothing. Then he turned back to me. "It's a body," he shouted back. "A woman."

CHAPTER 15

Within minutes officers from Archers Rest and Morristown were crawling all over my grandmother's home and backyard. The snow had stopped, but that made moving around only slightly easier. When I came back inside, I sat in the kitchen so I could have a clear view of the backyard. Oliver had put his tweed jacket over a chair and was doing the dishes. Eleanor worriedly brought blankets into the kitchen.

"Kennette will be cold when she comes home," Eleanor said.

Oliver took Eleanor's hand but said nothing. Like me, he probably didn't know what to say.

"I'm quite fond of her," Eleanor said. "Some people you can know your whole life and never feel close to. And others you just connect with right away." She looked toward Oliver and he smiled.

I wanted to say something but nothing would come out. I was irrationally angry at Barney for not being Lassie. I was angry at myself for letting her go out, and I was angry at Oliver for coming over and creating this stupid dinner party.

I got up, put my coat back on, and went outside. I saw Jesse and Chief Powell down by the river but they were in no hurry. It was clear that, whoever it was, the person was well past saving. Warm tears stung as they hit my cold cheeks.

"What's going on?"

I turned toward a vaguely familiar voice and saw a teal wool coat coming toward me.

I ran to her and grabbed her.

"She's okay! She's okay!" I shouted. "She's okay."

Jesse came running toward me and Eleanor and Oliver came out of the house, without their coats. Barney ran after them, jumping at Kennette and me excitedly. Kennette struggled to get away from me, and when she did, she looked at all of us as if we were nuts.

"What's wrong?" She looked from face to face, more upset than we were.

"Where have you been?" I yelled at her.

Tears welled in her eyes. "I lost Barney and when I went looking for him, I got lost. I couldn't see in the snow."

That was exactly what Jesse said had happened. But it was such a simple, logical explanation that I had been unwilling to believe it.

"Where did you go?" I asked, my voice still a full octave above normal.

Kennette was looking at all the fuss around her and seemed more confused than anything. "I went into this little sheltered area down river." She pointed away from the house.

"Why didn't you call?" I was still yelling. I knew how irrational I sounded but I didn't care.

"I don't have a cell phone," she said quietly.

"Come inside now," Eleanor said.

Jesse took my arm. "Get inside," he said quietly. "Get her warm. We'll get her story, but first she needs to calm down. We all do."

"Come with us," I said. "Everything's okay now."

"We still have a dead girl in the river," Jesse pointed out.

How weird that I had forgotten that.

"Do you know who she is?" I asked.

"Not yet."

"Can I see her?"

Jesse shrugged and pointed toward the body, now lying on the snowy ground near the water. I walked slowly over to the spot, nearly slipping twice. When I got to the body, I turned white.

"Oh my God" was all I could get out.

"What?" Jesse grabbed me and turned me away from the body. "Do you know her?"

"What's going on?" Powell walked over. "This is a crime scene."

"She knows the victim," Jesse said quietly.

I was shaking, surprised by my own reaction. Once I knew it wasn't Kennette, I had expected the woman to be a stranger.

"Let's get back to the house," Jesse whispered to me.

I nodded and Jesse pressed me against his chest and led me back to the house. Powell followed, barking orders at the other officers as he went.

Once inside I sat at the kitchen table, surrounded by Oliver, Eleanor, Kennette, and Barney. They all looked at me with panic in their eyes. Behind them Powell leaned against the door, as if blocking my escape. Only Jesse seemed calm. He crouched down in front of me and looked into my eyes.

"Nell, how do you know that girl?" he asked.

I took a deep breath. "From class. She's . . ." I looked up at Kennette and then Oliver before turning back to Jesse. "Her name is Sandra. She's in the art class Kennette and I take."

I quickly looked up to see Oliver's reaction. If there was one, it didn't show. He barely blinked.

"Poor dear," Eleanor said. "Did she fall into the river somehow?"

"If she did, she's the second woman to do that in less than a month," Jesse said flatly.

"Lily," I said, more to myself than anyone. "She's connected to Lily."

"We don't know that yet," Powell interrupted. "All we know is that two women ended up in the river. And one of them was two hundred yards from your house."

"Meaning?" Eleanor asked, a hardness in her voice that usually intimidated. But not this time.

"Meaning, ma'am," Powell said, "that perhaps she has a connection to someone in this room."

"She was my student," Oliver volunteered, "so I probably had more contact with her than anyone else. Though that doesn't amount to much beyond some constructive criticism and a little encouragement. Perhaps she became friends with Kennette or Nell. Her easel was next to Nell's."

"She didn't. She spoke to Oliver more than she spoke to me," I said as pointedly as I could.

"Well, Oliver," Jesse asked, "can you recall if she said anything about coming to Archers Rest?"

"No. Why would she?"

"Maybe coming to see you?" Powell offered.

He shook his head. "I'm always friendly with my students. I'd be happy to answer any questions, but I know almost nothing about her."

Powell turned toward Oliver and took out a notebook. "What did you know?"

"She wanted to be an artist, but she had minimal talent," Oliver said. "Obviously that upset her."

Is that why she was always crying around him? Another simple, logical explanation I hadn't thought of.

"Would she have any reason to come to this house?" Jesse asked.

"I have no idea," Oliver said, his voice steady.

"Had she been here before?" Powell turned to me.

"No, I barely knew her," I said. "I never told her what town I lived in, let alone what house."

Kennette nodded. "I meant to be friendlier, but I guess she just seemed so . . ." She paused. I could tell Kennette was carefully choosing her words. "She seemed uninterested in getting to know anyone."

Not entirely true, I thought. She was interested in getting to know Oliver. But I said nothing. Powell would take that kind of thing way too seriously, and for all I knew there was nothing more to it than a famous artist comforting someone who would never reach her goal. Except, I wondered, why did he give her money?

After Powell went back outside, Jesse took me into the living room and held me for a long time.

"What's going on?" I asked quietly.

"I don't know. Something bad."

"What's the connection between Lily and Sandra?"

"Nell," he pulled back and looked at me sternly. "There may not be one, except that they were both young women. Women about your age."

"A serial killer in Archers Rest?"

"I don't know. Whoever it was, there was a killer in your backyard tonight."

I nodded. "Maybe closer than that."

Jesse kissed me lightly. "I'll be back when we've finished up here. Allie is going to stay at my mother's tonight, so I'm going to stay here."

I smiled. "Not how I pictured our first night together."

"We'll have lots of nights together." He kissed me again and then left the room. I heard him walk out the front door, but I didn't want to go back into the kitchen so I sat on the couch and stared out the window into the lights from half a dozen police cars.

Suddenly there was a voice behind me. "We need to make up the couch for Oliver," Kennette said.

"He's staying?"

"Yes. He's very protective of your grandmother." She smiled.

"Jesse is staying too," I told her. And I was suddenly very glad he was.

"I don't know where we're all going to sleep."

I had a bigger question. With another dead woman washing ashore, this one only a few yards from the house, I wondered *if* we were going to sleep.

CHAPTER 16

It was more than an hour before Jesse came back to the house, and when he did, he was cold, tired, and in no mood to discuss the case. We had already decided that Kennette would stay with me in the guest room and Jesse would take the pullout sofa in Eleanor's office, where Kennette had been sleeping. Oliver went to sleep on the couch in the living room, and Eleanor went to her room with Barney.

By midnight the house was dark and quiet. Kennette was lightly snoring beside me and I was staring at the ceiling. How had Sandra ended up in the river right beside this house? The only logical explanation was that she had come to see someone, and the only someone she would have come to see was Oliver.

I went over every detail of the evening but nothing was unusual until Kennette disappeared. Then I remembered something. It was small and probably meaningless but I had to check.

I got out of bed as quietly as I could, though I had a feeling I could have jumped up and down and not woken Kennette. It was odd that she could sleep so peacefully when there was a killer on the loose.

I crept into the hallway and noticed that the door to Eleanor's office was open. It would have been fun, under different circumstances, to go to Jesse's room and wake him up. But that would have to wait for another night. I moved down the stairs and into the hallway to the kitchen, then stopped cold when I saw the light was on.

"Hungry?" Jesse was sitting at the table, staring at the back door.

"No, just couldn't sleep."

He nodded. "What was she like?"

"Sandra?" I asked.

I sat in the chair where Oliver had left his jacket, which still hung over the back. "She was . . ." I searched for the right word, "emotional." Then I told him how I'd seen Sandra and Oliver together and how she had been crying. And I told him about the scene in the ladies' room just days earlier.

"You don't think it was because she wasn't a very good artist?"

"The weird thing is that he praised her in class, over-the-top kind of praise. Something he didn't do for anyone else." I paused. "Except maybe Kennette, but Kennette is talented."

"And Sandra wasn't."

"Not to the extent he said she was. And if he was telling her she was so good in class . . . ," I started.

"Why did he tell us she wasn't?"

I nodded and leaned back, slowly slipping my hand into the pocket of Oliver's jacket.

"It's not in there."

I sat up, startled that I had been caught. "What's not in there?" I tried to play dumb.

Jesse smiled and opened his hand to reveal Oliver's phone.

"What did the text say?"

"You think there's a connection?"

"Well you obviously do, or you wouldn't have the phone," I said. "And you must have noticed that he seemed unhappy about the text and then went out for a cigarette not ten minutes later. Maybe she told him that she was outside."

"That's what I thought, but it says, 'Too soon to talk. Needs more time.' "

"What does that mean?"

"Don't know."

"But you know it's from Sandra?"

"Don't know that either."

I smiled. "Would you tell me if you did?"

Jesse shrugged. "I might. You would have a better idea of who Sandra wanted to see."

"That's just it. She could only have been coming to see Oliver."

"Except, how did she know he would be here?"

"Well who else?"

Jesse stared at me. I finally got what he was trying not to say. "You're crazy. Kennette wouldn't hurt anyone."

"You sure about that?" he asked.

Back in bed I tossed and turned while one of Jesse's prime suspects slept beside me. What did I really know about Kennette anyway? She never spoke about herself or her past. She didn't seem to have one. And wasn't it just as likely that Sandra was coming to the house to see Kennette—who lived here—as it was that she had come to see Oliver? I didn't like what I was thinking.

As soon as it was daylight, I got up and dressed. I wanted to take a walk down to the river and get as close to the crime scene as I could. I could hear Barney getting restless in Eleanor's room so I let him out. He would make good cover in case Jesse or Oliver, or I guess Kennette, wondered what I was doing wandering around.

But once outside, Barney had his own ideas. He didn't seem interested in venturing out into the woods, and who could blame him? The snow was more than a foot deep, and after last night's adventure, he'd probably had enough. But when I left Barney at the back porch so I could walk to the river, he started barking.

"Shh," I called back. Barney paced back and forth by the house. I knew the poor deaf dog couldn't hear me, and he probably felt left out, but I need to have a look around, so I kept walking.

I didn't know what I was supposed to be looking for. I thought maybe there would be a photo near this dead body the way there was by Lily. Maybe there was. But with all the snow it would have been hard to find. It was hard to find anything.

I could see where the body had been pulled onto the bank from the river. I could see where the police had walked back and forth. I could see an area that had been cleared where Jesse and the others had searched for evidence. And when I closed my eyes, I could see Sandra's cold, dead eyes.

Barney's barking was getting louder. I knew I would have to go back or the whole house would be awake.

"What are you doing?" I asked him as I petted his cold fur. "Did you go to the bathroom?"

Barney just wagged and circled me excitedly. I tried to calm him, but he just kept jumping at me like we hadn't seen each other for years. I bent down to quiet him, but instead he knocked me over onto the porch.

"Okay, Barney." It seems mean-spirited to get annoyed at doggy love, but I was getting annoyed. "If you don't stop this, I'll put you back in the house."

I struggled to get up, and as I did, I saw something. A dark spot on the white pillar holding up my grandmother's porch. I untangled myself from the dog and went closer. It was just a bit above eye level, so I could get right up to it. It wasn't just a dark spot, I realized. It had small clumps of something in it: hair. Long hair.

"It's blood," Jesse said. I had gone back into the house and woken him up, but in doing so I seemed to have gotten everyone else up as well. Eleanor, Kennette, and Oliver all came out to see what I had found.

"Is it from that poor girl?" Eleanor asked.

"Maybe," Jesse offered. "We'll have to get the state police to send a blood-spatter expert." He reached into his coat pocket for his phone and stopped. "Everyone just go back into the house. It's freezing out here."

The others followed Jesse's advice but I stayed outside. "If it is her blood, does it mean she hit her head on that post?" I asked.

"Several times and very hard."

"Hard enough to kill her?"

"Maybe."

"But that would mean she was killed two feet from my back door."
I said.

"Go inside, Nell."

"That's not possible." It didn't make any sense. "We would have
heard something," I said.

Jesse glanced at me, a look of slight irritation on his face. "I know
you want to help, but just go inside. I have officers on the way who can
deal with this." He walked over to me and took my hand. "Let's not
speculate. Let's just wait until we have answers."

I nodded. But how could I not speculate? The murder that had
started with a stranger in the river was now getting closer and closer
to home.

CHAPTER 17

After Oliver left to paint and Kennette went to open the shop, Eleanor and I sat in the kitchen. We were both too shocked to carry on a decent conversation. We kept starting sentences: "How could . . . ?" "Who would want . . . ?" But then we would stop. Whatever our questions were, we knew that for the moment there were no answers.

I would have been happy to crawl back into bed and get the sleep I hadn't gotten the night before, but I knew my mind wouldn't allow me to rest, so I sat there.

"That will be the girls," my grandmother said as the doorbell rang.

"Who called them?"

She ignored me and went toward the front door. I could hear Maggie, Bernie, Susanne, and Natalie talking in hushed and serious tones as they walked toward the kitchen.

"Oh, my dear, how are you doing?" Bernie leaned over to hug me, nearly dropping a plate of cookies in my lap.

"I'm okay. I'm worried about Grandma."

"I'm fine." Eleanor sniffed. "Honestly, I don't know what the world is coming to. It's so much worse than when we were young."

"Don't be an old woman," said Maggie, who sat next to me at the table. "The world has always been in trouble. We just didn't pay much attention when we were young."

"It wasn't at my back door." Eleanor shook her head. She looked for a moment as if she were about to cry, an unheard of event in my experience of her. Then she took a deep breath and said, "We need to set up in the dining room, so I'll need some help getting the machines downstairs."

Bernie and Natalie followed her out of the room, leaving Susanne, Maggie, and myself to stare out the window at the police team gathered around the porch.

"What are we setting up?" I asked. I'd been left completely out of the loop on this.

"Carrie's quilt," Susanne said. "We're cutting and sewing the top together today."

"No one told me."

"It will be a nice distraction," Susanne said. Then she sighed. "It's a shame the evening got spoiled."

"Never mind that," Maggie cut in. "Do you have any idea who could have done it?"

"None," I admitted. "But I do wonder why Sandra was here."

"You think she came to see someone?" Susanne sat up.

I didn't know if I should say anything. After all, it was little more than idle gossip at this point. But finally I said, "She spent a lot of time with Oliver."

Maggie gasped. "Please don't tell me you think he did anything?"

"I don't know."

Susanne waved me off. "He was with you the entire night. Eleanor told me."

"He went outside to have a cigarette. He was standing on the porch where . . ." I stopped.

"What do we really know about him?" Maggie asked quietly.

Susanne was having none of it. "He's a famous artist. One Google search and you would find a thousand things about him."

"There are a lot of things about a person that don't show up on the Internet," Maggie said. She leaned toward me. "When I was the town librarian, I got pretty good at doing research, even without the technology we have today."

"You think you could find out something about him?" I asked.

Maggie looked around. "I could try."

Susanne stood up. "Eleanor's happy. And you might dig up something that would upset her. Something that's no one's business."

"At this point I'm more worried about my grandmother's safety than her happiness. If Oliver is involved, then we have to know about it," I said.

Susanne stared at me for a long, hard moment. "If he's involved in this, then you think he's involved in the other one as well, don't you?"

I didn't answer but I didn't have to. Maggie and Susanne already knew what I was thinking. And I could tell that they were thinking the same thing.

✂

After a few minutes of silence we headed into the dining room where a cutting mat, two sewing machines, and an ironing board were already set up. There were yards of batik fabrics on the table, all in bright colors and patterns.

Susanne took a large folder out of her tote bag and placed it on the table. "By unanimous decision we're doing the second design. Since it's something I created myself, I decided to make plastic templates." She opened the envelope and pulled out the templates—circles and half circles in various sizes. "First we have to make the strip pieces for the backgrounds," she said. "We need one person to cut, two to sew, and one to press. I'll pin the finished ones together."

Eleanor looked at each of us. "Bernie and I will sew the strips. Maggie, you should press, and, Nell, you cut the circles." She had a way of speaking that dared anyone to question her.

I quietly took my place at the cutting area. Susanne showed me which template should be used with which fabric, and I did as I was told for about half an hour. The police investigation was going on right outside the back door, but I couldn't see anything from the dining room. When I had gotten far enough ahead of the rest of the group, I decided to make my getaway.

"Who wants some coffee and cookies?" I said to a room full of approving smiles.

I headed into the kitchen to put on the coffee. Through the window, I could see Jesse laughing with a large, friendly looking man. It seemed like they were taking a break from hard investigative work, giving me a perfect opportunity to interrupt.

As soon as I opened the back door to walk outside, Jesse shook his head. "Watch her, Jim," he teased. "She's the resident Sherlock Holmes."

"I'm Nell," I said. "I live here."

"Glad for the help, actually." Jim smiled and held out his latex-gloved hand. "I'm the resident blood-spatter expert."

"Did you find anything?" I asked.

"I told you," Jesse laughed. "Go ahead, Jim. It can't hurt."

"You're not a suspect are you?" Jim leaned in, his large round face barely containing a grin.

"I'm not the one to ask."

Jim winked toward Jesse. "She's probably strong enough to haul a body, but I'll tell her anyway," Jim said.

"Go ahead," Jesse said.

They seemed to be making a game of it, and I guess I would too if I spent my days looking at blood and dead bodies, but I didn't have time for games. There were quilters in the dining room who would want coffee any minute.

"What did you find?" I asked.

Jim walked over to the post where I had seen the dark stain.

"See here." He pointed to the stain. "That's blood. It's likely been caused by someone's head being hit against this post. Pretty hard too."

"So he hit her head against the post, which killed her, then he threw her in the river to hide the body?" I asked.

"Can't tell that," Jim said. "Can't say it's a man, for instance. But I can say that if it's her blood—"

"And that hasn't been determined yet," Jesse interrupted.

"Right," Jim agreed. "All we know is that she was hit on the back of the head. We know that from the examination of the body. And we know she was hit more than once. Probably several times."

I walked closer to the post, trying to see what Jim saw in the blood. "How can you tell?"

Jim bent his arms at the elbow and made fists with his hands. Then he began to pantomime a person banging a head against the post. It was eerie to think that something similar had happened only hours before—but for real.

"First contact breaks the skin," Jim said as his imaginary victim hit the post. "If it only happened once, there wouldn't be blood. So we know she was hit against the post twice." Jim pointed toward what looked like lines of blood over a splotch. "And this shows she was hit a third time because we have a crossing of the blood."

"And that tells us it was a pretty emotional situation," Jesse said. "Like maybe the suspect was angry or desperate. Maybe trying to keep her from going in the house."

"Wouldn't she have screamed?" I asked. "We would have heard that."

"We were in the dining room," Jesse said. "We were listening to music. And there was a storm outside. We all commented on the wind."

Jim turned to me. "And that's assuming she was killed while your dinner party was going on. I can't tell by the blood. I know it's more than twelve hours old, but I can't say it wasn't yesterday morning or even a few days ago."

"It wasn't a few days ago," I said. "It rained two days ago. Freezing rain. The whole porch got soaked, including this post."

"We'll get a better time of death from the autopsy," Jesse said.

"If he killed her by banging her head, why throw her in the river?" I asked.

The whole thing was just too unbelievable and no matter what they said, I couldn't make sense of it.

Jesse put his hand on my back. "We don't know if he killed her on the porch or if she died in the river. Maybe she was just unconscious and he put her in the river to finish the job."

Jim stepped in. "He, or she, also could have taken her to the river to dispose of the body. That's another thing the autopsy will tell us."

"He or she? Wouldn't it have to be a man to have been that strong?" I looked from Jesse to Jim.

Jim answered first. "Can't say. The victim was a small woman and so a stronger woman or a really angry one could have done it. But in dragging the body there would have been blood transfer."

Jesse looked at me and sighed. "Do you remember seeing blood on Oliver or Kennette last night? I don't."

I shook my head. "I didn't see Oliver's coat and I didn't really look at Kennette's." I turned back to Jim. "Where would the blood have been?"

Jim nodded and pointed to his own body. "Hands. Sleeves. Maybe around the face or chest, depending on the killer's height and how he, or she, moved the body. And of course on the shoes."

"I didn't look at anyone's shoes," I admitted.

"Why would you?" Jim offered. His face broke into a sympathetic smile. "It wouldn't have been a lot of blood anyway. Maybe just droplets."

"Kennette was gone for a long time before she returned to the house and she could have cleaned herself up. It's not like we were looking for blood," Jesse said.

I didn't like even the idea that Jesse was considering Kennette.

"Oliver went to the bathroom after his cigarette," I said. "He could have washed up in there."

"And it could have been someone who followed your victim here, killed her, and left," Jim suggested.

I hadn't thought of that, but if it were true, it still didn't answer the question of what Sandra was doing at the house.

Jesse grabbed my hand and walked me a few yards from Jim, who went back to work. Jesse's hand felt cold but protective and I was glad to feel his skin against mine. I leaned on his shoulder but he pulled away a little.

"You are really smart and I know you have a good mind for things like this," Jesse said. I could tell there was a *but* coming. "But I want you to understand that we really have no idea who did this. Or why," he said. "I know I keep saying this, but you could get in real trouble if you stick your nose in."

"I'm not sticking my nose in," I said defensively, but I knew he wouldn't buy it. "Okay, but it happened here. On my grandmother's porch."

"All the more reason to stay out if it."

"Unless it's Oliver."

"Especially if it's Oliver," he said. Jesse leaned toward me, brushing his cheek against mine. He whispered, "I just want you to be safe."

I nodded slowly and had just turned my face to kiss him when I heard a booming voice behind us.

"Is this how you conduct an investigation, Dewalt?" Powell was walking toward us, his boots plodding through the snow.

Jesse looked over. "Nice of you to join us."

Both men smiled but I knew it was the end of my trying to get information. However stern Jesse might be, I figured I could get around him, but not Powell. He seemed like a guy who didn't like people who broke the rules.

"I should go back inside," I said.

"Good," Jesse said. "Stay there and I'll come in later."

I walked toward the house. I knew Jesse was only trying to keep me safe, but I wasn't going to sit idly by while a killer came closer to me and the people I loved.

CHAPTER 18

I spent another hour working on the quilt and thought it was shaping up to be an amazing combination of color and movement. It started with a background of squares that were made from strips of fabric that had been pieced together, but Susanne's design called for a series of appliquéd circles and semicircles that swept across several of the background squares. The quilt had such a tremendous amount of energy that I named it *The Effects of Caffeine*.

While the group debated whether the circles should be added with invisible thread or a contrasting blanket stitch, I began to get restless. I went to the kitchen for another cup of coffee, but once there, I peered out the window. Watching Jesse and Chief Powell standing on the porch, deep in conversation, was too much to take. Was Jesse telling him that Kennette had time to commit the murder? Was he telling him about Oliver's strange relationship with Sandra? I knew that if I walked outside the conversation would stop. But I couldn't sew any longer. I was going crazy not knowing.

"I'm going to the shop," I announced.

"That's a good idea, dear," Eleanor said. "I'm sure Kennette could use a break."

"We'll talk later," Maggie said, then shot a glance at Eleanor, who appeared not to notice.

I nodded, and as I did, I caught a strange look from Bernie. Before she could say anything, I headed into the hallway and out the door. I knew I had ducked a conversation for the moment. But only for the moment.

✄

Despite the cold, wind, and snow, I decided to walk to town. On a nice day it would take less than ten minutes, but by the time I arrived on Main Street more than twice that time had passed and I was freezing. Instead of going straight to the store, I went to Carrie's soon-to-be coffee shop.

"Hey," she said as she unbolted the door. "Are you okay?"

"Fine. Cold," I said.

"Natalie called me about the girl at your grandmother's. I would have gone over but I had so much work to do."

"There's really nothing to do there. They're all sitting around eating cookies and—" I stopped myself. I had almost spilled the beans about her quilt.

"I'll get you coffee. I just made some." Carrie poured me a large mug. I took off my coat and dropped onto her couch. Even though it would be the fourth or fifth cup I'd have, I still felt like I needed the caffeine.

"I knew her," I said. "She took art classes with me."

"So Kennette and Oliver knew her as well."

I nodded. "Better than me. At least Oliver did."

"So you think it has something to do with Oliver?"

"I think it has to."

Carrie studied me for a long time. "You think she came to see him and he killed her to stop her from talking to your grandmother."

I sighed, relieved to be with a kindred spirit. "Finally someone who sees this the way I do," I said excitedly. "I think he was having an affair with her and he didn't want Eleanor to know. So when Sandra showed up at the house they had a fight and he killed her."

"How did he know she was going to be there?" Carrie asked.

"He got a text. It said: 'Too soon to talk. Needs more time.' "

" 'Needs more time,' " Carrie repeated, "*Needs*. Third person?"

I sat up. "Right. Third person. I need more time, but he *needs* more time."

"Or she," Carrie added.

"The person texting him was talking about someone or something else."

"And the text was from Sandra?"

"Don't know that. Maybe it was about Sandra."

"Then why would she go over to Eleanor's house, if she needed more time?" Carrie sipped her coffee. "If the text had said *needs to talk* . . ."

I knew where Carrie was going with this. "But it didn't," I said excitedly. "So Sandra would have been coming over to see him. Confront him."

"Or Eleanor. Maybe tell her something devastating about Oliver," Carrie said.

"What? Is Eleanor the other woman?" I sat up. That was a role I'd never imagined for her. But there was something else. "If she was coming over to confront my grandmother and Oliver didn't know, isn't it a stroke of luck that Oliver went out to get a cigarette right when Sandra arrived?" I asked.

"Unless she was waiting for him."

"But if she came over to confront Eleanor, why wait outside in the freezing cold? And why go to the back door?" I asked. "And why would Oliver kill someone because she was going to tell my grandmother a secret? This was their second date. If you can even call it that, considering Jesse, Kennette, and I were all there."

"So maybe she wasn't coming to see Oliver."

There it was. Sandra could only have been coming to see Kennette. And she had the time to commit the murder, drag the body to the river, and clean up.

"But why would Sandra have come to the house to see Kennette?" I wondered out loud. "What could their connection be? I've never even seen them speak."

"Well, you're not around her 24-7. And you did just meet Kennette a few weeks ago."

I knew she was right. "But what was so urgent that she had to meet Kennette at the house during a party on a Saturday night?"

"Maybe she wasn't coming to see Kennette." Carrie shrugged. "Maybe she was coming to see you."

I hadn't thought of that. Had Sandra changed her mind since the confrontation in the bathroom and decided to tell me what was going on with Oliver? And if she was, only Oliver would have reason to stop her.

I was getting whiplash from changing suspects so much.

We weren't really getting anywhere, and across the street I could see a steady stream of customers going in and out of Someday Quilts. I let Carrie get back to unpacking coffee cups and I headed over to the shop.

Kennette was chatting with Bill Vogel, an artist who drove up from Spuyten Duyvil once a month to buy fabric. He made large-scale pieces that were part sculpture, part art quilt and, I was told, sold for thousands. He swore by my grandmother's taste in fabric and would only buy from her.

"Heya, Nell." He kissed my cheek. "I love Kennette. Where did you find her?"

"She sort of found us," I said. "We take art classes together."

"Another artist?" Bill smiled at Kennette. "What's your medium?"

"We're taking a drawing class from Oliver White," she said. "He's wonderful."

"That's one word for him," Bill said. "How's it going?"

"It's interesting," I said, but I had a question of my own. "You know him?"

Bill shook his head. "Not him. His reputation."

"Which is?"

"He's temperamental. He's moody. He's a pain." He shrugged. "He's an artist."

"He's brilliant," Kennette added.

"That too," Bill said. "And he's worth a fortune. Or he was. I hear he's giving it all away to some school."

"Our school," I said.

"What a surprisingly generous move."

"Is it?" I asked. "I don't think he has any family."

Bill nodded. "Doesn't surprise me. Rumor has it that he has a bit of a problem with women."

"Meaning?"

"Love 'em and leave 'em. And not on the best of terms."

"That's not fair," Kennette jumped in. "You said you don't even know him."

Bill patted her shoulder. "Absolutely right. The man's work is amazing. Such emotion. Such depth," he said. "What else matters?"

My grandmother matters, I thought.

"I'll ring you up." Kennette grabbed the fabric bolts Bill was holding.

"Two yards of each," he called after her.

I grabbed Bill and pulled him toward the back of the shop.

"I need you to tell me something," I said.

He leaned in, smiling. "What?"

"When you said 'not on the best of terms,' what did you mean?"

Bill stiffened. "A lot of old rumors. Don't read too much into an old gossip like me."

I wasn't letting him off the hook that easily. "I don't care if he was a womanizer. I pretty much figured he was. What I want to know is whether you've ever heard that he had been violent with a woman."

I could see Bill squirm. "Oliver White is a very influential artist. And I have nothing but respect for him." He moved away from me. "Give your grandmother my love."

He walked to the front of the store, paid for his purchases, and left without looking back.

CHAPTER 19

During my Monday ceramics class I could barely concentrate. Several times the vase I was supposed to be forming spun off the wheel. When the teacher came over to help me, the clay splattered on her foot.

"I guess this isn't my strongest medium," I apologized.

"It could be if you focused," she said.

I picked the clay up off the floor and tried again, but my eyes were on the clock.

As soon as I had wrapped up my clay at the end of class, I was focused. I pushed ahead of the rest of the students and practically sprinted to the registrar's office, making it there just before they closed up for lunch.

"I'm a student here," I said, out of breath and looking, I'm sure, quite alarming.

"What happened? Is there a problem?" A man jumped from his desk and came over.

"No. No problem." I tried to calm down. I'd rehearsed what I would say and it was crucial that it sound relaxed. "I take a class with Oliver White. I just heard about the student who died." I took a breath. "Sandra."

The man nodded. "Terrible tragedy. I understand she drowned."

"Who said that?" I had to ask, even though I knew it made me seem too curious.

"The officer who was here earlier."

"Jesse Dewalt? About thirty, brown hair, glasses?"

"No. An older man. Looked military. I don't remember his name." He stiffened. "Why are you interested?"

"Oh." I backed down a little. "The police have been asking a lot of us questions."

"Us?"

"Those of us who knew Sandra." I made a kind of sad face that I'm sure looked fake. "I didn't get to know her as well as I would have liked, but I thought she was really talented."

"That's what Oliver said," he agreed. "So sad."

"We were thinking of sending a card and some flowers to her family, something for the funeral." I paused. "Do you have contact information?"

He looked at me for a moment then nodded. "Under the circumstances I guess it would be okay. I think it would be very nice for her family to know that she was part of the community of artists."

He walked into another room while I waited out front. Teachers and students were passing in the hallway, and I tried to keep one eye on the lookout for Chief Powell while not looking suspicious.

Several minutes passed and I started to worry. What if he came back with someone who questioned my intentions or wanted the whole thing to go through Oliver? But just as I considered leaving, he returned with a file.

"I'm sorry. I only have her home address. She left the in-case-of-emergency section blank."

"That's okay." I was improvising now. "I think she had a roommate. If you give me the address, I can ask her roommate about the family."

"Good idea." He smiled and wrote the address on a piece of paper. "It's very kind of you to do this."

I nodded. I don't think *kind* was the word Jesse, my grandmother, or the killer would have used.

✄

Sandra's apartment was about a five-minute drive from the school, in one of those large, nondescript apartment buildings that were built in the seventies. I'm sure it looked modern for about five minutes. Then it just looked soulless.

According to the slip of paper she lived in 11G, so I headed up the elevator and onto the eleventh floor. I hadn't quite figured out how to get into her apartment. I guess I thought it would come to me when I got there. Or maybe I'd get lucky and she would actually have a roommate. But no luck. I stood in front of the locked door, wondering what I should do next. Then I looked out the hallway window and got an idea.

I opened the window and climbed onto the fire escape. One step, though, and I realized it was rickety. Each time my foot moved, the platform creaked as if it might pull away from the wall at any minute.

"If I live through this, I'm calling the building inspector," I said as a threat to no one in particular.

I took a deep breath and tried to reassure myself.

Don't look down, I thought. I looked down.

I took another step toward Sandra's window.

If it's locked, I realized, I'm a complete idiot. The staircase swayed slightly underfoot.

A dead idiot.

I reached Sandra's window and pulled it up. It opened so easily, I almost lost my balance. I grabbed hold of the sill and climbed in.

Now what? I asked myself.

The apartment was barely furnished. There were her art supplies from class and a couple of half-painted canvases lying on the floor. I needed to satisfy myself one last time that Sandra was not the artist Oliver claimed she was in class. I went through the paintings one by one, studying them for anything that expressed a unique talent. I recognized each of them from class and they were, just as I remembered, nothing special. Oliver's second assessment of her was more likely—she had no future as a painter. I wondered for a moment if I did, but this was hardly the time for introspection. I left the paintings and got back to the task at hand.

Across the room an empty bottle of scotch and two glasses sat near a small TV. There was one wooden kitchen chair with paint spattered all over it.

What could I possibly find in here?

I walked into the other rooms and saw pretty much the same thing. In the bedroom an air mattress sat next to a bundle of blankets and a pile of clothes. The bathroom had a makeup bag and some toothpaste.

It felt like a squatter lived here—more like a hideout than a home. Maybe she was on the run from something. Or, to be fair, maybe she was broke and caught up in the romance of being a starving artist. It might have been that Oliver was just trying to help her out. It was something Eleanor would have done.

I walked into the galley kitchen and started opening cabinets. Nothing. To get at the last one, above the refrigerator, I had to use the wooden chair from the living room. I opened the cabinet and reached in.

"Oh my God." I jumped off the chair and took three steps back. I knew my heart was racing but I stopped myself from further retreat.

You're looking for a murderer and you let yourself get scared by a cockroach? I scolded myself.

I climbed back onto the chair and forced myself to look deeper into the cabinet. There wasn't just one cockroach but an extended family crawling around in the cabinet and, now that I was on the alert, on the floor as well. But there was also something else: a purple wallet in the back corner. I reached in.

"Yuck. Yuck," I said involuntarily as my hand moved inches away from a roach. I grabbed the wallet and threw it onto the counter.

Once down from the chair, I took the wallet into the living room. There were no IDs, no credit cards. Nothing in the billfold. I opened the change purse and saw just a few coins. At first glance there was nothing special about them, but when I looked closer, I realized they were Canadian. Lily had been from Canada. Could this be her wallet?

I went through the wallet one more time, checking every pocket. Deep inside the last one I felt something. A small piece of thick paper. I pulled it out. It was folded in half. When I opened it, I realized it was a black-and-white photo of a woman sitting on a bed. It looked a little like the photo Rich described. She was a woman about my age, sitting on a bed, wearing a polka-dot dress. But unlike Rich's description, this woman wasn't staring off into the distance. She was looking at the camera, smiling.

Still, it could be the same woman, and if it was, it would connect Lily's murder to Sandra's. I knew the only way I could confirm my suspicions was if Rich saw the photo. But that would be stealing evidence in a murder investigation.

Breaking and entering was one thing, but taking the wallet was another. If I did take the photo, I knew I couldn't bring it to Jesse because he would want to know how I got it. And based on the way he had treated Rich the night of Lily's murder, I wondered whether he'd ever show him this photo.

I stood staring at the wallet for several minutes before working out a compromise. I took the photo and threw the wallet back into the cabinet. I could show the photo to Rich, then return it to the apartment. It might only take a couple of hours. Then I could go to Jesse with Sandra's address. It was interfering, but only in a very limited way, and I could find out if he'd already been to the apartment and discovered what I had. I knew I was rationalizing a crime, but if Jesse had paid attention to Rich in the first place, I wouldn't have had to.

I put the chair back where I'd found it and left the apartment through the front door. I took the elevator down the eleven flights and walked to my car. I drove away in a haze. A few Canadian coins and an old photograph were the slimmest of ties, but in my gut I felt that Lily and Sandra must have known each other. The wallet wasn't Sandra's so it had to be Lily's. Who keeps their own wallet in a kitchen cabinet? That's where you hide something.

But what was the connection? Could they have met here or in Canada? And what was Lily's connection to Oliver? Maybe she was another wannabe artist that Oliver took under his wing.

I was so focused on the investigation that I almost went through a red light. Luckily I stopped just in time. As I was waiting, two police cars crossed the intersection in front of me. One was from Archers Rest and the other from Morristown. And they were headed in the direction of Sandra's apartment.

I could see that Greg was driving the Archers Rest car and Jesse was staring out the front window. Or did he look to the side and see me? I couldn't tell. I ran my finger across the photo in my lap, trying to convince myself that I had done the right thing. I took it as a good sign that no one in the Morristown car, including Chief Powell, saw me.

My relief was short-lived because now I had a bigger problem. Maybe I'd gotten away with busting into Sandra's apartment, but that was just the first part of my plan. How was I going to get the photo back into evidence without admitting what I'd done? Suddenly I realized that my enthusiasm, or what Eleanor would call meddling, might have jeopardized the entire investigation. It was the closest I'd come in days to seeing why Jesse wanted me to stay out of it.

CHAPTER 20

When I called Susanne, she promised to have Rich come to her place. What she didn't tell me was that Natalie, Bernie, Carrie, and Maggie would be there as well.

"We're Eleanor's friends, and if she's getting involved with a killer, then we want to know," Bernie said before I even sat down.

"I don't want to get you involved," I told them. "What I did was illegal."

Natalie put a cup of tea in front of me. "As of right now, we're accomplices."

I looked around. I could see the worry in their faces and they could probably see it in mine. I wasn't just concerned about my grandmother. There was a very real possibility that Jesse would lock up an entire quilting guild. But as I looked around it was obvious that nothing I could say would dissuade them.

"Okay," I agreed. "The first thing is this photo." I took the stolen picture out of my purse and handed it to Rich.

He stared at it for a long time. "It kind of looks the same, but the lady in this one is happy."

"Could it have been taken at the same time?" I asked.

"I guess so."

Bernie leaned into him. "Is it the same woman as in the other photo?"

Rich looked at the picture again. "I only saw it for a minute, but yeah. That's the lady. I remember the dots on her dress."

Susanne took the photo from him and examined it herself. "It looks a little like you, Maggie."

Maggie grabbed it. "I was never this beautiful," she said.

Carrie took it next. "Nonsense. You're this beautiful now."

Maggie waved her hand, but she blushed a little. "I was also pregnant for most of my twenties and thirties."

Bernie took the photo and laughed. "I don't know, Maggie. She's got that certain glow. Are you sure it's not you?"

"Okay, enough." Maggie grabbed back the photo and handed it to me. "Let's assume it is the same woman as in the photo Rich saw. What does it mean?"

I shook my head. "I'm not sure. What we do know is that someone took photos of this woman. One was found by Lily's body and the other was found in Sandra's apartment. I'd say that connects the two."

"So if we figure out who this woman is, we figure out the connection," Natalie said.

"Where do we start?" Bernie looked at me.

"We have to start asking questions," I said. "And if you guys are doing some of the asking, it won't seem so suspicious."

"One of us has to talk to Oliver," Susanne said.

"I'll do it," Bernie said. "I lived in Greenwich Village for part of the early sixties. Maybe we have some people in common."

"And somebody has to talk to Kennette," I sighed. I could tell they were all a little unhappy with that. "We really don't know much about her," I added.

Natalie nodded in agreement. "I'll take her to lunch."

"What else?" Susanne was getting into it now.

"Maggie, I need you to talk with my grandmother," I said. "You've known her the longest and she'll trust you."

"So get the dirt!" Bernie laughed.

"I'm going to find out what's going on with Oliver." Maggie looked at Bernie. "And try to get her to take it slow."

"Or break up with him," Carrie said.

"Let's not hang the man before the trial," Susanne scolded. "He's making her happy, and for all we know, he's completely innocent."

"That's the thing," I said. "*For all we know* Oliver is innocent. But we don't know. And if we're ever going to feel comfortable having him in Eleanor's life, we need to know who he is and what he's done."

"Well," Maggie said. "That might be more difficult than it appears."

We all turned to Maggie, who pulled a file from her bag. As she opened it we crammed together, all trying to see what she had brought. Maggie looked up at us, annoyed.

"Give her some room," Bernie said.

We each took a few steps back.

"As far as I can tell, Oliver White didn't exist until 1957," Maggie said.

"You didn't find any records of him in England?" I asked.

"Nothing. I found, through old immigration records, that Oliver came to this country in 1957, but I can't find anything in England."

"Why would he lie about that?" I asked.

"A prison record?" Natalie suggested.

"Don't get ahead of the story," Maggie scolded.

"He was in prison?" I practically shouted. "What did he do?"

"Hold on." Maggie had a tale to tell, and it was clear that nothing was going to get in the way. "There was nothing I could find about him before he came to this country. Once he was here it got easier. I checked through old newspaper files and starting in the late 1950s I found articles about him. He was an artist in New York."

"We know that," Bernie said impatiently. "Get to the prison record."

Maggie took a deep breath and continued. "I found several newspapers from that time, and I noticed that he seemed to have done a lot of group shows in alternative places from 1957 to about 1963. Then in '67 he did a one-man show that got good reviews. Apparently he was doing a lot of paintings of people taking drugs or alcoholics passed out. In one article he was quoted as saying that he wanted to immortalize the people that society forgot—"

"Maggie," Carrie called out. "What happened to him?"

"He disappeared out of the papers shortly after that show," Maggie said. "Then I started seeing his name again in the seventies as an established Hudson Valley artist, with paintings selling in the thousands."

"He was struggling. Then he disappeared," Natalie summed up.

"When he reemerged, he was rich," Susanne added. "How did that happen?"

"And what does that have to do with prison?" I asked.

"There was also this." Maggie pulled out a photocopy of a newspaper clipping. The headline was "Artist Arrested at Opening."

"What does it say?" I asked.

Maggie handed it to Natalie. "I haven't got my glasses."

Natalie took a deep breath "'A Greenwich Village art opening turned into a brawl last evening when emerging artist Oliver White was arrested for assault on Julie Young. According to witnesses, White approached Miss Young, allegedly his date for the evening, because she was speaking with another guest. The two got into a shouting match and White struck Miss Young, knocking her into a painting. Police were called and White was charged with assault, drunk and disorderly conduct, and resisting arrest. White was released on his own recognizance.'" Natalie looked up at us. We all looked equally stunned. She gave the paper back to Maggie. "It's dated March 11, 1967."

"Did he go to jail?" I asked.

"No. There's another article I found somewhere that says the woman didn't show up to press charges, so the whole thing was dropped," Maggie said.

"So he has a history of violence toward women," Susanne said flatly. "That tears it. Eleanor needs to know."

"That was more than forty years ago," Natalie said. "Nell, do you really think it means anything?"

"I don't know. I wish we knew more about him."

"We need to check his credit and tax records," Carrie said.

"I tried," Maggie told her. "All that stuff requires special permission. You have to be a police officer or a private detective to get that information."

"Or a banker," Carrie said. All our heads turned to her.

"Could you get that stuff?" I asked.

"I know where the files are. And I have the passwords I used when I worked on Wall Street. If they don't work anymore, I can always call in a favor."

"Isn't that illegal?" Susanne asked.

Carrie shrugged. "This is Eleanor."

Nobody could argue with that.

CHAPTER 21

I left what was once a quilt group but had now become my own personal crime ring. I was amazed and touched by how much they were willing to put on the line for my grandmother and, by extension, me. I knew that if we were really going to solve this case, I had to do the same.

I drove over to the Archers Rest Police Station and went inside.

"Heya, Nell." Greg came walking over. "Jesse will be happy to see you."

"Is he in a good mood?" This would be no time to confess if he was already angry.

"He's good. We've been out finding the killer."

"You've found the killer?" I couldn't believe it.

Greg smiled. "Not yet. But the point is that Jesse took me with him. He's letting me be part of the team and"—he leaned in—"I found something."

The wallet. He must have found the wallet. I told myself to look surprised.

Greg looked around then whispered, "We found this." He reached into his pocket and pulled out a man's watch.

I took it from him and examined it. The watch didn't seem particularly expensive or unique. There were no initials or anything engraved on it. Aside from a tiny piece of light blue rubber caught in one of the holes, it was just another cheap watch. There was nothing to tie it to one person. But it bothered me. It might be useless but why hadn't I spotted it?

"Where did you find it?" I asked.

"In the bedroom. It was wrapped up in the sheets."

I hadn't thought of looking there.

"Shouldn't it be in evidence?" I asked as I returned it to Greg.

"It will be. I just want to look at it for a while. See if it gives me a clue about the identity of the wearer."

"Well, you should be proud of yourself that you found it, Greg. I'm sure it will help with the investigation." I found myself a little jealous that Greg had uncovered a clue I'd missed.

Greg couldn't stop looking at his prize. "We searched the whole place. Dusted for fingerprints. Took pictures. It was so cool. Everyone else had already left the apartment when I checked one more time. I was never going to get promoted as long as I was out giving traffic tickets, but a murder investigation? It's just the chance I needed."

"What a lucky break for you," I said, hoping to bring Greg down to earth. But he would have none of it.

"I had to do something to get Jesse to see what a good detective I'd make," he continued. "I was getting desperate."

"Well you showed him," I said. "I'm sure he's very grateful."

Greg nodded happily and headed back to the front desk.

If the investigation was going well, maybe Jesse would be in a good mood about my little field trip to Sandra's apartment. Maybe. When I knocked on his office door, I heard his gruff "Come in," but it still took several seconds for me to work up the courage to open the door.

He jumped out of his chair. "Nell. This is quite a surprise. I thought you had ceramics class on Mondays."

"In the morning. I usually stay and work in the studio for a while, but I had something to do today."

"I'll bet I know what it was."

I knew I was turning red, but I hoped he wouldn't notice.

"You know?" I asked.

He smiled. "I drove by Susanne's house and saw Maggie and

Bernie headed inside. I figured you guys had some secret meeting that couldn't wait until Friday."

"You did?" I was starting to sweat.

"Carrie's quilt. The way you were talking about it the other night at dinner, I could tell you guys were anxious to get it started."

"You're quite the detective."

"I'm glad you're . . ." He stopped and seemed to start the thought all over again. "I think you are one of the smartest people I know, and if you wanted to join the police force I'd hire you in a second." He paused again. "But I'm glad you're leaving this up to me. I know how important it is to you to find the killer, so it means a lot to me that you're spending your time with the quilt group and not looking for clues." He paused a third time, even blushed a little. "I'm glad to see you have faith in me."

Ouch. There was no way I was saying anything now.

"No matter what I do," I said, struggling to find the right words, "it's not because I don't respect your abilities. I sometimes let curiosity get the better of me."

"But now with school and the shop and Carrie's mural and everything, you have enough on your plate," he said. A little hopefulness in his voice made me feel worse.

I nodded. "How's the case going, by the way?"

He laughed. "Okay. I'll tell you this much. We went to Sandra's apartment but we didn't find much."

"Really? Greg seems to think he's on to something with that watch."

Jesse kissed me. "He's not. We found some glasses and an empty bottle of scotch, and the watch was found in the bed. A young woman entertained a man at her apartment." He smiled. "I hear it happens all the time."

"But you must have found something: ID, money, a purse, or . . . a wallet." I hoped it sounded as if I were just coming up with the list as I spoke.

"We did find a wallet. Nothing in it."

"Not even money?"

Jesse laughed. "Okay. We found some Canadian coins in it."

"So Sandra was Canadian. Just like Lily."

"We're four hours from the Canadian border, Nell. I still have Canadian money from the last time I was in Montreal."

"In your wallet?"

He nodded. "I see your point." He leaned against his desk and put his hands on my hips. "When are we having our next date?"

"You seem pretty busy with the investigation."

"I've got practically the entire Archers Rest force on it. Plus Powell and several of his guys. I think I can take a night off."

"Saturday?"

He pulled me toward him. "Saturday."

We would have kissed but his phone rang.

I couldn't tell Jesse about the photo, but I couldn't hold on to it either. Once I left Jesse's office, I headed back over to Greg.

"Jesse thinks you did a really great job out there today," I said.

"Really?" Greg's smile took over his whole face. "That is so cool. I knew once he saw me in action he'd see what I can do. I would have done anything to get my chance to be a detective."

I nodded. "Well, you're on your way. He told me you found a wallet and he wondered if I could identify it. Maybe I saw Sandra with it at class or someone else."

"Gotcha. I'll get it."

While Greg was getting the evidence I took the photo out of my purse and folded it in half, the way I'd found it. I palmed it in my hand and waited. When he came back, he held a large, sealed evidence bag containing the wallet. This was going to be trickier than I thought.

"So do you remember seeing it?"

"I'm not sure. Can I look at it more closely?" Jesse would never fall for it but I was hoping Greg would. "I might be able to help you solve the case."

That did it. Greg grabbed a pair of latex gloves for me to wear, and I opened the envelope. I took out the wallet and started going through the empty credit card slots one by one. My plan wasn't going to work unless I could get Greg to look away, but he seemed fascinated by my examination.

I moved the hand with the palmed photo into position. "Can I see the watch again?" I asked. "Maybe it will jog my memory."

In the seconds it took for Greg to fish the watch out of his pocket, I pushed the photo into the slot. Then, after a few more seconds of fruitless searching, I found the photo.

"What's this?" I pulled it out and handed it to Greg.

"Wow. How come we didn't see this?"

"It was really jammed in there," I said. "But I have pretty small fingers so I guess I could pull it out easier."

Greg nodded but I couldn't tell if he was buying it.

"Why don't you tell Jesse you found it," I suggested. "You would have eventually."

"You wouldn't mind?"

"Not a bit." I gave him back the wallet. "But why don't you wait a couple of hours? Otherwise he might suspect something."

"You got it."

I started to walk out the door. Almost free. But I heard Greg's steps behind me.

"Hey, Nell," he said. "Thanks."

I smiled. If Jesse solved the case and Greg made detective, then it was a win-win for all involved.

The pressure I'd been feeling since I'd left Sandra's apartment was starting to fade away. Instead of obsessing about the case, maybe it was time for me to start worrying about my outfit for Saturday night.

CHAPTER 22

It was my day off but I stopped off at the shop anyway. I just wanted to check on my grandmother and find out what she was feeling. Since I'd arrived in Archers Rest, Eleanor had been my best friend, my confidant, and my mentor. But I felt that something subtle was changing between us. She was busy certainly, but I was busy too. It was nice that our lives were so full and happy at the same time. It was just that I still sought out her advice and friendship and she wasn't returning the favor. Whatever was going on with Oliver, I wanted her to share it with me.

When I got to the shop, though, I was surprised to see Kennette alone, pressing her drunkard's path quilt top.

"Where's Eleanor?"

"Haven't seen her." Kennette smiled. "Do you think we can work on quilting it Friday?"

"Sure. It already looks amazing." I looked down at the purple and blue quarter circles meandering across the quilt. Between the cool colors and the movement of the pattern, the quilt reminded me of waves in an ocean. "It's really turning out great," I said. "Do you know how you're going to quilt it?"

Kennette's eyes widened. "I haven't a clue. Is that going to be a problem?"

"My guess is that you'll get expert advice on Friday. Probably more than you want."

"They don't mind all my questions, do they?"

"Are you kidding?" I laughed. "They love it. If I ever get around to finishing my Christmas quilt, I'll go straight to the group for help on quilting."

Kennette smiled. "Why don't I finish ironing my quilt and then we'll work on yours. Maybe we can get both tops ready by Friday."

She had such enthusiasm that I found myself excited at the prospect. The shop was slow, so after her top was completely pressed, we sat and hand sewed sashes onto my remaining blocks and put the blocks together into a completed top.

I held it up. "I can't believe the top is finally finished." I stared at the pretty little wall hanging with all of my Christmas characters finally together in a quilt. "Thanks so much for helping me, Kennette."

"Oh please. You guys have done so much for me. I could never do enough to repay it." She seemed to be blushing a little. "I feel like I'm really making friends here. It's so cool. Natalie even invited me to lunch tomorrow."

I immediately felt like a heel. "That's great," I managed to get out.

"She's so nice. Everyone is so nice. I can't believe I met all of you."

"We are all fond of you too, Kennette," I said. "We're anxious to get to know you better."

She smiled but said nothing.

"I mean, it's like you just appeared out of nowhere," I continued. "We don't even know where you grew up."

"I was thinking the same thing about you. I mean, I know that Eleanor is from this area and so is Maggie. I don't know where Carrie grew up or Susanne. I think Bernie moved here with one of her husbands." She paused, only for a breath, and then looked at me, puzzled. "And you're not from New York originally, are you?"

"Pennsylvania," I said. "But I spent a lot of time here because of my grandmother."

"And then you lived in New York City?" she asked.

"After I graduated from college."

"That must have been cool."

"Yeah, I guess."

"And now you're here to stay," she said. "Especially once you marry Jesse."

"Well, I don't think Jesse and I are really at that stage."

"But you love him?"

"I wouldn't say love. I think we like each other."

"But you want it to be something more."

"I don't know," I stumbled. "And I don't know what Jesse wants."

"I can see the way he looks at you. You guys are meant for each other."

I was getting dizzy. Just who was digging for information here? I took a breath and regrouped.

"Have you ever been in love?" I asked.

Kennette shrugged. "Do you think Oliver and Eleanor are in love?"

"I don't know. I can see that you really like Oliver."

"He's an amazing artist. I wonder if I could ever be as good, don't you?"

"I guess." This was going nowhere. And just as I was about to change subjects once again and ask her about her childhood, a customer came into the store. Kennette ran over to help.

I watched her immediately befriend the customer and make her feel at ease. Kennette had charm and charisma, though it was wrapped in kind of a goofy package. And it was clear she had talent. Even the choices she'd made for her quilt showed that. It was hard not to like her and even harder to imagine her killing someone.

But that didn't mean she couldn't. As uncomfortable as it made me, I had to be open to the idea that anyone, even someone I liked, could commit murder.

"We got a shipment of fabric this morning," Kennette told me after the customer left. "I didn't know if I should open it so I left it behind the counter."

"Let's open it," I said quickly. The arrival of new fabric was a major event, because inside the box were all the possibilities for new quilts. If

Eleanor was going to take the day off, then she had forfeited the right to be here when the package was opened.

Kennette ran behind the counter and disappeared for a second, re-appearing with a huge box in her arms, which she set on the counter.

"Kennette, that thing must weigh a ton," I said. "You need to be more careful."

She just laughed. "I can handle it. I just can't wait to see what's in the box."

When we opened it, we were not disappointed. Fabrics for Easter and the Fourth of July were already arriving, as well as an entire line of soft romantic floral fabrics in faded shades of rose and green. Coordinating plaids and stripes had me already planning my next quilt.

Since Kennette was alone, I stayed at the shop to help. There were few customers and we debated closing up early. Then, an hour before closing, the shop door opened and an enthusiastic Barney trotted in. He immediately went around the shop, greeting Kennette, myself, and the customers. Behind him Eleanor breezed in, without explanation. She was surprised to see me there, but more than anything, she was happy. Really happy.

"How was your day?" I asked casually.

"Amazing." Her face lit up. "I went through the fabric catalogs for spring. There are some really beautiful collections coming out. I nearly bought everything."

"That's wonderful," Kennette jumped in. "Isn't looking at fabric fun?"

Despite my best efforts I rolled my eyes. Eleanor caught me and the smile temporarily left her face.

"What is with you these days?" she said to me.

"I thought you were working today," I said.

Eleanor looked at me as if she were confused. "I was working. I was buying fabric."

I nodded. My grandmother was lying to me. I knew it. I just couldn't prove it. And I knew there was no point in fighting about it.

"Well, it was slow today anyway," I said, "so if you did take the day off . . ."

The smile returned. "Maybe I will sometime," she said, "now that I have two great workers in you girls."

She giggled and went toward the classroom to set up for a trapunto class she was teaching that night.

Kennette walked over to me. "She's in a good mood."

"She said something about buying fabric," I told her.

"But you don't believe her?" Now Kennette had a smile across her face to match my grandmother's.

I shook my head. "My grandmother has been quilting my entire life, but I've never seen her giggle over it."

Kennette nodded her approval. For once I kept my opinion to myself.

CHAPTER 23

"She was late for work. Hours late," I heard Carrie say on the phone to Maggie, relating word for word what I told her about Eleanor's entrance into the shop.

After a few minutes of discussion, they seemed to reach an agreement. Carrie hung up the phone and came over to the wall where I was laying out my paints.

"Maggie already has plans to meet with Eleanor tonight, so we'll get to the bottom of this," she said solemnly.

"I don't think she's ever been late to work. I know it has something to do with Oliver," I said, the fear and anger evident in my voice.

"Which is okay as long as he's not involved in the murders," Carrie reminded me.

"Right," I said.

I wasn't sure I felt that way but I knew I was supposed to feel that way. After all, my grandmother deserved happiness more than anyone I knew. She had spent her whole life being there for everyone. Wasn't it time she had a little fun? Still, something in my stomach turned at the thought.

"The mural is coming along," Carrie said, changing the subject.

I nodded. The buildings were all sketched in and now I was focusing on the large coffeepot that would be at the top right of the mural, "pouring" the buildings into existence.

"I kind of like it," I said. "But it's nowhere near finished."

"Well, you have two weeks."

"I can't finish until you come up with a name for this place."

Carrie grunted and walked away. The shop was really shaping up. Carrie was getting the fixtures put in place. Her espresso machine was coming in the next few days, and she was in the middle of hanging a collection of mirrors and weird little paintings behind the counter. My favorite thing, though, was that Carrie was looking for a baker to make the muffins, cakes, and cookies she planned to sell. While she looked, I sampled. And when I took a break from painting, I rewarded myself with a slice of lime cheesecake.

"Coffee Corner," Carrie suggested as she munched on a brownie.

"Caffeine Fix," I offered.

"Java Hut," she countered.

"That's the worst," I laughed. "How about Caffeine and Calories."

"Great. How about just calling it Get Fat and Jumpy."

We were both laughing hard. The kind of laughing where it isn't even that funny but tears are rolling down your eyes and you can barely speak. It was the first time since the murders that I'd been that relaxed. If Carrie didn't have to pick up her kids, I probably would have stayed in the shop all day, safe from murders and suspects and my grandmother's romance.

But that wouldn't happen. Just as we were about to walk out of the shop, I saw Greg pacing outside Someday Quilts.

"What's he doing?" Carrie whispered to me.

We were still in her shop, staring out the window and well out of Greg's earshot, but I whispered back, "I'm not going anywhere until I find out."

"I have to get the kids. I'll go out the back so he doesn't get spooked." Carrie stood looking at Greg for another few seconds, then disappeared out the back of her shop.

It was funny to me how we had all become expert investigators so quickly. Or at least felt like we had.

I wasn't sure what to do. If Greg looked up, he would see me peering out at him from across the street, but he didn't seem to notice.

He didn't seem to be looking anywhere but at his feet. Was he contemplating taking up quilting but too nervous to walk into the shop? That would make him the talk of the quilt group. Did he have some news for my grandmother about the investigation? If there was news, I knew that Jesse would deliver it, not Greg. Maybe he was branching out, doing some investigating on his own. I stayed glued to my spot and waited for something—anything—to happen.

It took only a minute for Kennette to walk out of the shop. She was wearing the big teal coat my grandmother had given her and she looked happy and relaxed. I couldn't tell if she was surprised to see Greg but she quickly engaged him in what looked like a friendly conversation.

After a few minutes of chatting, Greg looked around and I instinctively ducked out of sight. Crouched on the floor and peering through a corner of a window, I saw Greg and Kennette move closer. Kennette reached into her coat and pulled out a large piece of what looked like rolled-up paper. Greg unrolled it and looked, nodding seriously. Then he rerolled the paper and tucked it into his coat.

They chatted for just a moment more, then Kennette whispered something in Greg's ear. Greg nodded, looked around once more, and darted down the street toward the police station.

Had I just witnessed a budding romance? Or was it something else? As soon as Greg was out of sight, I left the coffee shop and hurried across the street.

The class was starting when I walked in, so I found myself standing at the back, listening to Eleanor teach trapunto to the dozen or so women who had signed up, Maggie and Kennette among them. Trapunto is one of those advanced quilting techniques that actually looks harder than it is, at least that's the way Eleanor explained it.

"Trapunto," Eleanor said to the class, "creates raised areas in your quilt by using cording or small amounts of batting pushed in from the back."

She held up a small whole-cloth quilt with a pattern of grapes, leaves, and vines. As Eleanor explained it, the quilt is layered with batting sandwiched between the top and bottom, just like a regular quilt. Then the shapes, like the grapes and leaves, are outlined with quilting. So far it seemed doable. A soft yarn is pulled through the vines from the back of the quilt, raising them slightly in front. For the grapes and leaves, a slit is cut into the back and a tiny amount of batting is stuffed in, making the grapes rounded and seemingly soft to the touch. Then a second backing fabric is added to cover the slits at the back. Finally the quilt is tightly stippled, a quilting technique of random-looking loops. The effect is three-dimensional and very dramatic.

While the rest of the class started working on sample twelve-inch blocks, I slipped into the main shop. Barney was sleeping with his head on a bolt of fabric. He lifted his head as I walked past, but once he saw it was me, he went back to dreaming.

I went toward the office and quickly checked Kennette's coat. There was nothing in the pockets, not that I expected there would be. I went back to the front of the shop, flipped through the latest copy of *Quilters Newsletter*, and waited. Finally I got my chance when the class went on a break.

Kennette walked out of the classroom and toward the threads, then stopped, startled. "I thought you went home," she said.

"I went over to Carrie's to work on the mural."

Her face lit up. "How's it going? Can I see it?'

I nodded. "Soon. Anything happening around here?"

"Eleanor's class is really cool. I'm thinking of using variegated thread for my quilting. You should sit in."

"Not tonight," I said. "How was the afternoon? Did anyone stop by?"

"Customers." Kennette looked at me, confused. "Who were you expecting?"

"I don't know. I saw Greg hanging out by the entrance and I wondered what he was doing. I thought maybe he had come to see you."

Kennette's face went white. "Yeah. He stopped by to say hello. He's a nice guy, don't you think?"

"Yes. Very nice. And single, as far as I know."

Kennette smiled. "Oh, don't be silly."

"Why not? Two nice single people. I'm surprised no one thought of it before. He'd probably be interested in seeing your artwork, you know, and getting to know you. Did you invite him into the shop?"

"When?"

"When he came by today."

"No. I went out for some fresh air and ran into him."

"So it wasn't planned?" I asked.

"Why would it be planned?"

"I don't know. I thought maybe he wanted to see your artwork and so you showed him. Have you ever shown him any?"

I knew I was sounding a little nutty, but showing Greg her artwork was the only innocent explanation I could come up with for why she had handed him that rolled-up document.

"No," she said quickly. "Why would I show him something I've drawn?" She tilted her head the way a puppy does when he's confused.

I shrugged. I didn't want to push too far. "I just think you guys would be cute together."

"You're acting very strange tonight," she said, and walked to the back of the shop where she straightened out a few bolts of fabric until the break was over and class began again.

It was the sort of avoidance behavior that I knew well.

CHAPTER 24

As Barney and I were walking up the driveway of my grand-mother's house, I saw a delivery truck at the front door. When I got closer I realized a delivery man was standing at the front door, holding a vase of flowers so large it seemed to overwhelm him. For a second I got lost in the possibilities of a future full of romantic gestures from Jesse, but the deliveryman quickly brought me back to reality.

"Eleanor Cassidy?" he asked.

I shook my head. "No, but I can sign for her."

I brought the flowers into the house, put them on the kitchen table, and removed the cellophane that covered them. They were stunning. Two dozen plum-colored roses, just on the verge of blooming.

I didn't want to, but I found myself staring at the envelope that was addressed to Eleanor Cassidy. I knew who they were from. I knew that their arrival coupled with my grandmother's good mood meant she had spent the day with Oliver. I also knew that it was none of my business. For whatever reason she had chosen not to share this with me. Maybe she thought I would see her as too old for love. But I didn't. I'd be thrilled for Eleanor to be with someone who is as wonderful as she is—if such a man exists. It's just that I had my doubts that Oliver even came close.

I got up from the table and put on the kettle, but my eyes kept returning to the flowers. I sat down and stared at them. I tapped my fingers on the kitchen table while I watched the graceful way they bent their stems to fill the vase. I knew it was only a matter of time before nosiness, wrapped in concern, got the better of me.

I reached up and took the envelope out of its plastic holder. I held it in my hands. The envelope wasn't sealed so, after only a moment's hesitation, I opened it.

It read: "I can't stop smiling. Love, Oliver."

I sank down in a chair. I wanted to call the group, set off alarms, get everyone fired up and outraged, but I couldn't. It was the most romantic note I'd ever read.

It began to dawn on me that the sinking feeling in my stomach, the one that made me sick whenever I thought of Oliver and my grandmother, wasn't just fear. At least a part of it was jealousy.

When Maggie called, later that night, I knew what she would say.

"They spent the day together. At the house. If you understand me" was how she put it.

"I understand you."

"She's like a schoolgirl. She said she was nervous but once they—"

"I don't need the details," I interrupted. "She is my grandmother."

"Right. Well, even at our age we still enjoy intimacy."

"But she hasn't enjoyed it for almost fifty years," I said.

Silence.

"Has she?" I asked. "No. Forget I asked."

"She's in love with him. She didn't say it but I could hear it in her voice."

"I think he's in love with her too."

"What do we do?" Maggie asked.

"We keep doing what we've been doing. But we have to be very careful. If Oliver is the killer, then Grandma is going to get hurt, and if he isn't—"

"But she finds out we've been snooping . . . ," Maggie interrupted.

"There'll be hell to pay."

Maggie sighed. "Well, hopefully it will work out. I'll keep looking through the newspaper files and maybe we'll come up with something. One way or the other."

✄

The next morning I went into the kitchen early. Eleanor had come home after I was already in bed, so I didn't see her reaction to the flowers. They were still on the kitchen table, but I noticed that the card was gone. I was still a little hurt that she hadn't wanted to share her happiness with me, but maybe grandmothers and granddaughters can't be girlfriends. Still, I couldn't help but smile. Dinner dates, secret trysts, roses, and romantic notes. Murderer or not, Jesse could learn a thing or two from Oliver White.

I was thinking of calling Jesse to mention the gesture when I caught sight of a police uniform outside on the porch. Maybe I wouldn't have to call him, I thought. I opened the door.

"Good morning." Chief Powell smiled at me from the porch.

"Good morning. What are you doing there?"

"Making sure we haven't left anything behind."

"Any leads?"

Powell shook his head. "Nothing yet. I'm starting to wonder if it wasn't a serial killer on his way through town. I'm checking with the other departments in the state to see if they've found any girls in the river."

"I suppose it could be a serial killer, but that still wouldn't explain why someone from my art class ended up dead a few feet from my house."

"You're quite the detective," he said. "What's your theory?"

It was tempting but anything I said would get back to Jesse. "I don't have one."

He looked at me for what seemed a long time, then nodded. "I hope you don't mind me in your backyard. It's just that the snow is melting a little and I figured the killer might have left something. Technically, I guess I should have asked first."

"I don't mind." But I did, a little. Not that we had anything to hide. It's just that if the killer had left something, I wanted to find it. "I'm making coffee. When you're ready, you should come in."

"Will do," he said and went back to his work.

I closed the kitchen door and made the coffee as promised. I watched him out the window. He seemed to be looking at the ground around the pole where Sandra had likely hit her head. He walked from the pole toward the river and disappeared behind trees. I knew he was walking the path the killer must have walked while carrying or dragging the unconscious Sandra. But while the killer's footsteps were covered by falling snow, I could see where Powell was walking. He was definitely thorough, even if he was out of his jurisdiction. I could hardly argue with someone so intent on solving a case that they would break a few rules, even if Powell didn't seem the type.

I turned away from the window and sipped my coffee. Within a few minutes Powell was knocking at the window so I poured him a cup. I put a few muffins on a plate and set them on the table.

He sat, all friendly smiles and polite conversation—a huge difference from the military man who'd been in the kitchen on the night of Sandra's murder.

"Beautiful roses," he said. "From Jesse?"

"No. From . . ." I hesitated but I wasn't sure why. "Oliver. For my grandmother."

"Beautiful." He reached out his hand and rubbed his finger against one of the petals.

"You don't think Oliver's involved, do you?" I asked.

"I couldn't say."

"Couldn't because you don't know, or couldn't because you have evidence he is involved and can't reveal it?"

He laughed. "Jesse told me about you."

"He has?" It seemed a bit disloyal for Jesse to do such a thing. Especially since it made me the object of some kind of joke.

"In a good way," Powell clarified as he sipped his coffee.

"It's just that if Oliver is involved, well . . ." I pointed to the flowers. "He's getting pretty close to my grandmother. If it were your grandmother, I'm sure you would want to know."

"I suppose I would."

"Would you be happy if someone you loved was dating someone with Oliver's reputation? Someone who could be involved in the deaths of young women?"

Powell cleared his throat. "So you are anxious to get Oliver out of your grandmother's life."

"Well . . ." I stopped and looked at the flowers again. "If he's done something wrong, I am. My grandmother is a very special person. She's devoted her whole life to caring for her family and being there for her friends and anyone in town who needs her. She deserves a little happiness."

I could see Powell watching me intently and it made me blush. "She seems like a good woman," he agreed. "It makes sense that you want to protect her."

"Wouldn't you? I'm sure you have a mom or grandmother you would do anything for?"

He shrugged. "I'm an orphan."

"Oh." For some reason it put him in an entirely different light. "I'm sorry to hear that. How old were you?"

He hesitated, spending a little too much time eating his muffin, but then he took a breath and said, "My dad died when I was about four and my mom died when I was fifteen."

"Of what?" It was an impolite question, and I knew it, but it was out of my mouth before I could stop myself.

"My father was a drug addict."

"Really?" I couldn't hide my surprise. Powell was a straight-arrow, clean-cut guy. It didn't add up.

He ran his hand through his crew cut. "I guess becoming a cop was my way of rebelling."

"Or helping people," I suggested. "And your mother? Was she an addict as well?"

He shook his head. "She was killed. Murdered," he said quickly. "She crossed paths with the wrong people."

"Like Sandra and Lily."

He leaned forward. "I think there are bad people in this world and you have to weed them out or else they'll destroy innocent lives. That's why I do what I do."

I nodded. "I'm sorry about your mom. About your parents. It must have been awful."

"I know I can be a little pushy, but someone like you ought to understand why," he said. "I'm not going to rest until I have the right person behind bars."

"I do understand that."

He nodded and got up from the table. "I better get back to work. Thanks for the breakfast. Bachelors don't get a lot of home cooking."

"Anytime."

He stood by the door for a second, then looked at me. "If I did have a grandmother who was getting involved with someone I didn't trust, I suppose I'd look into his background. Especially if, as you say, he and Mrs. Cassidy are getting close."

"You wouldn't consider that interfering in a police investigation?"

"Not unless he's the killer."

He smiled and left. I sat alone in the kitchen with, almost, official permission to do what I was already doing.

CHAPTER 25

I sat through my color theory class the way I usually did, with one eye on the clock. It's not that color isn't an important part of an art piece. It's key. It's the theory part that left me cold. I wanted to do something—paint, quilt, solve a murder. And sitting through a two-hour lecture was keeping me from all of the above.

Though Powell hadn't exactly said it, he at least opened the door to my looking into Sandra's and Lily's murders. While I sat in class, I made a list of what I needed to know.

What connected the two women? I had a hard time believing their deaths, so close in time and place, were just coincidence.

What did Canada have to do with it? Maybe Jesse was right. Maybe those were just some leftover coins from a trip north, but who keeps foreign currency in their wallet?

Did the watch mean anything? Was it just an item forgotten by a man she knew or could it be the killer's watch?

And finally, why was Sandra killed near the house? Who was she coming to see and why?

As soon as the professor gave us our homework assignment, I was out the door. I got in the car and started driving with absolutely no idea where I should go. I felt like my car was mirroring my head. I just kept going in circles. I drove for twenty minutes, changing direction twice. Eventually I knew I had to stop and regroup. I stopped at a park and went for a walk. It was a beautiful winter day. The weather was slightly warmer than it had been a week before, though I could still see my breath and feel the occasional pinch of an icy wind against my cheek. As I walked I realized the answer to all of these questions started with Sandra. If I could connect her to Lily then maybe it would lead me away from Oliver. I knew I couldn't go to Jesse for answers but I could go to Sandra. I headed back to my car at almost a sprint and started driving with an actual destination in mind.

Because it was the place Jesse had first kissed me, the county morgue had an oddly romantic feel to it. At least on the outside.

Inside there was an imposing reception desk with a security guard.

"Can I help you?" he asked.

"Yes. I'm here to see Sandra. Her body was brought in the other day for an autopsy."

"Are you a relative?"

"Yes. Her sister."

"Last name?"

I knew he was asking for Sandra's last name but it suddenly occurred to me that I didn't know it. So I gave him mine, to stall. "Fitzgerald."

He looked through a list of names. I tried to see Sandra's name on the list but there were no first names, just first initials. From where I stood, looking at the list upside down, there were three or four names with the first initial S. I didn't think the guard would give me four chances to get it right.

The guard looked up, impatience creeping across his face. "No Fitzgerald on the list."

"Oh, sorry, I thought you meant my last name. Sandra and I were stepsisters. We had the same mother," I blathered, trying to think of a plan B. "We had different fathers so we have different last names. I guess you want Sandra's last name."

"That would be helpful, miss."

I laughed nervously. I was punting. "I guess it would. She was about midtwenties, blond hair—"

"Miss," he stopped me midsentence. "I don't look at the bodies. I just look at the names. Do you know your sister's name or what?"

I paused. Just as I was about to give up, I saw a large man walk out a door down the hall.

"Jim!" I called out.

"The last name is Jim?" The guard looked at me skeptically.

"No. That's Jim. He's the blood-spatter expert working on the case." I called again. "Jim!"

This time Jim turned around. "Hey," he said warmly. "I know you."

"I'm here to see you about Sandra." I was on thin ice because this could easily get back to Jesse, but it was my only way in. "Jesse asked me to stop by."

Jim laughed. "Really? Let her in Bobby."

I smiled at the security guard and walked down the hallway, following Jim to some unknown destination. The cold temperatures and the stark, sterile feel of the place had me a bit spooked. We turned and walked down a long hallway painted in two tones of gray and broken up periodically by swinging steel doors.

"So how's everything?" Jim asked jovially.

"Good. I guess."

"Jesse didn't send you, did he?"

I stopped. "I'm sorry. It's just that Sandra was found outside my house and I . . ."

Jim smiled and shook his head. "So what do you want to know?"

"How are things with you, with the investigation?"

"I don't know much more than I told you." He started walking again and I followed him until he stopped in front of a pair of swinging steel doors. "But I know the man who does."

He opened the door to a room that looked familiar. It was the same one where Lily's body was autopsied. It seemed strange that the hallways that seemed so creepy to me today were the same ones that I had walked with Jesse just weeks before. I guess I was so caught up in being with him that I didn't notice my surroundings.

"Dr. Parker, this is Nell," Jim said to a man in a white lab coat.

The minute the man turned around, I knew we'd met before. "I was here with Jesse Dewalt," I said.

Jim laughed. "Good. You two are old friends. Nell here is curious about Sandra Thomas."

Thomas. If nothing else, I had a last name.

"I was wondering if you knew how she died," I said.

Parker grabbed a chart. "Strangulation," he said.

"She wasn't drowned or killed by a bump to the head?" I asked.

"She did have internal bleeding, and she definitely hit her head against something," Parker read from the report. "It's possible she might have eventually died from the bleeding if she hadn't also been strangled."

"She wasn't drowned?"

"No. No water in her lungs. That indicates she was dead when she was put in the water."

Jim shook his head. "Somebody must have really wanted her dead. First he bangs her head, then he strangles her, then he dumps her in the river. The classic definition of overkill."

"Lily was given sleeping pills, tied up, taken to the river, and drowned. Sandra was strangled," I said. "If it was a serial killer, wouldn't he have committed the murders the same way?"

"There's nothing in the autopsy to suggest that the murders are related," Parker said.

"But the women were about the same age and they were found in the river only a couple of weeks apart. Both of them were murdered," I told him. "That can't be a coincidence."

"Yes it can," Jim offered. "And that's good news. If each of these murders was a stand-alone, then there isn't a serial killer on the loose and women in Archers Rest can breathe a little easier."

"I guess," I said, not totally convinced but with nothing tangible to offer as an opposing explanation.

"I have a meeting, so I have to go," Jim said. "Stay out of trouble, Nell."

"I am," I said a little defensively, before I realized he was just making fun of me. "I appreciate your help."

Jim nodded. He leaned in and whispered, "A murder on my property would have me poking around too."

I smiled. It seemed everybody understood my curiosity but Jesse.

After Jim left I turned to Dr. Parker. "Thanks for the information," I said.

"Anything I can do to help the Archers Rest police catch this guy."

Of course. He must have assumed I was with the police. After all, he'd met me first with the chief of police and then with a forensic specialist.

"Is it possible to have a copy of the reports? On Lily Harmon and on Sandra Thomas."

"I sent them over to Dewalt," he said. "But I can make you copies. Give me a minute."

He left me standing alone in a room with corpses lying on autopsy tables. They were all covered but, still, they were dead bodies.

When he returned, he handed me a folder. It was so easy that I started to worry.

"Thanks," I said. "I'll let you get back to work."

He smiled. "Anytime."

I was about to go, having already pushed my luck, when I thought of another question.

"Has anyone claimed Lily or Sandra?"

Dr. Parker frowned. "No. They're both still here. Sad isn't it?'

"All of it," I agreed.

I smiled at him, and then walked out the swinging doors, down the drab hallway, and past the surly security guard, clutching the photocopies of the autopsy reports. I felt as if I were getting away with the crown jewels.

Even though it was cold outside, the sun was shining and it was nice to feel a little warmth on my face. It might not have been as romantic a visit as when I was with Jesse, but it felt just as good.

Still, I couldn't stand there all day. I felt like I was one big step closer to finding the killer and I didn't want to waste the momentum.

The snow was melting, creating a dirty slush that made it hard to walk. When I finally unlocked the door and climbed behind the driver's seat, I knew my next move. I dialed Carrie.

CHAPTER 26

Within two hours Maggie, Carrie, Bernie, Natalie, and Susanne were all gathered in the cramped office of Bernie's pharmacy. I told them what I'd learned at the coroner's office and what Powell had said about Oliver.

"Maybe Powell can help with information," Susanne said. "It might be safer to get it from him."

"I don't think he's going to help," I explained. "I think he's just not going to stand in our way like Jesse would."

"Speaking of which, don't you think Jesse's going to be mad at you?" Natalie asked.

"Only if he finds out. And he won't," I said. "And if he does, all I'm really doing is looking into Oliver's background, which, as Powell pointed out, is what a good granddaughter would do."

"Well Eleanor will kill you," Maggie said.

"She'll kill us all," Bernie answered.

"Again, only if she finds out." I tried to calm them. "If Oliver is a good guy, she never has to know. And if he's not, then I'm willing to be in the doghouse for a while. But I understand if you guys want to step out of this."

I looked around. No one, it seemed, wanted to back out. In fact they voiced certainty that whatever we had gotten ourselves into, we were going to see it through as a group.

"The main thing is to find out if Oliver is good enough for Eleanor," Bernie said.

"On that front, I had a friend check Oliver's credit and it's excellent," Carrie told us. "In fact he seems to be worth more than fifteen million dollars."

"From paintings?" Maggie was astounded.

"From paintings and investments," Carrie said. "The interesting thing is that he lives very modestly. He owns a house, but it's small: two bedrooms, one bath. The only improvement he made was to convert the garage into a studio. He has an investment firm take care of his accounts: He doesn't touch the principal, and in fact he rarely even touches the interest."

"Wow," Natalie said. "That's a lot of money."

"Well, I hope he's innocent. Eleanor deserves a nice rich man for her old age." Bernie sat back in her office chair. "We could all use one. Does he have any brothers?"

"I've been looking into that," Maggie said. "The Internet is a wonderful thing. I found the number for a records office in London and called there. Apparently Oliver was married in 1954."

"Is he still married?" I gasped.

"Divorced in 1957," she said. Maggie smiled a cat-ate-the-canary smile. "But he wasn't married as Oliver White. His real last name is Lyons. Apparently he changed it when he came to New York."

"Do we know anything about the ex-wife?" Natalie asked.

Maggie paused. "It took a few calls but I found another marriage certificate for the ex-wife. It turns out she remarried shortly after the divorce. Then I found this Internet service that looks for lost friends. They found that she moved to Canada. I don't know what happened to her after that, but I can check if we need to."

"Canada," I repeated. "Maybe there is a connection to Oliver. Sandra had those coins."

Susanne frowned. "If they've been divorced all these years, what could she tell us?"

"Did you find his ex-wife's name?" I asked.

Maggie reached into her purse and pulled out a small notebook that looked like a detective's pad. "Her maiden name was Violet

Hammel. Then, of course, she became Violet Lyons," Maggie said. "And then she married a man named Gerard Kelly. So I assume she's Violet Kelly now."

"Did Oliver ever remarry?" Susanne asked.

Maggie shook her head. "Doesn't look like it."

"Does he have any kids?" Natalie's hand went instinctively to her slight bump.

"He said he didn't," I said. "At the school. He said he didn't have any family."

Maggie nodded. "It seems he may have told the truth about that. I contacted one of those Internet search companies to check birth and death records. Oliver had a brother who died at twenty-five, unmarried. There were no birth certificates in England, the United States, or Canada listing Oliver as a father."

"Okay, so he was divorced and had at least one bad dating relationship," Bernie said. "You could say the same thing about me."

"You were never arrested," Maggie said.

"Actually I was arrested twice. Once for protesting the Vietnam War and once for inciting a riot when I took off my top off in front of a bunch of sailors," Bernie said. "Sometimes I miss those days."

"Let's hope that Oliver's criminal past isn't any worse than yours," Carrie laughed.

Finding out about Oliver's past only made us more curious. As we talked through the evidence, one thing seemed obvious. Changing his last name made Oliver suspicious. Maggie promised to keep digging.

"There has to be more," she said confidently.

"I've got plans to meet with Oliver and Eleanor for dinner on Sunday." Bernie looked at me. "Maybe I can find out something."

"That's great," I said, "but there's also something else I need you to do." I pulled the folder out of my bag. "These are the autopsy reports for both women. Bernie, you're a pharmacist. I know that's not the same as a doctor but . . ."

Bernie grabbed the folder. "I'll do it. After all these years I know as much medicine as any doctor."

"And I'll see if I can find anything on Sandra and Lily," Carrie offered.

"Good idea," I said. "If we can find a connection . . ." I didn't have to finish the sentence. It was like when we made a quilt as a group. Everyone brought their separate talents, but they combined into one vision, one tangible outcome.

✄

As I headed to my car, Natalie chased after me.

"I forgot to say anything, since we were all caught up with Oliver," she said.

"Kennette." I realized what she was about to tell me. "You had lunch."

Natalie looked disappointed. "I tried. I really did. But somehow I ended up talking about how I met my husband and what baby names we were picking out and, well, everything except her."

"Believe me, I know." I smiled. "The same thing happened to me."

She looked relieved. "I did find out one thing, though. Kennette said her mother hates the idea of her being a painter. She said she envied you having so much support."

"Well maybe that explains why she had so little money and nowhere to stay," I said.

"Oh, she did have somewhere to stay. I remember now. I was trying to find out where she came from and the most I could get out of her was that when she first came to town she got a room with a girl she met, but then the girl ran out on the rent."

"Did she say the girl's name?" I asked.

"No."

"Did she say where the apartment was?"

"No. I'm sorry."

"It's okay. You did better than I did."

"Do you want me to try again? I really want to help." Natalie looked so sweet, so hopeful.

I grabbed her hand. "Let's have your mom try next. I think it's less suspicious that way. But you should find out if anyone's filed a missing-persons report on Sandra or Lily." I paused for a second, then added, "Or Kennette."

I got in my car and was about to put it in Drive when I realized Bernie was knocking at the window. As soon as I rolled it down, she stuck her head in the car.

"I couldn't say this in the house, obviously," she said. "But we'll be at the shop on Sunday at one o'clock sharp."

"I don't know what you're talking about, Bernie. Why are you all coming to the shop on Sunday?" I asked.

She sighed and slowly explained, "We're finishing Carrie's quilt top."

I nodded. "I'm sorry. I'm involved in so many conspiracies that I can't keep them all straight."

"Fun, isn't it?" She moved away from my window.

Was it fun? The sad, maybe sick, part about it was that, yeah, it was a little fun.

CHAPTER 27

Oliver was late to class on Thursday, and as we all stood behind our easels waiting, I wondered if maybe he'd made a run for it. There were rumblings among the class about a student who'd died. One girl heard that she committed suicide over a love affair gone wrong. Another said it had something to do with drugs. Kennette and I exchanged glances but were silent. I wanted to ask if anyone actually knew Sandra and had any real information about her, but based on the whispers I doubted I'd find what I was looking for. Besides, just as I was thinking of what I could say, Oliver arrived full of breathless excuses about trouble with his car.

"Before we start today," he said, "I want to talk about a student we lost over the weekend. Sandra Thomas. We still don't know all the facts about how she died, but we do know that she was a gifted artist and a sensitive soul, and it is a tragedy for her to have died so young."

I looked around. Everyone looked appropriately somber for about thirty seconds. Then a few hands went up, asking what still life we were going to paint in today's class. Oliver shook his head.

"Not yet," he said. "Sandra wanted to be a painter. Sadly that dream will never become a reality. But I want to keep her dream alive in my own way so I will be offering a scholarship in her name to two of the students in this class."

Whatever genuine sadness there was quickly dissipated as excited students starting planning for their shot at stardom.

"I will choose the students that I think show the most promise, which will make it very difficult since this is a very talented group of artists," Oliver continued. "I will make my decision at the end of the final class, in three weeks."

Everyone but me applauded at the speech. I was wondering if he would still be teaching the class in three weeks or if he would be in jail for the murder of the girl he was so beautifully eulogizing.

As we were packing up after class, Oliver looked my way. "Nell, if I could see you in my office."

I followed him down the hallway. He let me walk into the office first then closed the door behind me. I felt as if he was either about to share an important secret or silence me forever. Just in case it was the latter, I stood close to the door, waiting for him to say something. But he just sat and stared into his hands, seeming to struggle to come up with the right words.

I knew he was about to tell me that he had an affair with Sandra. I almost said it for him, but he looked up at me, finally ready to speak.

"I just wanted to say that obviously I cannot choose you for the scholarship, given my relationship with your grandmother." Oliver spoke quietly, as if he were nervous about hurting my feelings.

"That's what you wanted to talk to me about?" I rolled my eyes. "I couldn't care less about the scholarship."

He looked taken aback. "It's got nothing to do with your talent."

"No, it doesn't. It's got to do with your relationship with Sandra. All that crying, private meetings in your office. Whatever your guilt, I don't need you working it off by paying for my classes." The words came tumbling out of my mouth. I was angry. And I was surprised I was so angry.

And so was Oliver. "There was nothing romantic going on between Sandra and me," he said. "I assume that's what you are alluding to."

"Then what was going on?"

I could see a redness creep up from his neck, but I couldn't tell if it was embarrassment or anger. "She had certain ideas. Delusions, really. I felt sorry for her. But I did nothing I need to explain, even to the granddaughter of the woman I . . ." He stopped short of saying *love* but it was obvious that was what he wanted to say. And just the idea of the word punctured my anger.

"Maybe not," I admitted quietly. "But I would like you to explain the arrest for pushing your girlfriend into a painting."

He smiled. "You are every bit as inquisitive as Eleanor said."

He was treating the whole matter so lightly. I'd been waiting for answers, going over clues in my mind and coming up with nothing. Oliver had those answers and all he could do was smile.

"That's not an answer," I finally said.

He nodded. "You're right. I know you're worried about your grandmother and perhaps you have a right to be." He gestured toward a chair in the corner. "Sit down and I'll tell you everything."

I sat and waited. Oliver leaned back in his chair and took a deep breath. He appeared to be searching for a place to begin.

"When I was a young man," he started, "I was full of ambition and ego. I knew I had talent, and I was impatient to prove it to the world. I suppose that's true for many young people, except I was also angry and, at times, abusive."

"I know that you had a drinking problem," I said. "I know that you stopped sometime in the late sixties or seventies."

"I stopped that night. The night you were referring to. The young woman was my girlfriend and she was, like me, talented and ambitious. But she was troubled by demons even darker than mine."

"Does that mean drugs?"

Oliver nodded. "I'd say it was the sixties, but that would be an excuse. We let ourselves get caught up in the times and our youth and our terrible need to be someone. And in the process we both hurt people we loved very much."

"According to the paper, you pushed her."

"It was my first solo show. I was drunk. I was always drunk in those days. Julie was trying to make me jealous and it worked." He ran his hand through his thick white hair. "She and I were like gasoline and a match. And it just got out of control that night."

"I know you got arrested, but what happened afterward?"

He smiled and shook his head. "I sold out the show. Isn't that awful? There are always people with money who, what's that old saying? People who want to go slumming."

"How were your paintings slumming?" I asked.

"Well, an unknown artist has a solo show and gets arrested," he said. "Suddenly I was controversial. I was dangerous. It launched my career, I'm embarrassed to say. But it also got me to see that I had to change. I wanted people to like my work. Instead Park Avenue types bought my paintings as a way a way of rebelling without all the mess and complication."

"What happened to Julie Young?"

"I went by her place a few weeks after the show and brought her money. She was working on a truly amazing piece. She made large collages with fabric and things she'd found on the street. She was quite talented."

"What happened to her?"

"I lost track of her. It was better for both of us. At least for our mental health. I'm not sure if it was what was best for our work. There was something about the turmoil. It's a sad truth that after years of perfecting your technique you may find that your best work is behind you and you have to go to great lengths merely to find inspiration."

Oliver looked so sad and his explanation was so reasonable that I felt guilty for having pegged him as a killer. Unless he was one. I still didn't have all my answers, but I wasn't sure I should try and get them all in one day.

The problem with Oliver was that I liked him. I liked the effect he had on my grandmother, and I liked the idea of having such an interesting, talented, and accomplished artist as a friend and teacher. I wanted to believe his sad stories and innocent explanations.

"I guess I'll see you on Saturday," I said as I got up to leave.

"I'm glad we talked." He smiled shyly.

✄

I left his office and walked toward the main hallway. It was crowded with workers, making it difficult for me to get out of the building. Two guys nearly dropped a large crate on my foot as I waited to leave.

"What's going on?" I asked.

"We're bringing in the last of White's paintings for display."

"Display where?"

He pointed toward an open door at the end of the hall. "It's going to be a permanent gallery. Look for your tuition to go up to pay for it."

"I thought the paintings were a gift."

He frowned. "The paintings were. Security wasn't. Those paintings are worth a fortune and now the school has to install cameras and lasers and have twenty-four-hour guards. Some gift."

I nodded. Since the door at the end of the hallway was open, I decided to walk down and take a look. Whatever security they were planning, it had not been installed. Workmen walked in and out of the room without giving me a glance.

Most of the paintings were still on display from the night I'd met Oliver, and it looked like at least ten more were in crates, waiting to be added. I walked past *Nobody*, the painting of the woman lying in her own vomit, past the nudes of women he'd painted in the seventies and eighties, and toward *Lost*, the apparent treasure of his collection.

There she was, a woman in a dress that looked to be from the 1950s or early 1960s. She was sitting on a bed, staring out the window, deep in thought. It was as if she had forgotten that Oliver was there. There was, as in all his paintings, an element of sadness to it. But there was something in this one that the others lacked. There was a sweetness to it, even love. It made sense that this was the painting he considered his masterpiece.

I stared at it for a long time, looking at the details such as the fold in her dress and the way her hands rested on her lap. It slowly dawned on me that I had seen this image—or something very similar to it—before. And not just on the night of the gala but in the photograph I'd stolen from Sandra's apartment. Though the dress wasn't polka-dotted, it was the same dress. The woman in the photo was the woman in this painting, and her facial expression in Oliver's piece matched the one Rich described in the photo he saw on the ground. I was staring at a link between Oliver and the two dead girls.

But did it mean Oliver had killed them? Maybe Sandra stalked Oliver and stole the photo. Oliver had called her delusional, and he'd probably say the same thing if I told him about the photo. Or maybe there was a different answer, a darker one. Maybe Sandra had a connection to that photograph and through it to Oliver. And maybe Oliver did kill her to keep her from revealing that connection.

Every time Oliver explained away my suspicions, something happened to make me question him all over again. And while I was going back and forth, Eleanor was falling in love with him.

For the first time I thought about dropping the whole thing. I'd rather let a killer walk the street than risk my grandmother getting her heart broken. But I knew I couldn't. If Oliver was a killer, would he stop at two victims?

CHAPTER 28

"Amazing," Eleanor said. "I am amazed by these."

Kennette and I started the meeting Friday night with a little show-and-tell of the quilt tops we had finished. Kennette's drunkard's path was large enough to curl under for a nap and mine was a Christmas wall hanging, but they were both completed quilt tops ready to be made into quilts.

It was an accomplishment that for me had been months in the waiting.

"I'm not a junior quilter anymore," I pointed out. "So is there some kind of ceremony? Maybe champagne?"

"It's not actually finished," Eleanor said. "It's just a top. Lots of quilters make tops and then they sit unfinished for months."

"Years," Bernie agreed.

"Well not me," I protested. "This gets done tonight."

"Me too," Kennette said. "Except I don't know where to start."

The group quickly divided into teams. Carrie and Natalie helped me baste my quilt, while the others worked on Kennette's. Since they needed the large table in the classroom for their work, we stayed in the front and used the cutting table.

It gave me a chance to tell them both what I'd realized after Oliver's class.

"Just when I want to like him, there's something new that makes me suspect him," Natalie said, shaking her head and glancing toward the classroom.

"I just wish something led us away from Oliver," I said.

"But who would that lead us to?" Carrie asked.

Natalie and I looked at each other, and I could tell that we were thinking the same thing. It might lead us to the junior quilter in the other room, and none of us were happy about the idea.

"Hey, what are you talking about?" Susanne said a little too loudly, which I took as a warning that Eleanor and Kennette were on their way into the main part of the shop.

"We're done!" Kennette held up her large, pinned quilt.

"We're done with basting," Maggie corrected her.

"I know," Kennette said, smiling, "but I'm celebrating the process, like you told me to."

Maggie laughed. "Then you're doing a great job. Now you can celebrate quilting it."

"Don't get too far ahead," Bernie said. "We need to figure out a pattern for each of our young quilters."

I held mine up first.

"We don't want the quilting to outshine the wonderful paintings you've done, so I think we should keep it simple," Susanne said. As a quilt-show winner, Susanne was the one in the group that we deferred to on matters of design. "We should do a nice continuous line of holly leaves along the border and stitch in the ditch around each of the blocks.

"In the ditch I can do, I think," I told her. In-the-ditch quilting is a simple straight stitch on the seam line. The quilting is practically invisible from the front, but it holds the layers together and doesn't detract from the piecing.

"What do I do?" Kennette stood up and held her quilt up to Susanne.

"Allover," Susanne declared quickly.

"Absolutely," the others said as a group.

"Allover what?" I asked. I knew enough to know that an allover design meant one pattern across the entire quilt, whether it was a stipple or a specific design.

Bernie got up and walked as far from the quilt as possible. "Kennette is a fun, lively girl," she declared. "We have to do something fun with this quilt."

"Hidden messages," suggested Carrie, jumping up.

"Yes," Eleanor said, "but it can't look messy."

"We'll do a series of loops and stars. That way it will be easier to add in Kennette's name and whatever else we want," Susanne said.

With that the women excitedly headed toward the sewing machines. It was like the start of the Indy 500, without the cars and the fireproof uniforms. Sewing machines were flipped on, bobbins were wound, and Kennette and I were pushed into chairs and told to hit the gas—or rather, in the case of the sewing machines, to step on the pedals.

"What do we do?" she whispered to me.

"I have no idea."

"Nell, you just start sewing a straight line stitch right here." Susanne pointed to a corner of quilt. "Follow it to the bottom and then over and up again until you have the blocks quilted down."

"Then shout for help." Bernie patted my shoulder reassuringly.

"And Kennette, dear," Eleanor said quietly, "you're going to free-motion quilt."

"Which means we get rid of the feed dog." Bernie pressed a button and the feed dog—the moving piece of metal under the needle that helps feed the fabric through the machine and assures even stitches—disappeared.

"What happens then?" Kennette said, frightened.

"Well, you put your hands on the quilt a few inches from the needle and guide the fabric, making stars and loops," Natalie said. "You pretend you're drawing, which should be easy for an artist. It looks really easy anyway."

"Looks easy?" I said to Natalie. "Haven't you done it?"

"No," she gasped, her eyes wide. "It's really scary to free-motion quilt. If you do it wrong, you end up with a cluttered front and big loops of thread on the back."

Kennette got up. "I'm not doing that. I'll ruin my beautiful quilt."

"For heaven's sake, Natalie. You've scared her." Susanne shook her head and sat down in Kennette's place.

She put her hands on the fabric and pressed the pedal. The machine started to whir, and Susanne's hands moved in a slow and steady way, creating loops and stars just as she said. We watched in amazement as she quickly moved through the quilt, adding spark to an already lively design.

After about thirty minutes Susanne got up and stretched.

"I want to try," Kennette said nervously. "You can always tear it out, right?"

Eleanor disappeared and came back with a scrap of muslin and a small piece of leftover batting. She cut the muslin in half and made a quilt sandwich.

"A practice quilt," she said.

She put it down in front of another sewing machine, and Kennette, with Susanne's hands on top of hers, started making quilt designs on the practice piece.

"This is really fun." Kennette smiled. "Who knew it was so easy?"

"She's like this in class too," I said to Natalie. "She learns things in two seconds."

"What are you doing sitting there?" Susanne noticed me watching Kennette quilt.

"I'm done with my straight line." I held up my quilt to show her.

"Well then you need to do the holly."

"I'm not Kennette," I said. "No practice quilt is going to get me ready in five minutes."

"Not a problem, dear. You let me help you," Bernie said. She took my place at the machine and in twenty minutes had sewn a continuous line of holly leaves without once looking up.

"My quilt is finished," I said, and then I knew I was wrong. "Except for the binding."

"And the label. The label is crucial," Maggie pointed out.

Though I knew there were several ways to finish the edges of a quilt, I went for the one that I'd seen most often. Known as a French binding, it's really a long strip of fabric that is folded in half lengthwise, sewn to the front of the quilt, and then folded over the raw edge to the back. It puts two layers of fabric at the edge of the quilt, which, I was told, is the part of the quilt that gets the most wear.

I went to the cutting table and cut several two-and-a-quarter-inch-wide strips. With Carrie and Natalie reassigned to my team and helping, I sewed the strips together and then folded the newly formed long strip in half, lengthwise. After Carrie ironed the fold for me, I returned to the sewing machine. I sewed the raw edge of the binding to the raw edge of the quilt and then held up my really close-to-being-finished quilt.

"What now?"

"Hand sew the binding to the back," Maggie said.

"But you're on your own for that." Carrie pointed to the clock.

It was, amazingly, nearly midnight. We had forgotten about the time, the killer, our love lives, and the rest of the world. We had, once again, gotten lost in quilting. And I was sad to see it come to an end.

And so, apparently, was Kennette. While I left my quilt to be finished after a good night's sleep, Kennette opted to stay at the shop until she had quilted the rest of her drunkard's path.

"This way I can write my secret messages." She smiled.

"Maybe if we read the quilt, we'll learn a thing or two," Bernie leaned to me and whispered as we left Kennette behind.

"It may be our only choice," I agreed.

I laughed as I said it, but I wasn't sure I was kidding.

CHAPTER 29

"You look pretty." Kennette walked into my room just as I finished dressing for my date with Jesse. It had taken me three tries, but I was very happy with the patterned red wrap dress and tan boots I was wearing.

Kennette walked to my closet, ruffled through it for a minute, and held out a blue cardigan. "Is it okay?"

"Anything you want," I told her. "Do you have a hot date too?"

She laughed. "I wish. I'm going over to Susanne's for dinner. I think her husband is out of town, and she and Maggie are going to grill me."

"Grill you?"

"That's what she said. She wants to know everything about me."

"They did the same thing to me when I moved here," I said, trying to laugh it off. I silently hoped that Maggie and Susanne would be as successful getting Kennette's story as they had once been getting mine.

"Can someone help me with this bracelet?" Eleanor walked in the room wearing a new turquoise dress.

"You look . . . Wow," I said.

"Thank you, sweetheart." She was beaming. "Oliver and I are just going for dinner. I'm sure we won't be too late."

Kennette helped Eleanor put on her bracelet then stepped back for a look. "You both look gorgeous. Jesse and Oliver are very lucky." She grabbed the blue cardigan and a green floral skirt and headed out of the room.

Eleanor and I just looked at each other. "We're lucky too," Eleanor said.

"Because we have dates? I never thought you would say such a thing," I jokingly scolded her. "You were always so independent."

"I don't mean the men. We have each other. We have Kennette." She smoothed her dress. "We look really nice."

I laughed, and in the same moment I felt tears rushing to my eyes. "I hope he makes you happy because I love you and I want . . ." I couldn't hold back the tears any longer.

Eleanor rushed over and hugged me. "What's all this about? Honestly, such fuss over a new friend."

We sat on my bed and held hands. "I've always been happy, Nell," Eleanor said. "I'm just surprised that I enjoy Oliver's company so much. I'm so used to Maggie and the girls that I forgot what it's like to spend time alone with a man."

"How do you like it?"

"I think I like it," she said. "How do you like it?"

"You and Oliver?"

"Yes. I thought maybe you didn't."

"If he's good to you then that's enough." Even as I was saying it, I wondered if it were true. "It's just that you're being so secretive."

"I'm not being secretive," she said defensively. Then she sighed. "Maybe I am. I don't want you to think of me as a silly old woman."

"That could never happen."

Eleanor looked at me. "Fix your makeup," she said. "Jesse doesn't want to have dinner with a raccoon."

"Our moment of sentimentality has come to an end, I take it." I laughed.

Just as I spoke I heard the doorbell ring. Jesse wasn't due for another half hour so I knew it had to be Oliver. Eleanor winked at me and left the room. I listened as my grandmother went down the stairs and opened the door. I heard them greet each other, and I heard

Oliver spend a few minutes playing with Barney. When Eleanor left him to get her purse, I went down the stairs.

"Nell," he said. "You look beautiful. I take it you have plans with Jesse."

"He's taking me to dinner."

"Where? Do you know?"

"He didn't tell me."

"I'm taking your grandmother to a French restaurant near my home. It's quite romantic, and the food is almost as good as hers."

"Sounds lovely," I said.

"Well . . ." Oliver seemed nervous. "Wherever you go, I know Jesse will be proud to show you off."

"Thanks, Oliver." I blushed a little at the compliment, but I only had a moment and I didn't want to waste it. "I happened to walk into the gallery they're putting together at school. I had a chance to take a long look at *Lost*. It's amazing. Who was the model?"

"You are incurable," he said, a smile creeping across his face. "Someone in England. Years and years ago."

"Was her name Violet?"

Oliver blinked slowly but said nothing. Eleanor walked in with her coat and purse. Oliver took the coat from her and held it out. As she put her arms into the sleeves, he wrapped his arms around her.

"Turquoise is your color," he said to her.

They walked out the door and I watched them through the window. They held hands on their way to the car. He opened the car door for her. He even leaned in to give her a quick kiss before closing the passenger door.

A half hour later the doorbell rang again. I checked myself in the mirror, suddenly very excited about our date.

"Hey." Jesse walked into the house. "I'm starved. Are you hungry?" He walked past me into the hallway.

"Yes, I guess."

"Do you want Italian or Greek or what?"

"I don't care."

"Where's your coat?"

I was getting annoyed. "I look nice, by the way." I pointed to my dress.

"I told you that you look nice."

"When?"

"A bunch of times." Jesse paced impatiently.

"When?"

"I don't know, Nell. The last time I saw you," he said. "Can we go?"

I grabbed my coat, but my heart wasn't in this date anymore.

Jesse stabbed at his salad, grunting the occasional answer to my questions. After a while I gave up and ate my dinner as if I were alone. The restaurant was filled with happy couples chatting and holding hands across the table. Some looked nervous, maybe on a first date or about to propose. Some looked comfortable, like parents finally out for a night alone. Everyone was engaged in conversation except Jesse and me. Anyone looking at us would have assumed we were headed for divorce.

When I finished my coffee, I'd had enough.

"Can you drop me off at the shop?" I asked.

Jesse finally looked at me. "Why?"

"You're kidding, right? You clearly do not want to be here. I might as well salvage the evening somehow."

He reached over and grabbed my hand. "I'm sorry. I should have canceled."

I pulled my hand away. "That's your answer? What's going on with you?"

Jesse leaned in. "I had a bad day today and I've clearly been unable to shake it."

"Is it Allie?"

He shook his head. "No. She's fine. It's the case. I lost a piece of evidence."

"Not possible. You would never lose evidence."

"Thanks, but I might as well have lost it. Days ago I asked Greg to bring the watch he found to the lab for DNA testing. When someone wears a watch, their cells can come off onto the band. I figured it was a long shot but what the hell."

"He lost the watch? He was so excited about having found it at the crime scene."

Jesse seemed to be struggling to keep his voice low. "He not only lost the watch, he turned the whole thing into a circus. I found out that, instead of securing it in an evidence bag and bringing it to the lab, he's been carrying that damn watch in his pocket. Then after I chewed him out, he begged for a second chance and I was stupid enough to give it to him."

I knew Greg had been carrying the watch and I hadn't said anything to Jesse, which made me feel suddenly part of a conspiracy against him. But that might have led to a discussion about the photo, and I couldn't risk Jesse being as angry at me as he clearly was at Greg.

"I'm sure it will be okay," I said in a feeble and useless attempt to calm him down.

"He put the watch into an evidence bag, and it was supposed to take him twenty minutes to get to the lab, but when he wasn't back in two hours, I called his cell. He told me that first he ran into Maggie, coming out of the library, and they had a nice chat. Then he gave Kennette a ride from the shop to your place. And then, and I'm not sure why exactly, he went over to the Morristown Police Station to see if they needed anything taken to the lab."

"Did he take it out of the car when he was talking to all those people?"

"Take it out? He was showing off. He wanted everyone to know he was lead detective on the case."

"He didn't say that. Greg is maybe a little excited—"

"He told Powell that he was lead detective," Jesse said. "I look like a complete idiot. I had to listen to Powell tell me how important it was that evidence get to the lab right away. Thank God I took the

fingerprint evidence from Sandra's apartment into the lab for identification." Jesse threw his napkin on the table. "I'm trying to conduct a
murder investigation and I've got Barney Fife on the force."

The whole idea made me laugh a little, or it would have if Jesse
hadn't been sitting there and the watch hadn't been a possible clue to
the identity of the killer.

"Maybe we should call it a night," I said.

Jesse nodded and paid the bill.

Once outside the restaurant Jesse and I stood awkwardly. I didn't
know whether to say good night or continue the date.

"You look beautiful," he said. "I know I don't say it enough, but I
think it every time I see you."

"Eleanor isn't the only one with a romantic boyfriend." I smiled.

"What?"

"Never mind." I leaned in and kissed him lightly.

As I backed away, Jesse grabbed my hand.

"What are you doing?" I asked.

"Trying to make the best of a bad evening," he said, and he kissed
me.

"We can't stand here, in the street, kissing," I said. "It will be all
over town tomorrow."

He backed away. "Sorry."

I smiled. "I'm not complaining about the idea, just the location."

I took his hand and walked over to Someday Quilts.

The windows were covered with quilts, but we left the lights out
anyway and walked to the classroom at the back. I took an old sample
quilt off a pile of others and laid it on the floor.

"Should we be doing this?" Jesse said as we sat on the quilt.

"Don't you know by now that I'm always doing things I
shouldn't?"

Even in the darkness I could see him smile. I leaned in to kiss him,
and as I did I felt a shiver from his right side.

Jesse pulled away. "I have the phone on vibrate." He blushed. "Sorry." As he took the call I waited on the quilt, feeling more foolish than romantic. I wondered if it would be possible to get back to that feeling or whether we should call it a night. When he hung up the phone, I knew the question was irrelevant.

"You have to go," I said.

"Rain check?"

I nodded. I sat in the darkness for a long time after he left, my head swimming with pictures—Oliver and Eleanor, Lily's body on the ground, Sandra in the river, Kennette's encounter with Greg. It was exhausting to try to make sense of it all, but it was still easier to think about than my stalled romance with Jesse.

Then I got up and walked to the office, where I had stashed my nearly finished Christmas quilt. I sat in the shop and hand sewed the binding to the back of the quilt, being careful to miter each corner as I had been taught. Sometime after one in the morning, I sewed the last stitch into the binding and cut a piece of cream fabric. I ironed the fabric to some fusible webbing and then to the quilt.

Using a fabric marker, I wrote: "Nell Fitgerald's First Quilt."

Then I pinned the quilt to the announcement board at the front of the shop and stepped back. There it was—proof that I was a quilter.

And a reminder that anything, no matter how scary it seems at first, can be sorted out if you take it step-by-step. I just wasn't sure if I was thinking about quilting, the murder investigation, or my relationship with Jesse.

CHAPTER 30

I tried to sneak into the house at about two in the morning. The problem was that Barney had positioned himself right by the door and I had to push my way in.

"What's going on, sweetie?" I asked as I patted his head. "Shouldn't you be asleep upstairs?" He looked up at me, his eyes sad and tired. "You should go up because Grandma will miss you. She doesn't like to sleep without you."

Unless she wasn't here.

I walked up the stairs, with Barney close behind. I could see that her bedroom door was open.

"Grandma?" I said quietly. "Are you in there?"

There was no answer. I turned on the light. Her bed was empty. The bed was made, with a star quilt covering it and another folded up at the foot. The pillows were fluffed and a throw pillow sat in the middle. It was clear that Eleanor had not yet come home.

"I guess she's having a good time," I told Barney. I turned off Eleanor's light and headed toward my own bed. As I did I heard a sound coming from Kennette's room. I crept closer and listened. The light was out but it was obvious that Kennette was awake. I could hear her crying inside.

I opened her door and turned on the light. Barney walked into the room and jumped up on Kennette's bed. She buried her face in his fur and continued crying.

"What's wrong?" I asked.

She sat up and wiped tears from her eyes. "I'm fine."

"No you're not. Something is wrong." I sat down on her bed. "Did something happen at Susanne's tonight?"

She shook her head. "Susanne made roast chicken with baby potatoes. And Maggie brought key lime pie for dessert."

"That sounds nice," I said. "Did someone say something to you?" I was slightly panicked because I knew Kennette had been lured to Susanne's house to be pumped for information. Maybe they had pushed too far.

"They were so nice. We talked about everything, and Susanne showed me her quilts. Did you know that Susanne has won awards for her quilts and that she used to be a beauty queen?"

I nodded. "So you had a good time? Then what's the problem?"

"I just feel guilty because . . ." Kennette paused, then closed her mouth tight as if she was trying to stop herself from saying something. "I just really want to do something to pay you all back for everything."

I put my arm around her while Barney put his paws on her lap. "Believe me, I know how overwhelming it can be when everyone is so kind. But you don't have to pay anyone back."

"I guess."

She grabbed hold of the quilt on her bed and pulled it a little closer. Instead of the pinwheel quilt that had been covering the bed, Kennette was using her almost-finished drunkard's path. She seemed to have finished the quilting but not the binding.

As Barney moved around on the bed, I noticed that she had, as planned, put secret messages in the quilt. She had sewn a name. As I made a slight move to get a better look, Kennette snapped the quilt over her. But it was too late. I'd seen the name she'd sewn into her first quilt: Oliver White.

"Could you turn off the light?" she requested.

I nodded. Barney left the room with me, but rather than coming to my room, he headed back to his place by the front door. I guess he had no intention of going to bed until Eleanor was home and safe.

I, on the other hand, wanted to go to sleep. I didn't want to think about the murders. I didn't want to think about the quilt in Kennette's room, and I certainly didn't want to think of what my grandmother might be doing in the middle of the night.

When I woke up the next morning, I wanted to take Barney out for a long walk. I found him fast asleep at the front door. It was all the confirmation I needed that Eleanor had not come home all night. I didn't know whether to be happy for her or worried, but I didn't have time for either. I needed to open the shop. Sundays were always a busy day, and we also had Carrie's quilt top to complete. It would have been helpful to have Eleanor's full focus and energy, but I could hardly fault her. As I had found myself, it was alarmingly easy to get sidelined by romance.

I got to the shop minutes after our normal ten o'clock opening, and there were already three worried-looking women standing outside the door.

"We thought you weren't opening today," one of them said.

"No, sorry, just late," I told them.

"Eleanor never opens late," another woman said worriedly.

I smiled and tried to ignore the insult. I opened the door and let them in to wander around the fabric bolts as I started the computer and prepared for the day. Kennette came a few minutes after I did, having stopped at the bakery for muffins and coffee. She was dragging Barney behind her.

"I didn't want to leave him home," she explained. "He seems so out of sorts."

But as she said that, Barney lurched past her and headed to the shop's office. He was gone for a moment before he walked out again and, tail down, headed toward the classroom.

"Poor thing," I said as I sipped my coffee, "he's absolutely lost without Eleanor."

"It's kind of like she's cheating on him with Oliver," Kennette added. "I'm trying to fill in but I know I'm his second choice."

I took it as my opportunity. "But you might be someone else's first choice," I said. "I heard that Greg gave you a ride home."

She blushed. "He saw me walking and felt bad. It was really cold outside."

"Did you have a nice conversation?"

"We did. He was telling me about the investigation. Jesse must be so jazzed to have Greg's help."

"Well, Jesse says the investigation has certainly been affected by Greg's involvement," I said.

Kennette and I were kept busy dealing with customer after customer. I stayed at the cash register while Kennette cut fabric and tried to help on the floor. When Maggie and Natalie arrived, I put them to work helping customers. Soon Bernie and Susanne were also chipping in.

"Everyone's asking about Eleanor," Natalie told me as she waved good-bye to another customer walking out with yards of fabric and the promise of a new quilt.

"She didn't come home," I whispered.

Natalie's eyes widened. "Go Eleanor."

"Remember that she was with Oliver, and we don't entirely trust Oliver."

"Right," she said. "Still, I'd love to be having nights like that."

I patted Natalie's baby bump. "You already have."

Within minutes Bernie was at my side.

"She didn't come home at all?" she asked.

"And she didn't call," I said.

"Well I'll find out at dinner tonight." Bernie smiled. "They're both coming to my house, and they won't leave without my getting the full story."

"It's not a big deal," Maggie interrupted. "She's a grown woman. More than a grown woman. She has the right to do whatever she likes."

"Anything you want to tell us, Maggie?" Bernie smiled.

"That's enough gossip about Eleanor's romantic life," Maggie said. "Honestly, each generation thinks they invented sex."

Both Bernie and I suppressed a smile as Maggie walked away.

"I think I'll get to work on Carrie's quilt," Bernie said. She tapped Susanne and Kennette, and the three of them walked toward the classroom where we had planned to finish Carrie's quilt top.

I checked my watch. It was after one o'clock. There was no sign that the rush at the shop would be letting up anytime soon, but I was anxious for a break. Besides, Barney was hovering by the door, getting in the way of customers.

"If I took ten minutes, would you kill me?" I asked Natalie. "Kennette knows the register if anyone needs to check out."

"Go for it," she said.

I grabbed Barney's collar and led him out into the street. As I did I saw Eleanor jumping out of the passenger side of a police car. She was wearing the same beautiful turquoise dress she had on the night before, but now it was wrinkled.

"Grandma, what's wrong?" I said, but she didn't seem to hear me.

Barney ran over to her and wagged excitedly, but Eleanor brushed past him. Greg got out of the driver's side of the car and followed Eleanor, who was walking past me into the shop.

"Nell," Eleanor looked around and found Natalie. "Is Nell here?"

"Grandma, I'm right here," I said. "What's wrong?"

"Oliver," she said. "Oliver is in jail. And it's my fault."

"Go Eleanor," Natalie said.

CHAPTER 31

"He's not in jail," Greg said quickly. "He's been taken for questioning, that's all."

"Jesse took Oliver from a date to ask him about the murder?" Natalie sounded angry and confused.

Behind her, Susanne and Bernie seemed ready to storm the jail and break Oliver out. Our suspicions were one thing, I guess, but ruining my grandmother's date—that was intolerable.

"Not Jesse," Greg corrected her. "Chief Powell, over in Morristown. He called Jesse about it, and this morning Jesse asked me to pick up Eleanor, um, Mrs. Cassidy, and bring her here."

"Why didn't Jesse call Nell?" Bernie asked accusingly.

Greg shifted his feet. "I didn't ask any questions, ma'am. I'm not exactly Chief Dewalt's favorite person right now."

"It's okay," I said, though I was a little ticked off that Jesse hadn't called. "Someone get Eleanor a glass of water. And when you're calm, Grandma, tell us what happened."

"I'm perfectly calm," she snapped. "I'm just angry, that's all."

We closed the shop, pushing the customers out without the fabric they had come for. We all went to the classroom and sat around the big table, waiting for Eleanor to tell her story.

"We had dinner at a lovely restaurant near Oliver's home, so naturally he asked me if I'd like to see his place," Eleanor said.

"Are they still using that line?" Bernie laughed.

Eleanor shot her a withering look. "For heaven's sake, Bernadette," she said, "two people can enjoy each other's company without it turning into something sordid."

Bernie nodded. "Sorry. You went to his house . . ."

"Yes." Eleanor sipped her water. "When we arrived there was a police car from Morristown parked out front. That Chief Powell and another officer were just sitting there, waiting."

"They didn't have a warrant," Greg offered. "So they had to wait outside."

"Why did they want to look in Oliver's house?" I asked.

"Well," Eleanor said, "obviously they think Oliver has something to do with the death of that poor girl."

"Which one?" I asked, and immediately regretted it.

"The second one," Eleanor snapped.

"Aside from Oliver knowing Sandra, what would lead Powell to want to search Oliver's house?"

"How would I know?" Eleanor said. "And Powell wouldn't tell us."

"What evidence does he have that Oliver's involved?" I asked Greg.

"I can't say," Greg told me.

"Do you even know?" Maggie asked.

Greg blushed. "No, ma'am. Chief Dewalt didn't tell me."

Kennette, who had sat stunned through the whole conversation, looked at all of us, one at a time. "Oliver did not kill Sandra. It's not possible."

I smiled at Kennette. I admired her certainty and, out of loyalty to my grandmother, I found myself agreeing with her.

"This doesn't make sense," I said to Eleanor. "Did the police find anything incriminating in Oliver's house?"

"They didn't go into Oliver's house. They didn't have a warrant," she said slowly. "Greg just told you."

"That only means they needed Oliver's permission," I explained.

"I told Oliver that unless Powell explained himself he shouldn't let that man put one foot inside the house, so he didn't," Eleanor said. "And Powell arrested him."

"Not arrested," Greg corrected her again. "They took him in for questioning. And that's where they've been pretty much all night. Powell called Jesse last night."

"I just feel terrible," Eleanor said. "If I hadn't insisted that Oliver stand up to that bully, he could have let them search his house and this would have been over hours ago."

"Why didn't you call me?" I asked her. "I would have brought you home."

My grandmother stared straight ahead.

"Unless the police were questioning you," I added.

Still nothing.

"Powell was questioning you? What for?"

Greg coughed and we all looked at him. "Powell thought maybe your grandmother might have helped."

I jumped up. "This is nuts! Somebody take my grandmother home so she can get some sleep."

"Nell, I'm perfectly capable—" she started to say.

"Fine," I snapped. "I'm going to get some answers."

I stormed out of the shop. A group of women were waiting outside. Just as I was about to tell them to go home, Eleanor straightened her dress, took a deep breath, and walked to the door.

"I'm sorry for the confusion," she told them. "Come on in. We've got some lovely fabrics that came in just this week."

We exchanged glances. She was composed and ready for business. I, on the other hand, was looking for blood.

"What does he mean, hauling my grandmother into jail?" I burst into Jesse's office.

Jesse was at his desk, looking through some paperwork. He looked up at me and quietly answered, "He's trying to investigate a murder."

"Sandra's murder happened in Archers Rest. Assuming that

Oliver did have something to do with it, Powell doesn't have jurisdiction. Just tell him to butt out."

"Calm down, Nell."

"What kind of an answer is that? Are you afraid of telling Powell to back off?"

Jesse stood up. "Lower your voice and sit down." He stood within inches of me, but there was nothing romantic about our proximity. I knew he was making it clear that, at least in this office, he was in charge.

I sat down. As calmly as I could, I asked again, "How does he have the jurisdiction to investigate Sandra's death?"

"He doesn't."

"So why is he?" Every ounce of me was struggling not to scream.

"He's not. He's investigating Lily's murder. We found her just past Morristown, remember. She could have been killed in that town and floated a few hundred yards downriver into Archers Rest."

I nodded, but the information was slow to sink in. Sure I had suspected that Lily's and Sandra's murders were connected, but I had nothing except an old photo. Powell had to have something more.

"Why?" I asked. "Why does Powell think Oliver killed Lily?"

Jesse looked at me. The stern-cop expression slowly melted away and was replaced by the gentle smile of my friend. "You have every reason to be freaked out, with Eleanor getting dragged into this. I don't want you to worry." He sat next to me and took my hand. "Oliver is on his way home. I talked with Marty Powell this morning, and he admits that he was a little overzealous. But you have to understand that we're trying to solve two murders that may be connected."

"Based on what?" I asked.

"Based on confidential police information." Jesse kissed me on the cheek. "I was thinking that maybe you could come over for dinner on Wednesday. Maybe it's time you and Allie got to know each other better."

"That's your consolation prize for not telling me what you found out," I said.

"I take it that's a yes?"

I nodded and returned his kiss. I wasn't satisfied with his answer, but I knew if I wanted a better one, I'd have to find it myself. "I should get back to the shop."

We got up and he walked me from his office to the front door of the police station. As I was walking out the door, Susanne walked in.

"I just got a call from my sister," she said to Jesse. "What happened to Rich?"

"Breaking and entering," Jesse said. "Again."

"It was only at the school." Susanne sniffed.

"There's not a list of approved places Rich can break into," Jesse told her.

"Can I do anything?" I asked Susanne.

"We need to finish Carrie's quilt," she said. "I'll bail Rich out. He's a good boy. Just a little exuberant."

"Well, if he keeps this up, Susanne, he'll be exuberantly doing five to ten," Jesse said. He pointed the way toward the jail cells and winked at me, which I took as my signal to go.

"I'll call you later," I said. "Both of you." But they ignored me, already immersed in the latest crime wave to hit Archers Rest.

I walked out into an early February day that was cold but with a bright sun that felt almost hot on my face. When even the weather couldn't be clearly defined, why should anything else start to make sense?

CHAPTER 32

That evening Eleanor went to Bernie's for dinner as planned. She and Oliver, she said, had no reason to cancel any engagements. They were not criminals, despite what that Chief Powell might think. Kennette and I nodded each time she told us. I was afraid to even mention that Powell must have something on Oliver or else he wouldn't have moved forward the way he did.

What especially interested me was that Powell wanted to get into Oliver's house. He must have felt there was something in there that would prove Oliver guilty of at least one murder. And if Oliver was innocent, wouldn't he have preferred to let Powell in than to spend the night in a police station?

I knew I had to get into that house. Eleanor had written Oliver's phone number on a piece of paper she'd left in the kitchen, so I looked up his address by using a reverse-phone Web site. I told Kennette I'd be working on the mural for Carrie's shop and jumped into my car.

In less than half an hour I was standing outside Oliver's small house. It was like an English cottage, down to the roses planted in the front yard. The house looked sweet and innocent, but it had to be hiding something. I knew Oliver would be at Bernie's for several hours, so I would have time to find out what that secret was.

I checked his front door, and then the back. Both were locked. I checked each window. They were all locked. I tried each window again and looked for any way I might get in. No luck. Climbing onto a fire escape to get into Sandra's was, in retrospect, pretty easy.

I walked around to the back, where there was a converted two-car garage he used as his art studio. Instead of a roll-up garage door, there were two large swinging doors, like you would see on a barn. But unlike on a barn, these doors were padlocked. Even the small windows on either side of the building were locked. When I pulled myself up to look in the windows, all I saw was darkness.

"This is useless," I said to no one.

I was about to head home when I had an idea. I grabbed my cell phone and dialed.

"Natalie," I said. "I need your help."

In another forty-five minutes Natalie pulled up behind my car. She jumped out with a big smile on her face.

"This is going to be so fun," she said. "We're actually sleuthing."

"First we have to get inside," I pointed out.

We both looked toward the backseat of the car, where Rich was still sitting. Natalie waved at him and he reluctantly got out.

"I'm not going back to jail," he said.

"You won't," I promised. "Just get us in and then you can take my car for the evening. Natalie will drive me home."

He sighed and walked toward the house. Like me, he tried the front door and then started making his way around the side of the house. We followed, uncertain of what to do.

"I tried the windows," I told Rich.

"Uh-huh," he grunted.

He stopped in front of a window at the back of the house and pulled out a metal nail file. He moved the nail file along the window frame. Then for several minutes he moved the file in and out around the lock, while Natalie and I stood a few feet away, watching.

"Is your mom babysitting?" I asked Natalie.

"Yeah. She loves it. She was at my house in five minutes."

"Where did you say you were going?"

"I told her you needed Rich to break into Oliver's house."

"And she was okay with that?" I asked. It had been only a few hours since Susanne put up Rich's bail.

"She said he would probably be getting into trouble anyway. This way at least it's for a good cause."

Rich looked up from the back window he'd been working on. "Do you mind? This isn't a tea party. It's a felony. If you could keep the conversation to a minimum."

"It isn't a felony until we actually get in," I pointed out.

Rich shook his head and jiggled the window slightly, then he gave it a push and it opened. "Now you're in. I'm out of here."

I handed Rich the keys to my car, the price I had to pay for his expertise, and warned him repeatedly about drinking and driving. But he was on his way before I'd finished my speech.

"Stay here," I told Natalie. "I'll climb in the window and open the back door for you."

"Pregnant women don't get to have any fun," she said.

"Maybe you'll get lucky and the police will find us. I hear prison is fun."

I pushed my way up onto the windowsill and climbed in headfirst. Unfortunately it meant that I had to fall headfirst onto a hardwood floor.

"Are you okay?" Natalie called out when she heard the thump as I hit the floor.

"Shh." I got up and looked out the window. "Back door," I whispered.

I found my way in the dark to Oliver's back door and let Natalie in. We stood in Oliver's kitchen for several moments.

"What are we looking for?" Natalie asked.

"Something that links Oliver with Lily."

"But we didn't know Lily, so how will we know when we've found a link?"

"I don't know. We'll just have to figure it out."

While Natalie opened the kitchen cabinets, I looked through the drawers. Everything was simple and sparse. Even the refrigerator held only a few items. There was nothing that seemed even remotely suspect. Of course it would have helped if I knew what we were looking for.

I looked up at Natalie. "How about the living room?"

We moved from room to room, finding more of the same—simple decor but nothing unusual. The layout of the place was very basic. At the front was a small living room. It led into a hallway. On either side were two bedrooms, with a small bathroom on the right side and several closets on the left. At the back of the house there was a kitchen with a small dining area.

"Notice anything weird?" I asked.

"Nothing except the bare walls," Natalie said. "Don't you think he'd put up his own paintings somewhere?"

"Or at least a friend's painting or something," I agreed.

"It seems so uncreative."

I nodded. "The whole place is like a monk's quarters."

"I expected a bachelor pad." Natalie sounded disappointed. "You know, with all the talk about his having an affair with Sandra."

"Do you think Powell found evidence he had a relationship with Lily?"

"We should check and see if she was an artist or artist's model," Natalie said.

"That would give them a reason to meet," I agreed.

"But what about the photos?" Natalie asked. "I just don't see Oliver dropping a photo by his murder victims like some kind of serial killer's calling card."

"I suppose he wouldn't," I agreed. "Still, there has to be a connection between Oliver and both Lily and Sandra, or Powell wouldn't have dragged Oliver into the station."

Natalie looked at her watch. "Bernie will be serving dessert about now."

"Maybe she can stretch it," I said. "She can talk for hours."

But one phone call to Bernie's and we found that my grandmother and Oliver had already left, and Bernie had "lots to tell."

It took me a minute to explain that Natalie and I were still in the middle of committing a crime so her news would have to wait. If we were going to get out without getting caught, we only had a little time, and there was one place left to check.

We left the back door open and walked to the garage studio. We had found a key hanging by the door in the kitchen, and I hoped it would open the padlock on the studio doors. I put the key in the lock and prayed. It worked. I opened the lock and pushed one of the doors just a crack so Natalie and I could get inside.

At first the studio seemed just as ordinary as the rest of the house. There were paints everywhere, with rolled-up sketches, blank canvases, and half-finished, clearly abandoned paintings piled up against the wall. There was a chair sitting on an ornate rug, and it looked as though Oliver had recently posed a model there.

It was just as an artist's studio should look. I spent a minute imagining myself painting there, surrounded by oils and acrylics, and in my case, fabrics. But it was no time to get lost in fantasy.

I flipped through the paintings, most of them incomplete. Quilters often talk about their UFOs—quilts that are left unfinished mainly because the quilter has run out of interest or decided the idea wouldn't work. Looking through Oliver's studio, I realized that painters had them too. At the back of one pile was a piece that was completely different from anything else in the room. It was a bright collage of fabrics, found objects, and words on canvas. It was startlingly emotional and quite beautiful. I knew at once that the artist was Julie, the model for Oliver's *Nobody* painting.

I turned to show it to Natalie but she was leaning over, pulling at something heavy. I put the painting down and walked over to her.

"What's this?" Natalie asked as she pulled a covered painting from behind a desk. We uncovered it and stepped back. It was a large unfinished oil painting of a nude woman.

I knelt down to examine it. Something seemed strange to me, but I couldn't quite figure out why.

"You know who it looks like, don't you?" Natalie said.

I got up and looked at the painting from a distance. It hit me. Perhaps there was a little artistic license, but there was no mistaking the model in the painting.

And now nothing made sense.

CHAPTER 33

"Are you sure?" Carrie asked me.

"As sure as I can be," I said.

"Why?" Susanne seemed as bewildered as the rest of us.

The day after our trip to Oliver's, Natalie related our adventures to the rest of the group. I was supposed to be painting the mural at Carrie's shop, but I hadn't gotten much painting done because the questions our discovery raised were relentless.

"Did you have any idea that was going on?" Maggie asked me a second time.

"None," I admitted. "Not from his end anyway."

Bernie shook her head. "Kennette posing nude for Oliver? It just doesn't make any sense."

"She likes him," I said. "She makes no secret of that."

"But he likes Eleanor," Susanne pointed out. "And Kennette likes Eleanor. She wouldn't do that to her."

"It's quite tasteful," Natalie offered. "It doesn't really show anything, you know, private."

"But she's still nude whether it shows anything or not," I pointed out.

Maggie shook her head. "Don't be such prudes. He's an artist. He uses models. He probably thinks of Kennette as just another model, whatever she may or may not feel about him."

"So why keep it a secret?" Natalie asked.

We all sat silently, trying to come up with an explanation.

"Kennette is private," Susanne finally said. "Maggie and I tried everything we could think of to get information out of her the other night. We couldn't find out a thing."

"Maybe there's nothing to tell," Maggie suggested. "She's a young girl. She's full of hope and ideas and plans, but what kind of a past could she have? A high school boyfriend or a fight with her mother? We're all struggling to crack her like she's some great big mystery, but maybe there's nothing there."

"Except that she's posing naked for Oliver," Bernie said.

"What aspiring artist wouldn't pose for a famous man like Oliver?" Maggie asked. "Think of what you might learn."

Everyone looked at me. "If he weren't dating my grandmother, I guess I would too," I admitted. "And I might be shy about it, just like Kennette."

"That might explain why Kennette isn't mentioning it, but it doesn't explain everything. Natalie found the painting covered up and behind a desk," Carrie pointed out.

"Why would Oliver hide the painting," Maggie picked up her thought, "unless he wanted to keep it from Eleanor, who was supposed to come to his house the other night? And if he's hiding it from Eleanor, then Kennette's more than just a model."

More silence.

"Well we're not learning anything about Kennette, and I've been looking," Natalie jumped in.

"At least Oliver isn't shy about his past," Bernie added. "He was telling all kinds of stories last night."

"One thing at a time, please," Susanne cried out. "Honestly, we need to approach this with some organization. I feel like we're just going around in circles."

"Are you looking for someone to keep minutes and type up an agenda?" Bernie laughed.

"And maybe we should have refreshments," Maggie added.

"I vote for that," said Natalie.

"I think we're getting off topic," I suggested. My group of amateur detectives was turning into a social club.

Susanne stood up to address the group. "I'm just saying that we need to go in order. Like when we show quilts at the meeting. We each take turns showing our quilts and getting suggestions from the group," she explained. "And Eleanor keeps things from turning into chaos. There's no reason that solving a murder investigation should be any less organized than a quilt meeting."

With that, all eyes were on me.

"Okay," I said, looking at each face. I settled on the person that seemed the most impatient. "Then let's start with Bernie."

Bernie took a deep breath and leaned forward.

"Oliver said he came to the States looking for a fresh start after his divorce," she said. "He went straight to the Village because, well, that's where you went if you were an artist or creative type or just looking for some fun."

"And he said he got into drugs?" I asked.

"Yes." Bernie leaned forward. "He said he got on a downward spiral. He said he 'dabbled' in drugs, that was his word, but that alcohol was his choice for . . . How did he put it? His choice for self-destruction."

"And Eleanor was sitting right there while he told you?" I asked.

"The whole time."

"And then"—Bernie looked around, obviously holding the juiciest information for last—"he mentioned that he often painted near the river and once he had a model who fell in the river and nearly drowned. He said it was a scene he would have liked to have painted. He said he 'reluctantly,' and that was his word, helped her instead."

Bernie sat back and watched our faces. Like the others, I didn't know what to say. Oliver killing models to make great paintings was a motive that had not occurred to me. And if it were true, had that turned Kennette from suspect to potential victim?

"So where do we go from here?" Susanne asked, breaking the tension.

"I don't know," I acknowledged. "Anybody else have news?"

"I do," Natalie said. "Or rather, I don't. I contacted police departments in the neighboring states and Canada about missing-persons reports on the victims and Kennette Green. There were no missing-persons reports."

"They just gave you that information?" Maggie asked, surprised.

"No. I faxed them a request on Archers Rest Police Department stationery," Natalie admitted.

"Where did you . . . ," I started.

"I stole some for her when I bailed Rich out of jail yesterday," Susanne said matter-of-factly.

We all laughed.

"Between the two of you and Rich, I'd say we have our very own crime family," Bernie said.

Natalie glanced at her mom, who did not look amused, and then returned to her report. "I did find out that Lily Harmon is an alias. Her real name was apparently Lily Price. She had a dozen or so arrests in New York City and in Ontario for petty theft, shoplifting, and stuff like that."

"So Lily wasn't such an innocent victim after all," Natalie said.

"Would you kill someone for shoplifting?" Maggie asked. "That might not have anything to do with this."

"Well, it might have put her in contact with criminals," I suggested. "And one thing led to another."

"We don't have any criminals as suspects. We don't even know any criminals," Susanne said.

We all looked at her.

"Rich isn't a criminal," she protested. "He's a kid."

Susanne got up, as if she were about to storm out of the shop. Carrie coughed.

"Well, if I can go next," Carrie said. "I looked into Lily's and Sandra's financial background and there was nothing on Lily. I'll try the last name Price and see if I have better luck. And Sandra had a credit rating of 460, which is about the worst you can get."

"So Sandra was in financial trouble?" I asked. "We know Oliver was giving her money."

I looked around again. No one else seemed anxious to speak.

"So what's next?" Susanne asked, sitting back in her original spot.

"I guess we go back to Kennette," I decided reluctantly. "Carrie, if you can check into her financials—"

"If she has any," Carrie interrupted. "Has anyone seen her use a credit card?"

"Even so," I said, "it's all we've got." I sighed. "And I think I'll just ask her about modeling for Oliver and see what she says."

The others began to leave, some through the front door, others the back—just in case anyone was across the street, looking out the windows of Someday Quilts. I was just about to start work on the mural when Bernie came up behind me.

"I forgot to mention this, but I have bad news on the autopsy," she said. "I went through the reports on both girls and there wasn't anything we don't already know. Lily drowned and Sandra was strangled. They don't seem to have anything in common, except the killer."

"At least we think so," I said.

Bernie shook her head sadly. "They both seemed to have put up a fight, poor things."

"How do you know?"

"Well, Sandra had a few scrapes on her hands, so my guess is that she was hitting her attacker, and Lily's hands had been bound."

"By a rope," I added.

"No, I don't think it was. There were no fibers. It had to have been something metal or plastic. Anyway, she had bits of blue rubber under her fingernails. If it had been blue paint, we'd have Oliver, wouldn't we?"

As she walked out the door I stood frozen. I knew instantly that I had held the killer's watch in my hand. The watch Greg found in Sandra's bed and then lost.

CHAPTER 34

For two hours I worked on the mural and thought of how crazy things had become. I felt certain that if I could just figure out the connection between Lily and Sandra I could find the killer. And if I could find the killer, hopefully life would go back to normal.

When Carrie was ready to leave the shop to pick up her kids, I decided to leave as well. But rather than going home, I headed across the street to Someday Quilts. Just a few customers were wandering the store, and Eleanor was at the cash register, ringing up a sale.

"Need help?" I asked.

Eleanor nodded. "We've only got about twenty minutes until closing so we've got to get this group out of here."

"Where's Kennette?"

"She needed the afternoon off," Eleanor said. "It's been slow most of the day anyway."

Feeling for the first time today that I could do something within my comfort zone, I went toward the back of the shop to help a woman who stood staring at a bolt of brightly printed fabric.

"It's beautiful," I offered. "Can I cut some for you?"

She stroked the bolt, a technique I recognized as part of the quilter's courting process. First we fall for the look of the fabric—the print, the color. Then we begin to pet it, running our hands across the smooth cotton. It may seem odd to an outsider, but quilting is a tactile experience, and since quilts are meant to be snuggled under, it's important that the fabric feels right.

"I can't decide how much to get," she said. "I love it, but I don't know what I'm going to do with it."

"How large are the quilts you make?" I asked.

"Large enough for a nap, usually. I don't think I'm ready to make a bed-size quilt."

"Two yards at a minimum," I said confidently. "That way you can make borders and use some of it in the quilt blocks. But five yards if you want to use it for the back of the quilt."

She petted the bolt again. "I really love it," she said. "And I know if I wait a week it will be all sold out and I'll never see it again."

I smiled. "We usually order only one bolt of fabric," I agreed. "When it's gone, it's gone."

"I can't live without it, silly as that sounds."

"Not to a quilter."

"I know I'll use it," she said as she handed me the bolt.

"Five yards, then?"

She nodded.

As I cut the fabric I felt a certain amount of relief. Fabric has that effect. With each customer I helped, I ran my hands across the bolt and felt the cotton between my fingers, and just like the woman with the bright print, I fell in love with the fabric in my hands.

As we closed up the shop for the night I wanted nothing more than to stay there and cut fabric for myself and focus only on making a quilt. It seemed like a silly idea until I picked up a new arrival, a soft yellow floral.

"I want this," I found myself saying. "I want to make a quilt. And I want to make it now, tonight."

"I'll get some food from DeNallo's," Eleanor said, "while you pick out a pattern."

"You're going to help?"

Eleanor kissed my forehead. "I've been missing my granddaughter," she said.

I chose a simple Irish chain, a pattern of crisscrossing blocks that form diamonds in the quilt. I walked through the shop and gathered complementary fabrics, solids in soft greens and blues, a small floral in blues, and several choices from the collection of yellow florals as well as a yellow and green plaid. I hoped the quilt would be romantic and soothing.

Eleanor and I cut strips for the chain and sewed them together. Then we cut and sewed the strips to create the chain blocks. We cut the squares of yellow floral and added the strips at each side to create the background blocks. It was amazing how quickly two people, working side by side, could accomplish their goal. Within a few hours we had the quilt top I'd wanted. At six feet square it was large enough for a nap—or to hide under if I ever needed to run away from my problems again.

Although the entire time we had been working on my quilt I'd forgotten the murders and all the unanswered questions, as we finished the last block, those anxieties flooded back. I looked over at my grandmother, who had done so much for me and had been such a good friend, and I felt worried that in trying to protect her I was, instead, betraying her.

"How much do you know about Oliver?" I ventured as we pinned the top to the batting and backing.

"As much as you can know about a person after a few weeks," she said.

"But you love him."

She looked up at me. "Yes, I suppose I do."

"Isn't that kind of fast?"

"At my age I don't have a lot of time to waste on silliness."

"Is he worthy, though? Is he . . ." I couldn't find the right word to convey my suspicions without actually saying I suspected him.

"He's a good man. That much I know," she said as she put the last pin in the top. "Do you want to quilt this tonight?"

I shook my head. "Barney will be worried if we don't get home."

Eleanor folded up the quilt and put it in her office. "We can work on it again when it's slow," she said.

I walked over and wrapped my arms around her. "Don't get too caught up in him," I said. "Just in case."

She hugged me. "I won't, but you have to do me a favor too."

I looked into her beautiful brown eyes. "Name it."

"Don't keep finding reasons to push love away."

She kissed my cheek and headed out of the shop. I stood for a moment, confused. I wasn't pushing love away. At least I didn't think so. But as I followed behind her, I wondered if she knew something about me that I didn't.

CHAPTER 35

I walked over to the police station, which seemed quiet even for a cold January night. If Eleanor was right and I was looking for reasons to push love away, then that would stop now.

Greg was supposed to be manning the phones in the reception area, but instead he was furiously writing on a legal pad. When he saw me, he quickly put the pad under his desk.

"What's going on?" I asked.

"Not a thing," he answered.

"Well that's good news in the police business." I smiled.

"I guess. Though I wish we had something exciting to do."

"You have the investigation."

He grunted. I'd forgotten that he'd been frozen out because of the watch fiasco, but it wasn't a subject I wanted to get into.

"Jesse in?" I asked.

"His office."

I walked several steps before I took a quick peek back. Greg had the notepad out again and was hunched over it, writing.

I moved toward Jesse's office and saw that the door was slightly open. For a moment I stood outside and against the wall. I looked in as Jesse worked at his desk, studying papers as if he couldn't understand them. He had that stern, strong frown he'd worn when we first met. He was then, and now, so smart and so focused that I smiled just looking at him.

As he studied the papers his glasses slipped down his nose, and he reached up to push them back. Silly as it sounds, it made my heart leap. I'd always liked his laid-back professorial personality, but when I let myself, I realized I loved the way he was both capable cop and shy geek. I felt safe with him, and I knew I could be myself with him.

Things had been a little tentative, but that was only because of one dead body in the river, another on my back porch, and my grandmother's romance with a man who might be responsible for both. As soon as this murder investigation was behind us, I knew we could finally have the relationship we deserved.

I watched as he removed his glasses and rubbed his eyes. I couldn't wait a moment longer to talk to him, so I pushed the door open and walked inside.

"Hi," I said. "I know you're working, but I wanted to come by and see you."

Jesse looked up at me blankly.

I walked over to his desk and touched his shoulder. He moved away.

"Am I interrupting something?" I asked. "If I am . . ."

"No."

"Oh good." I smiled but I felt a little unsure. Still, I decided to press on. Jesse, I knew, was tired and overworked. He needed the break I could bring him. "I was hoping you were having a dull evening and we could hang out."

"I've got work," he said.

"Well take a break," I teased. I leaned down and kissed him, but he didn't kiss back.

I straightened up. "If you'd rather I leave . . ."

I waited, but Jesse didn't answer. I took a step toward the door. Jesse put his glasses back on and looked at me as if we had never met.

"Sit down."

His voice was flat, unemotional, all business. And it made me angry. Whatever was going on with him, he didn't have to take it out on me. I was about to tell him that, but I could see in his eyes that he wasn't in the mood to listen.

"What is it?" I said as I sat in the chair across from him.

He leaned back and looked at me. "The results on the fingerprints came back this afternoon."

"What fingerprints?"

"The fingerprints from Sandra's apartment."

I could feel the blood drain from my face. Jesse was watching me closely, and I was trying hard to seem interested but detached, as if the results had nothing to do with me. But I was actually searching my brain, replaying my little foray into Sandra's apartment. I didn't wear gloves; that much I remembered. But what had I touched? What was there to touch?

Then it hit me. The wallet. I had held it, opened it, searched through it. Of course he'd checked it for fingerprints. But I could say that Sandra had dropped it during class and I picked it up, looked through it for identification, and handed it back to her. Easy. He couldn't prove otherwise.

I tried to breathe again.

"So what did you find?" I asked as casually as my rapidly beating heart would allow.

"You." Jesse leaned back in his chair. It seemed as if he were trying to get as far from me as possible. "I found your prints on the window-sill and on several kitchen cabinets."

"How can you know that?" I stammered.

"I have them on file from the last time you interfered in a police investigation, remember?"

I remembered. "I knew Sandra," I said weakly.

"Not that well. Not well enough to be in her apartment, unless you would like to change your story."

"My story?"

"What you told me the night she was murdered."

"Yes, that's what I told my boyfriend. I wasn't aware that you were questioning me as the chief of police."

Jesse frowned. "Why were you in her apartment?"

"I'm not a suspect."

He sat up again and looked straight at me. "Yes, you are."

"You think I killed Sandra?"

"No." It was clear that he was getting angry but he was trying his best to keep it under control. "You are a suspect in a breaking and entering at the apartment of a murder victim."

His eyes never moved from mine but finally I couldn't stand his distance. My voice turned flat and I stared him down.

"Are you going to charge me?" I asked.

He slammed his fist on his desk and I jumped in my seat. "How could you do this? Are you an idiot?"

"What's that supposed to mean?" I raised my voice, the best defense being a desperate offense.

"I assume you were playing detective even though I'd asked you not to."

I lowered my eyes. What was there to say? He had me and he knew it.

"Yes," I said quietly.

Jesse's face went red and he seemed ready to kill me. "Let's get back to my question. What were you doing in Sandra's apartment?"

I looked at him, hoping for some understanding. "I wanted to see if there was anything that tied her to Lily."

"And?"

"And nothing." I took a deep breath. There was no point in lying any more. "I did find one thing. I found a photograph that was similar to the one that Susanne's nephew described."

"You found?" he asked. "Is it the photo that Greg said he found in the wallet after it was in evidence?"

I nodded. Jesse tapped his fingers on the desk and said nothing, though it looked as if he might explode at any moment. I waited for him to calm down. Actually, I hoped he would calm down, but it didn't seem likely anytime soon.

"I know you're mad," I finally said.

He clenched his jaw.

"And I was wrong," I said. "I knew that even at the time."

"Good for you."

"But she was found dead a few feet from my house. The main suspect is my grandmother's boyfriend. I needed to know."

"And I told you I would find out."

"Of course you will, but—"

"You don't belong in this investigation," he said.

"Neither does Powell, but for some reason you're letting him help."

Jesse's face went white. I'd gone too far.

He waved his hand as if to dismiss me. "I'm not going to charge you," he finally said. "You should go home."

I would have been relieved but there was a coldness in his voice that frightened me more than facing arrest.

"Let's not let this ruin things between us," I said quickly, softening my voice to that of a girlfriend trying to end a lovers' quarrel.

"Go home, Nell."

"I was wrong. I know I was wrong. But this is ridiculous. What we have—"

"We don't have anything. Not anymore."

"I'm not going anywhere until we talk about this," I said. Knowing that we were past the criminal activity and on to the relationship, I felt on more solid ground.

But Jesse didn't see it my way. He stood up and took my arm, pulling me from the chair.

"Go home," he said in a voice full of contempt.

He walked me over to his office door and led me out. Then he closed the door behind me.

I stood there, trying to think of the words that would change his mind. I could hear him walk back to his desk and get on the phone. I couldn't hear who he was talking to or what it was about. As I pushed my ear against the door, I realized that I was doing exactly what had angered him in the first place—sticking my nose in where it didn't belong.

✂

I walked past Greg, still writing on his legal pad, and out of the police station. The wind had picked up and it slapped me across the face. I thought about going back to the quilt shop and working on my Irish chain in the hopes of recapturing some of the peace I'd felt just an hour before, but I didn't have the focus for it.

Instead I walked in circles around town, looking at the closed shops and into the window of Moran's Bar. There were plenty of people inside enjoying the evening, but that just depressed me.

Instead I found myself heading toward the river, toward the very spot where Jesse had dragged Lily's body out of the water. Dead leaves and wet snow had reclaimed the area and there was no sign left of the tragedy that had happened there. But for me there was a new tragedy. I sat down on the cold, wet ground and let go of the emotion I'd been holding inside.

I cried for so long that I thought I would never stop, but eventually I didn't have any tears left inside me—just a hollow pain and the realization that I had betrayed Jesse's trust. I knew he felt that if I'd respected him I would have left the investigation to him. Somehow I had belittled his abilities when that was the last thing I'd ever intended.

But slowly the thought crept in my head—if he respected me, he would know that I couldn't just step over a dead body and leave it for others to fix. I didn't need or want to stand behind some man who would protect me from danger. I wanted to protect myself. If Jesse was looking for some damsel-in-distress type then he didn't really want me.

I stood up, suddenly aware of how cold it was. I wiped the tears from my face and started back toward the road.

I had made a mistake when I broke into Sandra's apartment. Jesse was right about that. But the mistake was not wearing gloves.

Next time I wouldn't be that stupid.

CHAPTER 36

I walked into class on Thursday determined to walk out with answers. I'd lain low for the last few days, still stung by my fight with Jesse. But now, with Kennette and Oliver about to be in the same room, I was back on the investigation.

"There's no still life," Kennette whispered to me as she got out her charcoal.

I looked down at the empty table where usually there was a display of fruit, pastries, bottles, or something that we could draw.

"Maybe he's bringing it with him," I whispered back. But just what "it" was, I didn't know.

"Good morning, class." Oliver walked in smiling. "I have a bit of a surprise for you today. You've all been doing such terrific work that I thought we would forgo doing a still life today and try something different. It's a bit more complex, but all I ask is that you take your time, focus your attention, and let yourselves find the emotion in the object."

The entire class stood at attention, confused and excited. Oliver was good at creating drama even when he wasn't painting. He pointed to the door and all eyes turned. In walked a young woman wearing a bathrobe. He directed her to the table and helped her as she climbed onto it.

It was clear that the "object" he wanted us to paint was a nude model. As we stood at our easels, the woman took off her robe and posed, one foot slightly turned and in front of the other, her hands laced behind her back. I stood with my charcoal in my hand, unable to decide where to start.

"Just draw boxes." Oliver was behind me and I found myself suddenly embarrassed that we were both looking at a nude woman.

"Boxes?" I asked.

Oliver lifted a ruler from my easel and held it in front of him. He squinted and seemed to be studying the woman.

"Look at the proportions and draw the figure as a group of boxes that correspond to the pose. Once you have the proportions correct, it will be easier to draw the lines and shapes." He handed me the ruler.

I nodded and held the ruler up as he had. But instead of figuring out the proportions of the model, I was trying to watch Oliver as he spoke with Kennette. Though it was difficult to see without being obvious, I could hear what they were saying just behind my easel.

"I'm not sure I'm ready for this," Kennette said to Oliver.

"You are one of my most talented students. Just take it one step at a time."

"But she's naked," Kennette said. "I know it's stupid . . ."

"You have seen a naked woman before." His voice seemed tired. "And in this case she is merely a model. Nothing more. She is not a nude woman. She is not even a person. She is a series of curves and shadows; a way for you to express your emotions. I have every confidence that you will be able to do that."

Oliver moved on and I turned and smiled at Kennette, who smiled shyly back. It was despicable of me, but I realized that Kennette's nervousness about the model was the perfect opening to ask her about the painting in Oliver's house.

That would have to wait, though. I needed to focus on drawing the model and at least have something to show at the end of the class. I held up my ruler and squinted as Oliver had instructed. I determined the proportions of the head, the torso, the arms, and the legs. I lightly drew my boxes and then reshaped them to form the curves of the female form. I found myself staring at her and seeing only shadows and lines.

Halfway through the class, I realized that I was seeing the model exactly as Oliver described. To an artist, she wasn't a woman: She was an object.

But I guess a killer would feel the same way.

As soon as class ended, Oliver disappeared. I hadn't yet decided who I would speak to first, or what I might say, but since I was left with only Kennette, I turned to her drawing. As always, it was an amazing work—simple yet emotional.

"You nailed it," I exclaimed.

Kennette frowned. "I felt a little silly drawing a nude woman with Oliver standing there."

"Really? Drawing nudes is an important part of learning basic art skills."

"I know. I guess I'm just being silly."

"Besides, Oliver used hundreds of models in his work. If he weren't dating my grandmother, I'd pose for him. Wouldn't you?"

Her eyes widened. "God, no. I can't even imagine it." She rolled up her drawing and stuck it in her bag.

"I guess it would be weird," I said, trying to think of a new direction to take the conversation. "After all, we've become friends with him."

"Exactly," she said.

"And I know you like him," I said.

"Who doesn't? It's not like he's just any old artist. He's famous. He's won awards. He even got an LSA Fellowship." She looked at her watch. "I've got to get to the shop. You don't look ready to go, so I'm going to grab the bus. Okay?"

Without waiting for my answer, she grabbed her bag and sprinted from the room. I followed close behind but lost her in the parking lot. Since there was now no point in hurrying to the shop, I went back into the school and looked for Oliver.

He wasn't in his office or in the teacher's lounge. I went back to the classroom, wondering if he'd returned there, but he hadn't. I walked over to the dean's office but no one had seen Oliver. There was no place left to check except the exhibit hall, so I headed over there, but what were the odds he'd be staring at his own paintings?

Good, apparently. I found Oliver looking at some of his earliest work. Paintings of homeless people and drug addicts in the late 1950s and early 1960s. He seemed lost in memories, and not happy ones either, based on the tears welling up in his eyes.

"Oliver," I said quietly. "Are you okay?"

He jumped. "Heavens. Yes." He wiped his eyes. "Yes, Nell, fine. Caught up in the past."

I walked close to him to see what exactly he was looking at. It was a painting of a young man, unshaven and unwashed. He held a knife in his hand as if he were about to strike, but the eyes were blank. On the whole he was more sad than menacing.

It struck me all at once. "It's you," I said.

He nodded. "Many years ago."

"I'm sorry." The words came out of my mouth. "I mean, you look so sad that I'm sorry you ever felt that way."

"So am I. Thank goodness I'm much happier now."

"I guess my grandmother has something to do with that."

Age and pain seemed to fall away from Oliver and he grinned widely. "That she has. She's a lovely woman, your grandmother. Wise and smart and kind. I imagine she's always been that way."

"As long as I've known her."

He nodded. "What she's doing with a man like me, I can't imagine."

"Meaning?" This was my opening. This was where he would confess, I felt it in my bones.

Instead he sighed. "A tired old has-been."

"You are a famous artist, a working artist," I tried again. "You use models from the school, don't you? You still paint and you still sell your work, so how could you be a has-been?"

Oliver took a few steps and stopped again. This time between *Nobody* and a painting of an unhappy woman unbuttoning her shirt.

Both had shiny little gold-plated signs that read: "On loan from the Oliver White Collection." I stared at the paintings for a moment before I realized it was the same person in both paintings.

"Is this Julie Young?" I guessed. Since he had more than one painting of her, it seemed logical that she was someone he'd had a relationship with, and Julie Young—the woman he'd pushed at the gallery opening—was the only name I knew.

He nodded. "That's her. She was quite beautiful, or would have been if drugs hadn't taken away her beauty."

"Your models are still quite beautiful," I said. "I'm kind of surprised I don't recognize them, though, from around school."

"So am I. I use a lot of the advanced students. It's a good learning experience for an artist to try one's hand at being a model. You learn about your own body as you pose. Especially how uncomfortable it is to stand in one position for a long time." He smiled. "But it's also extra money. And true to the cliché, there are a lot of starving artists out there."

Suddenly my mind went in another direction. "Was Sandra one of your models?"

Oliver seemed startled at the thought. "No. Why would you ask me that?"

"I was walking down the hallway," I lied, "and I saw you give her some money. It was the day she died."

Oliver stiffened and took a deep breath. "You must be mistaken, Nell. I did no such thing." He looked at this watch. "I have to go. A patron of the arts has commissioned a painting from me and I really must set to work."

But I had one more question. "What's the LSA Fellowship?" I asked.

Oliver stopped and turned. "Are you interested in attending the London School of the Arts?"

"No," I stammered. "Kennette."

"Well, she's certainly got the talent for it. Fellowships are extremely hard to come by, but I'd be happy to recommend her."

"Did you get one?"

Oliver paused. "I haven't thought about that in years. I did receive the scholarship, yes. I wasn't able to take advantage of it, though. I was leaving for the States." He took several steps toward the door. "I'll have to chat with Kennette about this next time I see her."

"Well, she might be interested in work as a model, if you're interested. To make extra money." I threw it in, hoping for some reaction.

But there was only puzzlement.

"Really? She's a bit shy, don't you think?"

Then he was gone. I was left in the room with the unhappiest moments of his past on display. And a thousand new questions.

CHAPTER 37

I drove to the nearest Internet café and grabbed a coffee and donut, and then one of the computers. I might have waited until I got home and used my own computer for free, but I couldn't wait.

I searched for the London School of the Arts. It had a splashy Web site and the names of several prominent English artists among its graduates. As he admitted, Oliver White wasn't among them. Neither was Oliver Lyons.

I searched the LSA Fellowship recipients. The list went as far back as 1918, but Oliver wasn't there. Of course he said he'd turned it down. So I went back to the search engine and typed in "LSA Fellowship" and "Oliver White." No hits. I typed "LSA Fellowship" and "Oliver Lyons." Nothing.

I tried again. I searched both of Oliver's names crossed with "fellowships," "awards," "education," and "London" in separate searches. While there was plenty about the accolades he received over the years, there wasn't one hit for the London School of the Arts.

I leaned back in my chair and gulped some coffee. How had Kennette known about the LSA Fellowship? Had she been searching through his past like I had? Or more likely, had he mentioned it when he was painting her?

And that brought me to another question, why were they lying about it? I couldn't imagine Eleanor caring about Kennette posing for Oliver. She wasn't a prude. She understood that artists need models, and even with Kennette's obvious crush on Oliver, my grandmother wasn't so insecure as to let a little bit of modeling make her jealous.

There had to be another reason. And since I couldn't ask either of them without admitting I'd been in Oliver's house, I had to figure out another way. But after sitting there for almost an hour, I still hadn't come up with an idea.

Frustrated, I drove toward home but without any intention of actually going there. I didn't have to work and I didn't feel up to going to Carrie's, though I was tantalizingly close to finishing the mural.

I wanted to see Jesse. I did ask myself if I was jonesing to see him because I couldn't, and because I hate being told what to do. But in my heart I knew it was simpler than that. I just wanted to see him. Aside from our potential relationship, Jesse had been a reliable and supportive friend. I liked the way his mind worked and I liked to talk things over with him—how things were going at the shop or in class or just anything. If we were sitting next to each other on the couch, he would stare off into space as I talked and I'd be absolutely sure he wasn't listening to a word I was saying, but then suddenly he'd comment on it. And days later, when I'd forgotten the bulk of our conversation, he'd bring up a tiny little piece of it.

Except, of course, if I talked about the murders. That was something that was clearly off-limits. And it made me wish all the more that I could tell him what I was learning, and that instead of being angry at me, he'd be happy to have me on the case.

But that wasn't going to happen, and I was at an impasse. I felt as though I were going around in circles. I found one clue after another, but instead of leading me in one direction they were leading in all directions. It was Kennette. It was Oliver. It was a stranger. It was a friend. The women knew each other. Their murders were unconnected. Everybody—Jesse,

Powell, Kennette, Oliver, even me—seemed to have a secret, and I was no closer to finding out which one led to the killer.

I really needed more help than the girls could give, but without Jesse, I had no official channel through which to get it. Then, as I stopped at a red light in Morristown, I realized I finally had a destination. I parked in front of the police station and went inside.

"Chief Powell?" I asked the desk sergeant.

"Wait here," he directed. "I'll call him. What's your name?"

"Nell Fitzgerald."

I looked around the impressive station. There were marble columns near the front door, large plaques honoring officers over the years, a framed poster announcing a detective exam on March 1, and the city emblem inlaid in the tile floor.

This was definitely a more formal operation than the Archers Rest Police Department, but that made sense. Morristown was more than twice the size of our little village. We shared a fire department and a high school with them, as well as some other city services like garbage collection. It was almost as if Archers Rest was Morristown's little brother, though I doubt any Archers residents would have admitted it. The only thing that reminded me of Archers Rest was the large poster announcing a fund-raising effort for bulletproof vests: bake sales and rubber bracelets and apparently anything they could think of to raise money. Archers Rest was always short of cash for even the most vital of police services.

"Nell." Powell's voice startled me.

I reached out my hand and he shook it vigorously.

"Do you have a minute?" I asked.

"Absolutely. Come back to my office."

He motioned for me to follow him down a long hallway to a door at the end. Once inside he pointed to a chair and then sat on the other side of a large desk. He took a bottle of scotch from his desk and put it in a bottom drawer.

"What can I do for you?" he asked. "Not in any trouble I hope."

"Not today." I smiled. I watched him for a second as a smile broke across his face. Once he warmed up, he really was quite nice in a drill sergeant sort of way.

"How's Jesse?"

I hesitated but what was the point? "Pretty annoyed with me."

Powell nodded. "The fingerprints."

"He told you?"

"No. I was waiting for him to but, no, he hasn't said anything." He leaned forward. "It actually made me curious. Finding fingerprints on the windowsill was a terrific lead. People don't usually enter an apartment from a fire escape."

"I'm aware of that," I admitted.

"Well never mind. Once I realized that Jesse hadn't told me who the fingerprints belong to because they were yours, it all fit together."

"How did you realize that?"

"I asked Greg to send me a copy of the report."

"That's pretty sneaky. He's supposed to get Jesse's permission, isn't he?"

He laughed. "I would have thought you would admire that move. Besides, withholding information like that is suspicious."

"You didn't think Jesse was the killer?"

"I think everyone's the killer. Haven't you figured that out yet?"

"I guess I do too," I said.

If I was going to get anything from him, I knew I needed to give him something in exchange, so I told him about Kennette's secretive behavior and her knowledge of the LSA Fellowship.

"And I have a feeling there's more going on between Oliver and Kennette than they are letting on," I finished.

I wasn't about to tell him about my visit to Oliver's house. One episode of breaking and entering might amuse him; I couldn't take the chance that he'd feel the same way about two.

"You're really stuck on Oliver being the guy," he said.

"More like I'm trying to prove he isn't. You're the one who called him in for questioning."

"For all the good it did me," he snorted. "Tell me why an innocent man refuses to cooperate in an investigation."

"He said he wouldn't help?" I asked.

"He told me that Sandra was a student, nothing more, and he had no knowledge of Lily Harmon. He was adamant about that."

I didn't ask him if he knew that Lily's real name was Price. I assumed he did but didn't want me to know. Instead I suggested a simple explanation for Oliver's behavior. One I wasn't sure I believed.

"Maybe he's telling the truth," I said.

"Then why refuse a consent search at his house?" Powell volleyed back. "Why refuse to provide fingerprints or DNA for comparison?"

"You have DNA of the killer?" I asked, stunned.

This was a huge break that Jesse had never mentioned. And the thought that he had kept it from me stung.

"No." Powell said excitedly. "Not the killer. The victim."

"That makes no sense. Why would . . ." And then it hit me. "You think Oliver and Sandra were related?"

Powell stared at the floor, shaking his head repeatedly as if he were trying to decide something.

"Okay," he said eventually. "Maybe there are a few things you should know."

He got up from his desk and walked over to a filing cabinet. He took out a box and walked back to the desk.

"This really is something I shouldn't be sharing with you," he said. "I can't stress that enough. I expect you to be discreet with the information."

Well that's a mistake, I thought. I had five amateur detectives waiting for any information I could find.

"Absolutely," I lied.

CHAPTER 38

There were newspaper clippings, gallery flyers downloaded from the Internet, photocopies of photographs—all about Oliver. I could barely look away from them I was so fascinated by the sheer volume of paper. But I had to know.

"Where did you get these?" I finally asked.

"Lily." Powell grabbed a chair and pulled it next to mine. He started going through the papers until he found one he obviously wanted me to see. It was a marriage certificate for Oliver Lyons and Violet Hammel.

"Why would Lily have all this?" I asked.

"She was his granddaughter."

"That's not possible. He never had any kids."

Powell got up and went to his desk. He opened a file and handed me a slip of paper.

"It's a birth certificate," I said. "It shows that Violet Kelly and Gerard Kelly had a daughter named Rachel on September 23, 1957, in London, England." I handed him back the certificate. "I know Violet is Oliver's ex-wife, but all this proves is that she remarried and had a family. There's no tie to Oliver."

"There is, if that little girl was actually Oliver's daughter. Oliver's divorce from Violet was finalized three days before she married Kelly. And the girl was born only two months later."

"You think Oliver walked out on his pregnant wife?" I asked. "Then she just married some other guy."

"It was 1957. She may not have felt like she could raise a kid on her own. How would she support it?" Powell tapped the paper. "And Oliver skipped the country."

"Still, it seems pretty cold to leave your pregnant wife to fend for herself."

"Doesn't he seem like the type to you?"

I paused. Maybe not now. Now he seemed happy to be in the classroom or with my grandmother. But fifty years ago, based on everything I knew about him, I had to admit, he did seem the type.

"But this is just speculation," I pointed out. "Can you prove Lily was Violet's granddaughter?"

Powell shrugged. "I'm working with Canadian authorities to get the birth certificates for Rachel's children. Then I can at least prove Lily's relationship to Violet."

"But that doesn't prove Oliver's related."

Powell shook his head. "But because Rachel's birth certificate lists Gerard Kelly as the father, I'd need DNA from White to prove that he's actually Rachel's father—and therefore Lily's grandfather."

"Why not get DNA from Rachel?"

"That only proves she's related to Lily," Powell said, "and that's taken care of. I need Oliver to confirm the rest."

"Does Oliver know that's why you need his DNA?" I asked.

The whole situation was puzzling. I'd come in here looking for information about Oliver's night of interrogation, but this was more than I had bargained for.

"The night I tracked down where Lily had been living, that was the night I brought Oliver in. I showed him all of it," Powell said. "I explained that we found this among Lily's things. He didn't seem interested."

"He denied it?"

"No. He just sat there staring into space. He didn't ask any questions. He didn't answer any. He certainly didn't cooperate. Strange for an innocent man, don't you think?"

I did. "But why would Oliver kill his granddaughter? Maybe he would kill a lover, like Sandra, if they were lovers," I said, "but why kill his granddaughter?"

"That's why I wanted a consent search of his house. I wanted to find first, evidence that Lily or Sandra or both had been there; and second, a motive," Powell said. "I know in my gut that he's hiding something in that house."

I searched my brain for anything that might fit what Powell was searching for. There was only one suspicious item—the painting of Kennette. But even if I'd been willing to tell him I'd seen it, it would hardly help find a motive for Lily's death.

"Can't you just get a warrant?"

"Not enough probable cause. If I can't prove a connection to Lily, then I can't get a warrant to search the house. And if I can't search his house, I can't get the connection. It's so damned frustrating."

"You said you found the certificate among Lily's things," I remembered. "Where did you find Lily's things?"

"She had a small apartment near Peekskill," he said. "She was subleasing it from some guy, so the whole thing was illegal. That's why it took so long to find. She had a roommate but that person was long gone when we arrived. The place was trashed, but I found these."

"It has to mean something," I agreed. I just didn't know what.

I got up to leave but I had one nagging question.

"Was Jesse involved in any of this?"

Powell nodded. "Sure. Obviously it's technically his case. He brought his people to Lily's apartment. In fact they were there before I even arrived on the scene. But he didn't think there was cause to bring Oliver in for questioning."

"So you did that on your own?"

"And as I guess you have found out, Chief Dewalt does not care for people doing things behind his back."

That made me smile a little. It was nice to know I wasn't the only person in the doghouse over this case.

"Can he force you off the case?" I asked.

Powell smiled. "No. After he calmed down, he was just interested in the information. Jesse's a stand-up guy but he's a little cautious. I think he secretly appreciates it when someone else jumps into the fray."

"I hope so."

Powell patted my shoulder. "Give him time. Then when he's ready, you tell him what you've learned and he'll listen."

"And he should be grateful," I added.

"Don't push it."

As I left I made a promise to share anything I found with Powell, and he generously offered me the same. I knew I was lying and I assumed he was as well. But even if he only shared a little, and only when he hoped I'd offer something in return, it was still more than Jesse was doing.

It had been a confusing conversation, with more maybes than actual proof. But I walked away with a possible connection between Oliver and Lily. That was more than I'd gone in with. I already had a connection between Oliver and Sandra. If Oliver really was guilty of murder, then it seemed to me that he needed one motive—one reason both women had to die.

And if there wasn't one motive, then I needed to find two killers: someone who had killed Lily, perhaps because she was Oliver's granddaughter, and someone who had copied elements of the first murder to kill Sandra.

Just thinking about it exhausted me. Finding one killer looked to be nearly impossible. I didn't even want to think about the odds of finding two.

CHAPTER 39

"He killed Sandra because she wanted his money. And he killed Lily because she wanted his money," Natalie offered. "That's one motive."

"Oliver doesn't care about money," I pointed out.

"But he cares about his reputation," Susanne offered.

Natalie, Susanne, and Natalie's son Jeremy sat with me at a diner in Morristown an hour after I'd finished my meeting with Powell. While we waited for our sandwiches, I recounted what Powell had said. I knew it meant telling the story again to the rest of the group, but they weren't available and I couldn't wait.

"I think the best news is what Powell said about Jesse. That once Jesse has calmed down he'll forgive you for all of this meddling," Susanne offered.

"Let's stay focused," I said.

Although I did think it was good news that Jesse might be willing to get past our difference of opinion, I didn't think there was any point in even entertaining the idea until the murder was solved.

"What is Oliver's reputation anyway?" Natalie asked, pulling me back to the subject at hand. "And how does having a granddaughter, or an affair with a beautiful young woman, tarnish his reputation? He's an artist. The more scandal the better. I mean, look how his career took off. He got arrested and sold out a show."

"I agree," I said. "And it's possible that he wasn't having an affair with Sandra. We've only been guessing at that."

"Then why were they so cozy together?" Susanne asked.

I was about to shrug my shoulders when it hit me. The kind words. The crying in the parking lot. The money.

"Maybe Sandra was his granddaughter," I said.

"Did she kill Lily?" Susanne asked. "And if she did, then maybe Oliver was protecting her, but somebody got to her when Oliver was at Eleanor's dinner party with you."

"Maybe," I said. "Or maybe Oliver killed Lily. Sandra knew and was blackmailing him, so he killed Sandra."

"He killed his own granddaughter?" Susanne seemed alarmed at the idea.

"He didn't even know her," Natalie pointed out. "He didn't care enough about his daughter to stick around for her birth, so why should he care about his granddaughter?"

"Then why would Oliver kill her?" Susanne asked.

"I got it," Natalie jumped up, alarming Jeremy to the point that he burst into tears.

Susanne grabbed her grandson and held him tightly.

"Lily was Oliver's granddaughter. Powell's right about that," Natalie said. "But Sandra killed Lily and Oliver killed her."

I sat back and went over the details in my head. Sandra could have killed Lily. "That has to be it," I agreed. "Oliver killed Sandra because she killed Lily."

Susanne turned her attention from Jeremy to us.

"If he killed the woman who killed his granddaughter, it was rage and grief, not cold-blooded murder," Susanne said. "If that's the case, it's okay. He could still be with Eleanor."

We both looked at her.

"He'd still go to jail," I pointed out.

"Only if we tell," Susanne said. "And if Oliver was driven to do what he did, then why should he spend the rest of his life in jail? And why should we break Eleanor's heart?"

We looked at one another in silence.

"Because he's a killer," I finally said.

"Besides, if we're figuring this out, don't you think that maybe Jesse or Powell will figure it out?" Natalie asked quietly.

Susanne nodded sadly, but she had punctured a hole in our excitement. By trying so hard to find a link between Lily and Oliver, Natalie and I had both forgotten what such a discovery might do to Eleanor.

We sat eating our lunch in silence, trying to find a way to solve the murder without hurting my grandmother.

"We don't really know what happened. Powell's just guessing and so are we," I pointed out. "We have no idea whether Oliver was Lily's or Sandra's grandfather. And even if he was, we have no idea if Oliver knew. And even then, we don't have a motive for why he would kill either woman."

"So what do we do?" Natalie looked as overwhelmed as I felt.

"We take it step-by-step. First we have to prove that Oliver was related to one of the victims," I said. "Then we have to see if it leads us to a motive."

"And if it was rage over the death of his granddaughter, can we let sleeping dogs lie?" Susanne asked.

I swallowed hard. "No. If he's the killer we turn him in, no matter who it hurts." I turned my eyes to a now comforted Jeremy, sleeping in his grandmother's arms.

The next evening I brought the chairs into a circle for the quilt meeting. I put on the coffee and rang up the last of the day's sales. It wasn't until I turned the Open sign to Closed that I noticed I was being watched.

"What?" I jumped when I saw Eleanor out of the corner of my eye.

"You are a million miles away," she said.

"I'm just thinking," I said, trying to think of a topic I could safely claim to be thinking about.

"I know exactly what you're thinking."

"What?" I said slowly. With all the skills she had, I wondered for a moment if it was possible my grandmother could read minds.

"Honestly, Nell, if you're going to get like this every time a man breaks up with you, you'll end up a nervous wreck."

"Every time?" I repeated. "How often do you expect it to happen?"

She rolled her eyes. "The world does not revolve around men."

"Spoken like someone who gets roses every other day." I pointed to yet another arrangement Oliver had sent, which Eleanor kept at the register.

She smiled. "What did you do to Jesse anyway? I ran into him yesterday, and I thought he was going to break a world speed record trying to get away from me."

"He thinks I don't respect what he does. You know, because I asked about the investigation."

Partial honesty was a good plan, I decided.

"Well the girl was found right outside our door," Eleanor said. "She was a classmate of yours. And they hauled Oliver in for questioning. You have every right to be curious."

I hadn't seen that coming. Buoyed by her indignation, I went on.

"Jesse thinks I should just stay out of it and leave the whole thing to him."

"You should."

A hundred and eighty degrees in two seconds. How did she manage that?

"You just said I had every right to be curious," I pointed out.

"Curious, yes. But not to interfere." She raised an eyebrow at me, making me feel like a child caught up after bedtime. "I would think you were smart enough to realize this, but a killer is by definition a dangerous person. And dangerous people are best left to the police."

"Well at the moment one particular dangerous person is wandering around. And the police have no idea where he or she is."

"Just as long as you stay out of his way." Eleanor grabbed my hand. "That's all I care about. You have to be careful."

"So do you, Grandma."

"What trouble could I get in? I spend my days in a quilt shop." She smiled.

"So do I," I reminded her, "and according to you and Jesse I'm always getting into trouble."

"At least I'll have my eyes on you tonight." She winked.

"No you won't. I'm helping Carrie in her shop so she doesn't come to the meeting. And you guys are supposed to be finishing her quilt. It's just a few days until the opening."

"Has she figured out a name yet?"

"Don't ask her or she might snap. And then there'll be another murder in this town," I laughed.

CHAPTER 40

"Seriously, what are you calling the store?" I asked. "You need to put up a sign."

"I know," Carrie grunted. "I have the sign guy waiting to paint and he's getting very impatient."

"Just go by the address," I suggested. "I know several places in Manhattan that are known by their building numbers. You would be 118. That's simple."

"It's boring."

I stepped back. I had just put the finishing touches on the mural. It was almost exactly as I had pictured it. A large coffeepot pouring out a city skyline that was part New York and part my imagination. In front was a small coffee shop with a tiny Open sign in the window.

"If I'm not going to put the name of the shop on the mural, I guess I'm done," I announced.

Carrie and I took a moment to stare at the finished mural.

"I'm in love with it," Carrie exclaimed. "It's everything I could have wanted and more." She jumped over and hugged me. "Sign your name."

I mixed several colors until I had a nice dark brown; then I dipped my brush into it and moved my hand to the mural's lower right-hand corner. For some reason my hand wouldn't stop shaking at the idea of signing my name. Finally, I wrote "Nell Fitzgerald."

"You're a real artist now," Carrie said.

"I know. It kind of gives me the jitters."

Carrie moved back and started jumping up and down. "That's it. That's it! That's what we're calling this place: Jitters."

I could see the relief in her face as she finally figured out the puzzle she'd been grappling with for so long.

"I have to call the sign guy and tell him or he won't have it ready for Tuesday," she said.

I was about to join in her celebration—at least Carrie had found an answer to one of the problems we'd been facing these last few weeks—but something out the window caught my eye.

"What's wrong?" I called out as I ran from the coffee shop to Someday Quilts.

"I don't understand it," Eleanor said.

"He was fine a minute ago." Kennette stepped back toward the door.

I knelt down. Barney was barking and jumping up and down angrily at nothing, and there seemed to be little any of us could do to comfort him.

"We're going to be here awhile, and I thought that he needed some company, so I brought him from home," Eleanor told me. "But the minute we got here he started going crazy. Honestly, I don't know what's wrong with him."

I looked up the street. There were a few teenagers at the corner, but they weren't even looking at us. I turned the other way. A car was parked a few yards away. I could see that it was occupied but it wasn't under a streetlamp so I couldn't see who was inside.

I wrapped my arms around Barney, a gesture that normally meant I would get covered in licks. This time he strained to get away from me.

"What is it, fella?" I whispered, even though I knew his deafness had progressed to the point where he probably couldn't hear a word I said. "It's okay. Grandma's okay. Kennette's okay. I'm okay."

"Try taking him down the street and see if he calms down,"

Eleanor said. "He probably smells a squirrel or something. Poor thing. His other senses are probably heightened now, and he can smell everything in sight."

"Probably," I said, but there didn't seem to be any squirrels on the street, and there usually weren't. They tended to overrun Eleanor's backyard and any other open space, but on Main Street there were too many people and too few trees to attract much in the way of wildlife. And in any case, I'd never seen Barney get this upset over a mere squirrel.

Still, I took my grandmother's advice and grabbed Barney's leash.

"Why don't you come with me," I said to Kennette, "in case he gets away."

We walked him toward the car parked down the street. Barney strained at the leash and it was hard to keep up with him. Kennette stayed a few steps ahead, apparently afraid of what Barney might do. As frightening as it was, I was glad I had an excuse to see who was sitting inside the car.

I only had to walk a few feet to realize that it was a Morristown Police car. I pulled Barney to a stop and leaned in.

"Hi," I said. "What are you doing here?"

"Waiting," Chief Powell said. He nodded toward a building where two men stood talking in the darkness.

"Heya, Nell," said a voice from the passenger seat.

I leaned in farther. "Hi, Greg. What is this, a policemens' night out?"

Barney, who had momentarily calmed down, began barking again. Powell and Greg both got out of the car.

"What's wrong with Barney?" Greg went to pet him but seemed to think better of it.

"I have no idea. Something has spooked him," I said.

Kennette moved to the front of the police car, away from the conversation. I noticed Greg look at her but he didn't so much as say hello. Powell seemed to notice it too, because he walked over to Kennette.

"I met you the night of the murder," he said. "You're the art student living with Mrs. Cassidy and Nell."

"Kennette Green." She shook his hand.

"What's your story?"

"I don't have one." Kennette shifted uncomfortably. "I mean, I'm a friend of Nell's and I take classes. Nothing interesting."

"You like Oliver White?" Powell nodded in the direction of the two men standing in the dark.

"Who doesn't?" Kennette asked.

Powell shrugged. "Seems like a friendly guy. Seems like a lot of women like him. I just wondered if you were one of them."

Either Powell was a great judge of character or he somehow knew about the painting in Oliver's studio. I tried to catch his eye, but he was too interested in Kennette to notice me. Besides, I had my hands full trying to keep Barney from running off.

"I think he's a great artist and a great teacher, and you don't have to like him to think that," Kennette said. "Even Nell thinks that and she doesn't like Oliver at all."

I found myself turning red. "I didn't say that," I told her.

"No, but you act like it, and I think it really bothers Eleanor," Kennette said.

Her tone was soft and sympathetic but her words were like knives. I may not have trusted Oliver, but I didn't want my grandmother knowing that.

"I think Oliver is a great guy, actually," I said. And at that Powell looked over at me. "I love his class and I couldn't be happier that he is so interested in my grandmother. It shows he has good taste."

The two men in the darkness started walking toward us. As they passed under a streetlight, I realized it was Jesse and Oliver. They headed to the front of the police car where Powell, Greg, and Kennette were standing. Barney, who had settled down, suddenly broke from me and ran, barking, toward the group. I lunged to catch him but it was too late. Jesse grabbed the dog and pulled him back.

"What's up, buddy?" Jesse crouched next to Barney and seemed immediately to change the dog's mood. He was now licking Jesse and wagging his tail.

"Has he lost his mind?" I asked. "A minute ago he was freaking out."

"I think it's Oliver," Kennette announced. "He was by the shop earlier, and I think Barney is jealous of him and Eleanor."

Oliver leaned over the dog but didn't touch him. "I'm not trying to take your place, old man," he said. "I know I come second."

I wanted to stay and find out what Oliver and Jesse had been talking about, and why Powell and Greg weren't included in the conversation, but Barney had finally returned to normal. I took the opportunity to grab his leash and lead him away from the men. Kennette followed at a slight distance. Once we got back to the shop, Barney didn't join the group of quilters, though he was an honorary member. Instead he walked into the office, his tail between his legs, and lay down on a quilt near Eleanor's desk.

"Crisis over?" Eleanor shouted to me as I hung up my coat.

"I guess so, but he seemed really unhappy," I said.

"Except when he saw Jesse. He really likes Jesse," Kennette offered.

"Well Barney's a good judge of character," Eleanor said. "If he doesn't like someone there's a reason. And if he does, well, that's good enough for me."

"I wish he were a good judge of quilts." Susanne shook her head. She pointed to the nearly finished quilt meant for Carrie's coffee shop, now pinned to the design wall.

"It looks good," I said.

"It looks okay," Natalie countered.

I took a step back and closed my eyes, then opened them again to get a fresh look. The quilt was really beautiful but there was something missing.

"It needs a bit more quilting," I offered. "And something else, something structured. There are a lot of circles and swirls but maybe it needs some boxes."

"You should paint them," Maggie suggested. "Use fabric paints. That would add a nice bit of texture."

With the enthusiastic agreement of the crowd shoring me up, I gathered some paints and added a few small strokes to the quilt. I stepped back. I didn't want to go overboard.

"That's it," Bernie declared. "A little more quilting and it's done."

"Can I do it?" Kennette asked. "I want to add a little something of my own."

The women grabbed Kennette, led her to a sewing machine, and handed over the quilt to her. While Bernie and Susanne fussed about her, Maggie and I stayed in the front of the shop. I told her about the scene up the street.

"Jesse is building a relationship with Oliver," Maggie concluded.

"Why?"

"They already know each other from Eleanor's dinner party, so if Oliver were going to trust someone enough to give him information, it would be Jesse."

I nodded. "It makes me feel like Jesse knows something we don't."

"Let me look into it," Maggie said.

"How?"

"Well, just like Jesse is using his kind nature to lure Oliver into a confession, I can use my crankiness to lure Jesse into telling me what's going on."

I smiled. She was probably right. When it came to revealing information, Jesse may have been immune to my romantic charms, but I didn't think he stood a chance against Maggie.

CHAPTER 41

I stood in Someday Quilts, waiting. Behind me, Eleanor, Susanne, Kennette, Natalie, and Bernie were lined up. The only one yet to arrive was Maggie.

"She knows it's at eight o'clock, right?" Bernie asked.

"Of course she knows," Eleanor said.

"Well we're going to be late if we wait for her," Susanne pointed out.

"One more minute, then we go," Eleanor said. "She's not usually late."

Outside, I saw a figure hurrying up the street.

"She's coming," I said. "Grab the stuff."

Maggie was breathless when she grabbed my arm. "We have to talk," she said.

I nodded, but before I could say anything, Eleanor broke us apart. "We said we'd be the first to arrive, so let's go," she said.

And just as she said it, white twinkly Christmas lights lit up Jitters. We walked across the street and opened the door, the first official customers of Carrie's coffee shop. Inside, Carrie's husband was pouring champagne, and her kids were eating cupcakes on the big velvet sofa.

As we said hello, others started coming in. Oliver arrived with a box the size of a notebook. Greg and another officer from Archers Rest stopped in and helped themselves to coffee. A few neighbors and friends from town began to fill the place, making for quite a party.

"I'm a wreck," Carrie confessed. "I don't know how you felt when you opened Someday, Eleanor, but I feel like I'm going to faint."

"You'll be fine, dear. You've probably just had too much caffeine," my grandmother said. "I assume you have some herbal tea here."

Carrie laughed and headed behind the counter with Eleanor following close behind. I looked around the place. It was exactly as Carrie had once hoped it would be: the funky furniture, the mismatched art pieces, and the giant mural on the back wall.

"It's cool," I heard someone say behind me.

I turned around to see Jesse smiling. His daughter, Allie, ran from him to play with Carrie's children, so he and I were left standing together, looking at the mural. He put his arm around me.

"I'm really proud of you," he said. "It's so imaginative."

"Thanks," I said. "I'm proud of myself too."

I leaned into his arm for just a second before I was interrupted.

"Now," Susanne said, "before it gets too crowded."

The women of the quilt group gathered together in the center of the coffee shop. Maggie held a box out for Carrie.

"A little something from us. From all of us," she said, nodding toward Kennette who stood at the edge of the group.

Carrie began to get glassy-eyed. "I hope it's what I think it is," she said. "I've been holding a space for it." She ripped open the box and pulled out the quilt we had made. At that she started crying. "Oh my heavens. It's so beautiful."

Her husband grabbed the quilt, and he and Jesse held it up over the blank wall. Against the soft mocha color, the bright batik fabrics really popped. The circles and swirls gave the quilt movement, and my small blocks of painted fabric added a nice, hard contrast to the soft lines everywhere else on the quilt. Though it had started as Susanne's vision, it became a group effort as we pinned, sewed, quilted, and painted together. I noticed, as I looked at the quilt up close, that Kennette had managed to quilt in a secret word: "Jitters."

"We did good with this one," I said to Kennette as we stared at our creation.

"It's so great," she said. "I like the idea of giving a quilt to someone even more than I like the idea of making one for myself. It's like giving away a part of yourself."

I smiled. "I think that's why we do it. What could be more personal than turning an idea into an object?"

"I'm humbled by it myself," Oliver said as he joined us. "I brought a little something for Carrie and now I feel a bit embarrassed to give it to her with such talent in the room."

"I noticed the package," I said. "What's in it?" I pulled Carrie away from the quilt. "Oliver has something for you," I said.

Oliver blushed a little, then handed her the box. Carrie unwrapped it and took out a framed sketch of a woman looking into the distance, a coffee cup in her hand.

"Oh my God," Carrie said. "You can't possibly give this to me."

"I drew it for you," Oliver said. "I'm kissing up to Eleanor's friends so they'll like having me around."

"Well, it's working." Carrie kissed Oliver on the cheek then rushed off to show the others.

"An Oliver White sketch is worth a couple thousand dollars," I said to him.

"Eleanor's worth more than that."

At that Kennette burst into tears and disappeared into the ladies' room.

"Should you see if she's okay?" an alarmed Oliver asked.

"She'll be fine," I said. I had something more important to do than comfort Kennette's broken crush. "Do you want some coffee or something?"

"Lovely."

"If you need to grab a cigarette, I'll bring it out to you," I offered.

I watched Oliver exit the shop as Carrie made two cappuccinos. All she could talk about was Oliver's generous gift, which was already hanging behind the cash register.

"Maybe we should just let things be," she whispered to me. "He really is such a nice man. He couldn't be the killer."

"You're easily bought," I said, and grabbed the two coffees.

"Here's to you and my grandmother," I toasted as soon as I walked outside.

"I'll drink to that." Oliver took a long sip of his coffee and smiled. "I wasn't sure that you liked the idea very much."

"I want her to be happy," I said. "And I think you make her happy."

"It's strange at this point in my life to be feeling like a schoolboy," he said, smiling, "but at least now I have the common sense not to let anything stand in the way of love."

"I guess I could use some of that."

"He's a good man, your Jesse," Oliver said. "But I sense he likes structure and stability. He just needs to get used to having someone with your spirit in his life."

"I get the sense he'd prefer it I let go of some of that spirit," I admitted.

"Don't. Don't change that, Nell. Not for Jesse, not for anyone. It is what makes you such an interesting and talented artist."

I couldn't hide my surprise at the compliment. "Thanks, Oliver," I said softly. "I feel so privileged to have been taught by some of the best artists around, you included."

I looked through the window and saw the women in the quilt club laughing and enjoying the party.

"Oliver, we need you inside for a photo with the local press," said Carrie, popping her head out the door. Oliver dropped his cigarette on the ground and went inside. I hesitated for a moment, then picked up the cigarette, extinguished it, and put it into the plastic bag I'd brought along just in case. I dropped the bag into my coat pocket. I felt bad about it, but I told myself it was the only way I would know the truth.

"What are you doing out here?" Jesse opened the door.

"I was talking to Oliver," I said quickly. I wasn't sure if he had seen me grab the cigarette, but if he didn't say anything about it, I wasn't going to. "It's freezing out here."

Jesse grabbed my hand and led me inside. We found a spot near the back and sat. We held hands and looked around as the place filled up, but it was clear we were both struggling to think of something to say.

"The mural is great." Jesse smiled.

"You said that, you know."

"I know. I just think anything I say will get us into trouble."

"You can ask about school."

"But that leads to Oliver and the investigation. So does a discussion of your grandmother or my job or pretty much anything," he said.

"So then, you like the mural." I laughed.

Jesse leaned in and kissed my cheek. "I get that maybe I overreacted a little. I still think you were wrong, and I think you should really stay out of things that are dangerous."

I found myself ready for another fight. I let go of his hand. "Are you apologizing or telling me off again?" I asked.

"Sorry. I'm . . ." He paused. "I'm not doing either, really. I'm just hoping that maybe we can figure out a way to get things back on track now that we both admit to being wrong."

I hesitated. It wasn't my intention, but I guess I had admitted to being wrong. I nodded and rested my head on his shoulder. The evening was turning out to be far better than I'd even hoped. And better than Carrie had hoped. The place was getting crowded. People seemed to be enjoying the party and to be impressed with all the hard work she had put into the shop. I could see Oliver and Eleanor standing with Bernie near the front. Natalie was helping Carrie pour coffee. Susanne was helping Carrie's husband hang the quilt. And Maggie was looking around the room. I caught her eye and she smiled, then nodded toward the ladies' room.

"Excuse me for a second," I said to Jesse.

I followed Maggie toward the bathroom and we ducked inside. There was a pile of crumpled tissues on the sink that I assumed belonged to Kennette, but she was nowhere in sight.

"I brought you something," Maggie said, handing me a slip of paper. "It's Violet's phone number in Canada."

"How did you get this?"

"I tried to find her through normal channels, you know, directories and Internet searches and a people-finding group, but they all came up empty. So I got it from Jesse."

"He gave you Violet's phone number?"

"Not gave. Not exactly. But I figured if Susanne could steal stationery, then I could steal this." Maggie took a breath. It was clear she was very excited and wanted to tell the story without leaving anything out. "We were in his office, having a nice chat. I saw files on his desk with Sandra's and Lily's names on them. I asked him to get me a cup of tea, and then I rifled through his desk."

"And he didn't catch you?" I had inspired quite a crime wave in my fellow quilters.

"No. But I don't think we'll need it. Jesse knows," Maggie said. "He knows who the killer is."

"He does?" I was shocked. "Who is it?"

"He wouldn't say. What he would say was that he believes he can bring the right person to justice soon."

"When did he say that?" I was just sitting with him. Why hadn't he told me that the case was nearly solved?

"I went to see him this afternoon. I told him I was worried about you and Kennette and Natalie and all the young women in town. And he told me that I had no reason to worry. None of you were in danger."

"But he didn't say he knew who it was." I got the feeling Jesse was just reassuring a worried citizen.

"No." She smiled. "But it was the way he said it. He knows the killer isn't attacking random women. He knows the murders are connected. I think he's closing in."

I wanted to be relieved. I could just sit back and wait until Jesse wrapped up the case and then the biggest obstacle to our romance would be removed.

And yet I knew I'd be unable to do it.

CHAPTER 42

"You will testify that this belonged to Oliver," Powell said as he put the cigarette butt into an evidence envelope.

"Yes, if it links Oliver to Lily," I agreed. It had been less than twelve hours since I'd confiscated some of Oliver's DNA, and yet I'd changed my mind about turning it in a dozen times. Finally handing it over in Powell's office should have made me feel better, but it only filled me with the feeling that I was somehow betraying my grandmother.

"I'll call in a favor and get the DNA processed right away," Powell said. "If Oliver's not related, then we're back to square one, but at least you'll be relieved. I didn't realize you liked the guy so much."

"You mean the other night?"

"That was quite a glowing review."

"It was for Kennette's sake. I don't want her telling my grand-mother I have doubts about him."

Powell nodded. "Well here's hoping for her sake that this cigarette removes any motive Oliver had for Lily's murder."

"But if it's not Oliver, then who is it? Do you have any idea?" I was thinking that if Jesse really was close, then he must have shared his thoughts with Chief Powell.

But Powell shrugged. "We have DNA evidence so we'll see where it leads. After that, I don't know."

I nodded as if I believed he were right, but I suspected that he wasn't sharing the whole truth with me. That was fine, because I was holding back from him too.

✂

I walked out of the police station and headed for my car. I wasn't going anywhere, but it was the only place I could find that would give me the privacy I needed. As soon as I closed the door, I dialed my phone.

It rang. And rang again. I didn't want to leave a message but was beginning to think I'd have no choice when a woman finally answered.

"Violet Kelly?" I asked.

"No, she's sleeping," a friendly woman said. "This is her daughter. Can I help you?"

"This is Rachel?"

"Who is this?"

I had two options, mentioning her daughter and finding out if she knew her child was dead, or mentioning her father. Either way was a minefield.

"Do you know who Oliver White is?" I asked.

"Are you from the police?"

"You've talked to police?" I asked.

"Why? Who are you?"

"I'm . . ." I hesitated just long enough to sense a change on the other end of the phone.

"Are you a friend of his or something?" Her tone had turned hostile. "Look, if you are a friend of his, tell him I will never forgive him for what he did to my mother, or to my daughter."

And then she hung up.

I sat back in the car. I was sure now. Jesse was convinced Oliver was the killer. Powell seemed to be as well. In fact it seemed obvious.

Except I kept coming back to something Oliver said to me in class: "Let yourself be wrong." Something about Oliver being the killer felt too easy. Or maybe it was just that as I got to know Oliver and saw the effect he had on my grandmother, I wanted to be wrong.

✂

When I walked into class on Thursday, I watched Oliver unpack a box of small wooden figures. He was so friendly and relaxed and seemed to genuinely enjoy talking with the students. Gone were the pretentious speeches of the early classes. Now he had gotten to know everyone by name and was as much a cheerleader as teacher, seeing something to praise in everyone's work. When I forgot about all that was happening outside of the studio, this was my favorite class.

"Since quite a lot of you seemed to feel intimidated by our live model, I've decided to take a step back and introduce you to these," Oliver said as he held up one of the wooden figures. "They are a tried-and-true way to practice drawing the human figure in poses. Not as much fun as the real thing, but this way we can focus on proportion without getting hung up on nudity. You'll each get one, and you will use it to draw three poses, focusing on the basic human form. No need for great artistry here, just technique. For those of you who cannot avoid great artistry, feel free to embellish."

As he said it, his eyes went to the easel behind mine, where Kennette usually worked, and I realized Kennette wasn't there. She had been making her self scarce in the couple of days since Carrie's café had opened. I hadn't been able to find her when it was time to drive to school, but I assumed she'd get the bus. It had never occurred to me that without me to give her a ride she wouldn't come to class, and I felt horribly guilty about it.

"No sign of our Kennette, I see," Oliver said as he handed me one of the wooden models.

"I don't know what happened to her."

"She'll come next week, I hope. It's our last class and I have a surprise for her." His eyes twinkled and he moved on before I could ask what he meant. Instead I focused on what was in front of me—a tiny wooden man. I made him stand with one arm on his hips, with one leg bent, and then with his legs crossed over each other as if he were meditating. I found it easy to focus only on the proportion, the line, and the shadow without adding the emotion that's hard to escape with a real model—and in life. Maybe that was my problem with the investigation. I felt like the answer was out there, in hard lines and cool shadows, but I couldn't get past my emotions and see it.

It didn't help that halfway through class my phone beeped. When I checked, I saw that it was a text from Powell. It read: "It's a match."

I looked up at the happy professor at the front of the class, advising one of the students on a new pose for his wooden model. It was odd. Now that I had exactly the information that could finally finish this investigation and answer the questions I'd been nagged by for weeks, I felt, well, disappointed. I had wanted to "let myself be wrong" but there was little doubt that I hadn't been.

"Why the long face?" Oliver smiled at me as I gathered my things after class. I had been slow to finish; I'd lost my motivation after the text message. Now nearly everyone in class was already gone.

"You're Lily's grandfather," I said flatly.

Oliver turned white. "Why don't you come to my office?"

I followed him out of class, down the hall, and into his office without either of us saying another word. Once he closed the door behind me, I realized I'd left my purse, and my cell phone, back in the class. A decision I deeply regretted. I positioned myself near the door in case I needed a quick escape.

"I'd ask you how you know something like that but obviously you have a very curious mind," he said.

"So you don't deny it?"

"No. It was brought to my attention recently. Too late for me to do anything to help the child."

"After she was dead?"

"Apparently. Though I didn't know it at the time. Sandra was acting as liaison. She told me about Lily and showed me a photo of my former wife, Lily's grandmother. But she told me that Lily wasn't willing to come see me," Oliver sighed. "Sandra was trying to talk her into it."

"Sandra sent you the text. The one about needing more time."

He seemed confused, but then nodded. "How have you figured this all out? I thought I had hidden it well," he said. "Sandra told me about Lily, not that she was dead, but that she was my granddaughter, after the first class. She told me Lily was angry and didn't want to see me. Sandra was quite upset about it. She said she needed money to help pay for expenses—Lily's expenses. Perhaps I was gullible but I thought she was trying very hard on my behalf. I think now that she wasn't."

If Sandra had killed Lily, which now seemed likely, then Oliver was giving himself a good motive for having killed Sandra. Maybe Susanne's hope that Oliver had killed out of grief over the loss of his granddaughter was true. And maybe it was reason enough to let him off the hook. The only problem was that Powell now had evidence against Oliver, evidence I'd supplied.

"Do you think Sandra was conning you?" I asked.

He shrugged. "I think that's a fair assumption. She knew I had quite a bit of money and that I was donating it to the school. Of course the papers hadn't been finalized yet."

"And you backed out of the deal." I suddenly remembered the signs that read "On Loan" in the gallery.

"I chose several of my more personal paintings to remove from the endowment. If I had a family, then I wanted certain paintings to go to them."

"Why care now? You abandoned your wife and daughter more than fifty years ago."

Oliver sank into a chair. "I did."

"Is that why you killed Sandra, because she killed Lily?"

Oliver looked up at me. "You think Sandra killed Lily? Oh God, if Lily came here looking for me and died as a result, then . . ." His voice trailed off.

The man who only twenty minutes before had been so happy, now seemed broken and old. I wasn't afraid of him, nor was I willing to be the one to call the police, but that didn't mean I liked any of his answers.

"How could you do it?" I asked.

Oliver just shook his head, "I thought the past should stay in the past. I guess that's not possible."

"I think you should stay away from my grandmother," I said.

He nodded. "I'm sorry, Nell. I did not intend to cause you, or Eleanor, any pain."

It was an unsatisfying end to a puzzle I'd been working on for more than a month. I walked out of his office, and the school, feeling as though I was somehow guilty too. Not of murder, obviously, but of stirring up ghosts and breaking my grandmother's heart. And somehow, at least at that moment, my crime seemed worse than Oliver's.

CHAPTER 43

When I got to the shop, I noticed that it was quiet. One customer was finishing up her purchase as I walked in. Bill Vogel, the artist from Spuyten Duyvil, was pulling bolts of bright solids that had just arrived.

"I'm doing something Amish but not," he was telling Eleanor. "It's a whole new direction for me."

Eleanor was listening, but she didn't seem enthusiastic. "You're always testing boundaries," she said flatly. It was unlike her to be anything but excited about what might happen to her fabric once it left her shop. But Bill didn't seem to notice.

"I suppose artists are always testing boundaries." He smiled. "That's what makes great art."

"Perhaps it's not such a great quality in people, though," Eleanor said. She looked up and saw me standing near the front counter. "Ring up Bill, will you, Nell?"

I nodded. As I finished Bill's sale, I noticed that Barney was following Eleanor around. When she walked toward the office, he followed. When she walked to the cutting table or the checkout desk, or to straighten a bolt of fabric, he followed. I knew what it meant. He was worried. And it made me worried too.

"What's going on?" I asked.

Eleanor looked at me. Her eyes had the glassy brightness of someone who had just been crying.

"Slow day," she said. "I'm thinking of making kits of that Irish chain you've been working on. You picked really lovely colors, and I think the customers would like it. Of course you need to finish it."

"You're rambling."

"Am I? I thought I was making a point. Well you would know better than I, Nell. You seem to know better than anyone about everything."

Ouch. "You talked to Oliver."

Eleanor picked up a twelve-inch acrylic ruler as if she were about to slap my hand with it. "Why do you feel the need to protect me? I've been around awhile, you know. I've done a fair job of keeping myself fed and clothed without your help."

"He was lying to you."

"About what?"

"Well, he killed someone for starters."

"Which he admitted?"

"Not exactly."

"But you have proof?"

"Not really," I said. "But it adds up. I know that Lily, the first victim, was his granddaughter. I know he abandoned his pregnant wife in England."

"She was not pregnant with his child. At least that's what she told him. She said she had an affair with the man she later married. So he left. Maybe it was foolish, but they were young and the marriage was difficult. When he discovered that the child was his, he tried to find them, but Violet had remarried, the child had a father, and Oliver felt that perhaps it was best to leave things alone. It nearly destroyed him to let go of his only child. That's why he took up drinking."

"He told you that?"

"The first night we had dinner."

I hadn't expected that. I had worked so hard to uncover all of it that I assumed it was a secret. "But he's lying about his name. Maggie found out—"

"So that's what all those secret meetings were about."

"You knew we were meeting secretly?"

Eleanor laughed, but there was no joy in it. "At Bernie's pharmacy, at Susanne's house, and Carrie's. Honestly, Nell, I know all your cars, all your schedules."

I was losing, so I changed tactics. I sat on the stool near the cash register and shrugged. "We were trying to protect you, whether you needed it or not. And we found out that Oliver's last name—"

"Is Lyons," she finished the sentence. "He changed it to White when he came to the States because he felt like a new life needed a blank canvas. Nothing sinister in it."

"I told him to stop seeing you," I admitted. She knew everything else. There was no point in hiding it.

"I'm aware of that," she countered. "I told him that you don't have the authority to determine who my friends are, but he already felt that somehow his past and my . . . 'lifetime of decency,' he calls it, make him unworthy of me. I thought we were finally getting to a place where he was making peace with it. But now he feels that without your blessing it would be a mistake to continue our friendship."

Even if I was right, even if Oliver was a killer, it crushed me to see the look in my grandmother's eyes.

"I'm sorry," I muttered.

She dismissed me with a wave of her hand and walked toward the office, with Barney close behind. I sat in the shop, hoping that no other customers would come in for the rest of the day. As upset as Eleanor was, I knew she would never close the shop early for anything as mundane as a broken romance, but I couldn't stand to wait on anyone, and I couldn't bring myself to leave.

Within minutes the door opened.

"Where were you today?" I asked.

"I wanted to finish this." Kennette pulled her drunkard's path quilt out of a bright pink backpack. "I wanted to finish the binding."

She held up her large, colorful quilt with a meandering path of blues and purples.

"It's really beautiful," I said.

"I can't believe it's mine. It's like what you said about Carrie's quilt.

It's a little piece of my imagination turned into reality. And now I want to give it to someone special."

For a second I thought she was going to hand it to me, but instead she stuffed the quilt into her backpack.

"That's new," I said.

She held up the bag. "Yeah. I used to have one just like it but it got lost. Now that I have a paycheck, I figured I'd get a new one. Good for traveling. Of course now I need traveling money."

"Are you going somewhere?"

She smiled. "I think so."

"But we have one more class with Oliver."

"That's okay. It's not like I was going to be an artist or anything."

"But you're so talented."

Kennette wasn't listening anymore. She was watching Barney circle by the office door. "Is Barney still upset?"

"No. He's fine. He's just worried about Eleanor. She and Oliver broke up. Well I sort of broke them up. Long story," I blurted out.

Kennette dropped her bag and rushed back to the office. I could hear her talking to Eleanor but I didn't want to listen. Instead I walked out into the street and watched as people gathered in Jitters, drinking coffee without a care in the world.

I decided it was time for one final meeting of my group of detectives before we handed the investigation, or what was left of it, over to Jesse and Powell and went back to being quilters.

CHAPTER 44

"This was not how it was supposed to turn out," Susanne said quietly.

"But he didn't admit it," Natalie protested. "Maybe he's innocent."

"He has exactly the motive we thought he would," I pointed out. "Just because he didn't confess doesn't mean he didn't do it. It just means he's smart enough to try and keep himself out of jail."

"Well, I thought being a detective would be more fun," Bernie sighed.

Meeting at Carrie's coffee shop had gotten more complicated since it opened. Lucky for her, the café was already a popular hangout, but it made it hard for us to speak openly. We were stuck whispering in the corner near the front, waiting for the velvet couch to open up.

"What now?" Maggie turned to me.

"We let it go," Carrie answered. "We've done enough damage. I mean, it would have been bad enough if Jesse or Chief Powell found this out, but for Eleanor's friends to have done this to her . . ."

"And she knew we were up to something." Natalie smiled. "You have to give her props for that."

I nodded but I wasn't really listening. I had gotten into the bad habit of keeping an eye on the entrance to Someday Quilts, but at the moment it was paying off.

"I have to go," I said suddenly. I handed Carrie my coffee and ran out the back door.

I went down the alley to the end of the block and peered around the corner so I could see Someday Quilts. I had just seen Kennette walk out of the shop, look around, and then stuff an envelope in her coat. Or, really, Eleanor's coat. She had been acting weird lately, all the disappearances and then not showing up at Oliver's class. And she was leaving town. Now, after all we had done for her, was she stealing money from my grandmother?

As I watched from the corner, she walked toward me, looking around nervously. She got within inches of me and I pushed up against the wall. If she turned the corner, we would have run into each other and I would have to explain why I was there. But Kennette didn't see me. She just kept walking up the street and toward, of all places, the police station.

I let her get several yards ahead, and then I followed. She seemed about to go up the stairs and into the station when she paused. I hoped she'd turn around and go somewhere else so I could stay on her trail. I knew that there was no way I could follow her into that building without encountering Jesse, and I wasn't brave enough for that.

Just as it seemed I might be out of luck, she turned toward the parking lot. She walked over to one of the five squad cars that belonged to the Archers Rest Police Department. After looking around one more time, she opened the driver's side door, slipped behind the wheel, and disappeared from view.

"What are you doing?" I muttered. I wanted to run over and stop her from apparently stealing a police car, but I was too confused and too riveted by the scene to do anything.

My eyes kept darting back between the police station and the cars, waiting to see if anyone would come out and find her before she inexplicably committed a serious crime. Then, just as suddenly, Kennette's head popped up. She slid out of the car, looked around once more, and closed the door.

I ducked into the pizza place and watched her walk from the police station back toward the quilt shop. When she was far enough ahead of me, I left the pizza place and followed her as she went back toward the shop. I stopped in front of Carrie's coffee shop and watched as she ducked back into Someday Quilts.

I was tempted to go into the shop and confront Kennette then and there, but I came up with what I hoped was a better plan. I dialed my phone, and on the third ring I heard Bernie pick up.

"Go over to Someday and watch Kennette. Watch everything she does. Don't let her leave the shop. I'll explain later."

Before she had a chance to respond, I hung up. I darted back up the street toward the police station. It seemed quiet outside. I glanced at the window to make sure there wasn't anyone about to walk out the door, but there didn't seem to be much activity. When I felt sure it was safe, I headed toward the parking lot and to the police car Kennette had broken into. I slowly opened the door and slid behind the driver's seat. Just as Kennette had done, I leaned down in the seat. But then I ran out of ideas.

"What were you doing?" I asked no one.

I felt around under the seats. I found two candy wrappers and the cap of a pen. I moved my hand further back. At the tip of my fingers I felt a thick piece of paper. Maybe it was the envelope that Kennette had stuck in her pocket when she walked out of the shop. I stretched my hand and reached as far as I could, grabbing the paper between my fingers. I slowly pulled it out from under the seat.

"What are you doing?"

I froze. I didn't need to look to know who was talking to me. There didn't seem to be much chance of escape so I straightened up in the seat and, before I dealt with the man outside the car, I quickly looked at the paper in my hand. It was a crumpled parking ticket.

I rolled down the window.

"Hi," I said, a forced smile on my face.

"Hi?" Jesse snapped. "Tell me what you're doing."

"I found this," I held up the ticket as if it were a prize.

Jesse yanked me out of the car and slammed the door behind me. He grabbed the envelope out of my hand.

"You lost a parking ticket?" he barked.

"I didn't say I lost it. I said I found it."

"Oh, you're on the case, aren't you?" His voice dripped with sarcasm. "My favorite detective is busy following the clues. I thought we were past this."

"I'm being a concerned citizen."

"So, what kind of clue is this ticket?"

"It's not a clue, but . . ." Suddenly I decided not to tell him anything. Either way I was in trouble, so why help him? I stood there looking defiant and feeling stupid.

"Nell, I could put you in jail for this."

Suddenly I noticed something scribbled in pen on the ticket that made me feel my adventure hadn't been for nothing. "There's some writing on it," I said.

Jesse turned the ticket around and looked at it. "March 1," he read. "Mean anything to you?"

I shook my head. Maybe it had all been for nothing.

"I'm going to guess that some cop ripped a parking ticket out of his book to use as a notepad," Jesse said. "They really shouldn't do that. It screws up the numbering system."

"Well then you should probably go inside and talk to them about that."

He smiled, but he didn't look happy. He took a deep breath. "Nell, I'm going to assume that you weren't planning to steal the car, but this is unacceptable. If you want to work out your Nancy Drew fantasies, then go over to the high school and find out what's in the mystery stew. But stay out of my way."

"So you're not going to charge me; you're just going to lecture me."

Jesse slammed his fist on the hood of the car. "Why are you doing these crazy things? Why can't you just work in the shop and go to school?"

"And be a good girl?" I countered. "Because I'm a grown woman, and grown women have minds of their own."

"You know my wife was a grown woman but she wasn't meddle-some and dangerously unpredictable."

I paused, took a breath, then looked him in the eye. "I'm not your wife. I'm me. I'm sorry that's not good enough for you."

I turned to walk away with my words hanging dramatically in the air. But I had taken only one step when Jesse grabbed my arm.

"You're under arrest," he said quietly.

✄

"This is ridiculous," I said for the thirtieth time as Jesse walked me into the only cell in the jail. "You can't possibly arrest me."

"I can do whatever I want. I'm the law around here," he said. He twirled the keys in his hands, smiled a little, and walked away.

"Hey, Nell, I figured you'd end up here." I turned around in the cell to see Rich sitting on a bench.

I couldn't help but laugh.

"Honestly, I think you spend more time here than you do at home," I said to him. "What was it this time?"

"The library."

"What were you trying to steal at the library?"

"I don't steal anything. I do it just to prove I can. And because the guys bet me. It's my walking-around money."

"More like your bail money."

He shook his head. "I know. And the worst part is that I have a date tonight."

I sat next to him on the small bench.

"Is she cute?" I asked.

He blushed. "I've been working on this for months," he said, "and Blimper has his eye on her. If I don't get out of here, I'm toast."

"That's too bad. But relationships are hard, even without jail com-ing between you, so maybe you're better off."

"You know Chief Dewalt's just trying to protect you," Rich of-fered. "I think he's a tool, but he cares about you, and I think he's worried about you getting yourself killed. I would be if, you know, I dated someone like you."

I smiled. "Well, thanks. I think."

Since it was pretty clear there wasn't any point in trying to figure out how to get back on Jesse's good side, I focused on the question I still had left: What was Kennette doing in that car?

I got up and walked to the cell door and rattled it, just in case, but it was locked. I tapped my fingers on bars. I'd been in jail for less than ten minutes and I was already trying to figure my way out.

"I have an idea how we can both get out of here," I said. "But you have to rat me out."

CHAPTER 45

I lay back on the bench and stared at the ceiling. Maybe I was dangerously unpredictable, and if I was, then I should be able to use that to my advantage.

"Do you want some coffee or something to eat?" I looked up to see Greg standing outside the cell.

"Why? Am I going to be here awhile?"

Greg opened the cell and walked inside. "I hate to tell you this, but Rich is out there making a deal with Jesse. If Jesse lets him off the hook for breaking into the library, then he'll give Jesse a story about you."

I sat up and pretended to be surprised.

"Like what?" I asked.

"Seems like you broke into somebody's house."

"Did Rich say whose house?"

"I don't think he knew. Did you find anything?"

I shifted a bit on the bench. I didn't want to confess to Greg. I had a bigger fish in mind. "I didn't say I broke into anyone's house. Rich could be pulling Jesse's leg."

Greg nodded. "It's just that you have gotten really involved in this investigation and I'm wondering what you found out."

He sat on the bench, only inches from me. I tried to move but there was nowhere to go.

"Unfortunately," I admitted, "I haven't really found out anything. Powell can tell you."

"You've been talking to Powell?"

"Yeah. So have you," I pointed out.

Greg looked at me, then at the open cell door. We could both hear footsteps in the hallway.

Jesse leaned against the door. "Nell, you're coming with me."

"Where?"

"Do you really care? You'll be out of here."

I got up and walked into the main police station. Rich mouthed a thank-you, and I mouthed back, "Tell Susanne." He nodded and headed out of the station. I followed Jesse to a police car. Greg walked behind us, and in a moment that struck me as both odd and funny. Greg got in the back of the squad car while I, still technically under arrest, got in the front passenger seat next to Jesse.

"Where are we going?"

"To the site of your latest break-in."

"And where would that be?"

Jesse glanced at me. "You can drop it, Nell. Rich told me all about it."

I nodded. I couldn't believe how easily Jesse had fallen into my trap.

"I do have one question," Jesse said. "Why do you want Susanne to know we're on our way to Oliver's house?"

There was no point in pretending anymore. "Get ready to build a bigger jail, because they've all been helping me try to solve the case."

"The whole group?"

"Except Eleanor and Kennette."

"You have a bigger investigative department than I do," Jesse laughed. "Though you should probably call Eleanor and Kennette and get them over here as well. We might as well have the whole gang in on the fun."

He was in a strangely happy mood for a man who had been ready to wring my neck not twenty minutes before. I decided I was better off not asking why. I might as well enjoy the freedom while I had it.

✂

Oliver answered the door, looking tired and confused. Three Morristown Police cars were parked out front when we arrived. Powell and his men were standing outside the house. Jesse didn't seem surprised or even interested in their presence. Greg, though, immediately went over to say hello.

"I have reason to believe that Nell broke into your house looking for clues," Jesse told Oliver. "I'm wondering if I can fingerprint your place."

Oliver looked at me. "No need. If you find fingerprints it's because Nell has been an invited guest to my home and my studio."

I smiled a half smile at Oliver. Why he was protecting me, I couldn't guess, but it didn't matter.

"So there you go," I said to Jesse. "No break-in."

"And therefore no permission to enter his home and conduct a search, so neither of us got what we wanted," Jesse said.

"You knew?"

"I'm not as bad a detective as you think."

"Powell must think so, otherwise he wouldn't have his guys watching the house."

"Yes," Oliver said. "Why are they here? None of them will tell me."

"Powell's waiting for a search warrant based on the DNA match he found from a cigarette you discarded at Carrie's party," Jesse told him.

Oliver immediately looked at me, first confused and then disappointed. "I suppose that just seals it, doesn't it."

"Except you aren't guilty of either murder," Jesse said.

Oliver smiled. "Not according to our girl here."

"So let us in for a search and maybe we'll get to the truth," Jesse offered.

Oliver opened the door wide, and as he did, Natalie's van pulled up with the rest of the quilt club inside. Eleanor pulled up behind them in her car, with Kennette in the passenger seat.

"What's going on?" Eleanor demanded as she got out of the car.

"Oliver's agreed to let us look through his house," I told her.

At that Powell and his officers ran up the pathway and into the house, ahead of me, Jesse, and Oliver.

It took about a half hour for the police to go through Oliver's house. Like Natalie and me, they found nothing unusual. Then Oliver offered Jesse the key to his studio, and we all walked out and watched the men open the doors widely, letting light into his dark, private space.

For about ten minutes the police searched Oliver's studio, while the rest of us stood in the driveway and watched. I could see Natalie looking over at Kennette, waiting for any sign that she might be nervous. The painting of her had been safely tucked back behind the desk, but it was only a matter of time.

I watched as the cops spread out across the room, each taking a corner and meticulously searching it. Jesse was looking through Oliver's paints and prop box—items he used in the backgrounds of his paintings. Greg was going through paintings that had been piled up against the wall, and Powell was staring at the one misfit in the group, Julie's collage, which I'd accidentally left in the open when Natalie and I searched the studio.

"I found something," Greg shouted.

He held up a small painting, and Jesse, Powell, and the other cops rushed over. I strained to see what it was, but I couldn't imagine what would make that one painting significant.

Jesse grabbed Greg's sleeve and walked him out to the driveway.

"Hold it up," he told him.

Greg held up a painting that seemed oddly familiar. Certainly nothing special but something I knew I had seen before.

"It's not mine," Oliver said. "I think that's fairly obvious."

"It's Sandra's," I suddenly realized.

"What's Sandra's painting doing here?" Oliver asked.

"Maybe she was here," Powell said. "You were close. Nell can testify to that. And you gave her money. Maybe Sandra was conning an old man for his money, which would have been perfect except that your granddaughter showed up. Your fortune and your paintings were now going to go to Lily. Sandra killed Lily. You killed Sandra."

"That's absurd," Eleanor said. "You really have no idea what kind of man this is."

Oliver smiled at her. "Even if all of that is true, why would I have a painting of Sandra's?"

"A souvenir," Greg offered. "Maybe she gave it to you as a gift."

I looked at the painting again. "After she was dead?" I asked. "Besides, it wasn't here when Natalie and I . . . , well, when we searched the place. And I know that painting was in Sandra's apartment when I . . . looked through her apartment. It was something she painted in class. I'd swear to it."

"Hold it up again," Jesse said to Greg. "Take another look, Nell, just to be sure."

Greg shifted his arms and held the painting up again. I looked at the painting but it was something else that caught my eye. Greg's sleeve had moved slightly down his arm to reveal a light blue plastic bracelet, the kind worn to show support or raise money for causes.

There it was. The sign about the police fund-raiser. The bottle of scotch. The dead mother. The intense desire to "solve" the case. And the perfect patsy—me.

"It wasn't Oliver," I said. "He's being framed. And I guess I've been helping."

Jesse walked over and stood directly in front of me as if shielding me from everyone else. "Why do you think that?"

"I don't know why I didn't see it. Julie is your mother," I said. I looked at Powell. "The woman in the painting *Nobody*, the woman who made that collage you were looking at."

Everyone's eyes instinctively went to the collage. Powell laughed.

"Nell, you've gone off the deep end," he said.

Oliver walked over to collage and picked it up. Powell grabbed it from his hands. He held it close, then took a deep breath and let it slide to the floor.

"He shouldn't have it," Powell said quietly. "He shouldn't have anything that belongs to her. He murdered her."

"You're Marty?" Oliver said. "When I knew your mother, you were such a slight boy. I didn't recognize you."

"Why do you think Oliver murdered your mother?" Maggie stepped in.

"They were drunks together. My mother became an addict, out of control, and he just left. Just like he walked out on his wife. My mother had no one to help her. I tried but it wasn't enough."

"She died of a drug overdose more than ten years later," Oliver said.

Powell nodded.

"That's not murder," I said. "And it doesn't justify your killing Lily for revenge."

"*He* killed my granddaughter?" Oliver lunged at Powell, but Jesse stopped him.

"She was just like you," Powell spit out. "She was a nothing. I picked her up for shoplifting, and she had a backpack full of stuff about you: pictures, articles. It was pathetic. She told me her grandfather was a rich artist and he'd pay the bail."

"So you dosed her with sleeping pills?" Jesse asked.

"I needed to think," Powell said. "I needed to bring this man to justice and I needed time to figure out how to do it."

"By what . . . stealing his money?" Bernie asked.

"I don't care about his money. He took my family away from me. Why should he get to have a granddaughter, when I lost my mother because of him? I wanted him to suffer, to think he had a chance of finding her and then to know that she was gone forever."

"And to go to jail for it as well," Susanne chimed in. "So you killed that poor girl?"

"But you had a family," Oliver said, tears rolling down his eyes. "You had Alessandra. I remember hearing that she was born months before your mother died."

Powell shook his head. "My sister had my mother's weak character.

She was supposed to get you so excited about a family reunion that the truth would be devastating. But she couldn't go through with it. She even started to think you were a good man."

"Sandra," I said. "Sandra was your sister?"

"Half sister." He nodded. "She decided to tell you everything, Nell. To get you to help put me away. She thought I was obsessed." He laughed. "She was too young to remember what it was like when Mom was well. She only remembered the bad stuff. She thought we were better off without her."

"Was that your watch in her bedroom?" I asked, but I almost didn't want to know the answer.

"She stole it." Powell spat out the words. "She was always stealing. She even stole the photo from Lily's body that was supposed to frame White. She was a worthless thief and liar. And then suddenly she wanted to tell the truth." Powell let out a hollow laugh. "I had to stop her before she ruined everything."

"So now you spend the rest of your life in jail?" Eleanor said sadly. "And what did you gain?"

Powell smiled. "The great Oliver White lives the rest of his life knowing that his granddaughter drowned in a cold river because of him."

I looked at Oliver, who seemed on the verge of collapse.

"But she didn't," Kennette said suddenly. "I'm his granddaughter."

Oliver spun around and looked at Kennette, in her bright teal coat and brown plaid pants. "I'm Violet's granddaughter and Rachel's daughter. I came looking for you because I wanted to be an artist just like you."

"Why didn't you tell me?" Oliver stared at her, seemingly unable to take it all in.

"I didn't think that you could love me, because you didn't love my mom," she said. "My grandmother said you were incapable of love, but when I saw how much you loved Eleanor, I knew that wasn't true."

Oliver wrapped his arms around Kennette and held her for a long time; both were crying and causing the rest of the quilt club to cry as well. I looked over at Powell, completely destroyed by the reunion.

Jesse cuffed him and handed the prisoner over to Greg, who smiled happily but kept a firm grip on Powell.

"How did Lily get your stuff?" I asked Kennette once Oliver had let her go.

"I rented a room from her in an apartment in Peekskill and she stole everything I had. I couldn't pay the rent or even buy food. I would have gone home but I wanted to prove to my mom that I could be an artist."

"You can be," Oliver said. "You are."

"I don't think my mom will agree," Kennette said. "She thinks that being an artist will make me a bad person, and when she found out I was taking classes from you, she told me you would ruin my life."

"She's pretty angry but I think she'll understand if the two of you talk to her," Jesse offered.

I turned to Jesse. It took me a moment to realize what he had said. "You knew?" I asked. "When did you know?"

"I found out that Violet was living with her daughter in Kitchener. Lily had a surgical scar on her right side. Rachel confirmed her daughter never had surgery. She also told me her daughter's name was Violet Kennette Campbell," Jesse said. "I knew Powell was going to lie about the DNA and I wanted to be able to counter him."

"You knew Powell was the killer?" I couldn't believe Jesse had figured it out before I had.

"I was pretty sure"—he smiled—"but I needed you to prove it. I just don't know how you did."

"Greg helped me."

We all looked at Greg, who looked sheepishly around.

"I solved the case?" He looked around bewildered.

I nodded. "Couldn't have done it without you."

CHAPTER 46

The day after my final class with Oliver, I arrived early at the shop. A shipment of fabrics arrived, so I spent the morning putting them away. I knew I wouldn't have time in the afternoon, once the party got started.

By one o'clock Bernie and Maggie had arrived, homemade treats in hand. Carrie brought coffee from across the street. She'd left the shop in the capable hands of her only employee, Rich.

"He's not a thief," she said. "And if I ever lose my keys, he's the perfect go-to guy."

"And maybe with some spending money he won't keep betting he can break into things." Susanne smiled.

"Here's hoping," I laughed. "Unless we need him again."

Natalie brought photos she'd taken at Carrie's opening, made into a photo album for each of us. Susanne brought sparkling grape juice so Natalie could join in a toast. Eleanor had stayed up late the night before, making fried chicken, with plenty left over for the road. I didn't bring anything, just an old pair of jeans and a sweater so she would have a change of clothes.

Oliver and Kennette arrived just minutes after we'd set everything up.

"This is for me?" Tears rolled down Kennette's face. "Why did you do this?"

"You have been a joy to befriend," Eleanor said. "And we will miss you."

At that the room broke out in hugs. While Oliver stood back and watched, his granddaughter was pulled into the group with each woman offering her love and her good wishes.

"You can all visit me in London, anytime," she said. "It's going to be really scary going to the London School of the Arts. I won't know anyone. I wish Nell were going with me."

I smiled. "I think I get all the adventure I can stand right here."

"But think of what we'd learn," Kennette pleaded.

"I will be Nell's personal coach," Oliver stepped in. "There will be no slacking off with me around."

I laid my head on his shoulder. "I like that idea, Grandpa." I winked.

He blushed. "You think you're making a joke, but maybe not, if your grandmother will have me."

"Oh that's enough now," Eleanor interrupted.

"Then we'll be kind of like sisters," Kennette jumped in excitedly.

I grabbed her hand. "We kind of are," I pulled at her sweater. "I mean, you're already borrowing my clothes all the time."

Bernie handed out the sparkling grape juice and we all made toasts to wonderful friendships and to quilting. And to Kennette's bright future at LSA. We ate the chicken and cakes and looked through the photos.

Several times women came to the door and knocked, but we just pointed out the Closed sign and went back to our party. As much as it pained my grandmother to deny a quilter her fabric, some things are more important.

After a couple of hours, Susanne wrapped up some of the leftovers and handed them to Oliver. "You have a long trip ahead of you. You'll get hungry."

"And don't forget this." Eleanor picked up Kennette's blue and purple drunkard's path quilt. "This is very special."

Kennette looked at it for a long time, stroking the fabric. "I want you to have this," she said to Oliver. "It's a part of me, made into something real. Quilters think it's really important to give away quilts."

He began to tear up as he took the quilt. "It's more than I deserve, but I'll treasure it every day." He held up a wrapped painting. "And I have something for you."

Kennette opened the painting. It was the portrait of Kennette that Natalie and I had found in the studio.

"Grandma," she said. "She is so beautiful."

"It's not you?" Natalie asked. "She looks just like you."

Oliver looked at the painting. "She does. I don't know why I didn't see it before. I guess I was so focused on finding Lily that I didn't see what was right in front of me. A bad quality for an artist."

"I'll treasure it," she said.

"Well it's only one of several you will eventually inherit," he said. "I worked out a deal with the school to pay for security of my exhibition if they allowed me to withdraw *Lost* and several other works from my gift. I want those paintings to go to my family."

Kennette hugged him again. The two stood holding each other for a long time before Oliver finally stepped back.

"We have a long drive back to Kitchener. And I have a lot of catching up to do with your mother and grandmother."

Kennette went around the room for one more hug.

"You don't have a quilt now," I said.

"That's okay."

"No it isn't." I hurried to the back room and returned with my Irish chain.

"I can't take that," Kennette protested.

"I'll make more," I said. Then I looked around the room at the others. "They'll force me to."

Oliver kissed Eleanor as we all exchanged glances. "I'll be back in a week. I just want to see if there's a chance for my daughter and me to find a way back to each other."

"I'll be here," Eleanor said.

Once outside I realized that Jesse and Greg were waiting by Oliver's car. Jesse shook Oliver's hand and the two men launched into a good-natured argument about soccer. Greg gave Kennette a long hug.

"Thanks for your help," he said.

"But you won't be taking the detective's exam in Morristown, so I didn't really help."

"Is that what you were doing?" I asked. "You were helping him study?"

"We didn't want the chief here to know about it," Greg admitted. "It would have meant that I'd have to leave Archers Rest and work for Powell. And that's a bust now. Not that I'd leave anyway."

"I told him that if he stops buying fund-raising bracelets from competing police departments, losing evidence, and planting paintings as favors to a killer, then I would consider letting him study for detective." Jesse smiled.

"If he hadn't," I pointed out, "I wouldn't have figured out it was Powell."

"I didn't lose the watch, though," Greg offered. "Powell must have stolen it from me when I showed it to him."

"You're not helping yourself, Greg," Eleanor said.

We watched as Oliver gave Eleanor one last hug and then he and Kennette got into the car. The rest of the group headed across the street to Jitters, but Jesse and I stayed in front of Someday Quilts.

"Hi, old friend," I said.

He nodded.

"I know I should apologize about all my interference but . . . ," I started.

"You don't need to apologize. You followed your heart. That's who you are."

"And you like that about me." I smiled.

He smiled back. "Very much."

"So, are we back to where we started when this whole thing began?" I asked flirtatiously.

"If you mean friends. Yeah, I think so."

I pulled back. "So you can't forgive me for getting involved in the case?"

"It's not that. Well, it is a little. It's just that I'm not ready, I guess. I know I have to be more flexible and more open if I want to be in a relationship again. But I'm a play-by-the-rules guy and you," he said and laughed, "well, let's face it, you're not."

"Not just me," I said, pointing to Susanne, Maggie, Eleanor, Natalie, Bernie, and Carrie, who were all standing outside Jitters.

"No, you're right about that. Who knew quilters were such a dangerous bunch?"

"I did." I smiled.

"Friends?" Jesse asked.

"Friends."

I kissed Jesse on the cheek, and as I did, he put his hand on the small of my back. We stayed close, our cheeks touching, for almost a minute.

It wasn't over between us, I thought. It would just take its own time. And just like making a quilt, if I got too caught up in getting to the finish line I'd miss out on all the fun along the way.

I pulled away from him and headed across the street to my fellow detectives and the less-dangerous but just as exciting adventure of planning a brand-new quilt.

Clare O'Donohue

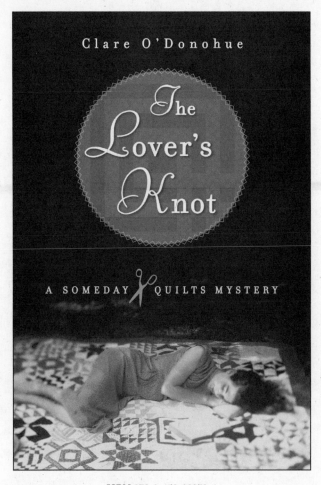

Clare O'Donohue

The Lover's Knot

A SOMEDAY QUILTS MYSTERY

ISBN 978-0-452-28979-6

Available wherever books are sold.

Plume
A member of Penguin Group (USA) Inc.
www.penguin.com